PRAISE FOR
Kernel of Truth

"A wry, witty voice that had me laughing out loud, a truly puzzling mystery plot, and a popcorn shop setting that earns its place with clever clues aplenty. *Kernel of Truth* is as ingenious as Bec's Tuxedo Coco Pop Fudge (and as irresistible). Bursting with delights."

—Catriona McPherson, award-winning author
of *The Day She Died*

"Kick back, pick up a snack and enjoy this entrée into the Popcorn Shop Mysteries. The heroine is delightfully sarcastic, but with a sweet spirit, and she refuses to give up on her dreams. The supporting cast runs the gamut from a potential love interest to a flaky ex-husband, and readers will be charmed by each of them."
—*RT Book Reviews*

"[A] fun start to a new series, popping with a protagonist full of heart and a great poodle sidekick."
—Open Book Society

"This book is brilliantly written with fun, quirky characters. It's got a wonderful setting, a believable crime and a smart woman with extreme determination. I thoroughly enjoyed reading it, and am so excited for this series to take off."
—Marie's Cozy Corner

"Kristi Abbott plunges the reader headlong into a mystery that is full of red herrings, and yummy food and recipes . . . Read *Kernel of Truth*—you won't regret it!"
—Fresh Fiction

Berkley Prime Crime titles by Kristi Abbott

KERNEL OF TRUTH
POP GOES THE MURDER

Pop Goes _the_ Murder

KRISTI ABBOTT

BERKLEY PRIME CRIME
New York

BERKLEY PRIME CRIME
Published by Berkley
An imprint of Penguin Random House LLC
375 Hudson Street, New York, New York 10014

Copyright © 2017 by Penguin Random House LLC
Penguin Random House supports copyright. Copyright fuels creativity, encourages
diverse voices, promotes free speech, and creates a vibrant culture. Thank you for buying
an authorized edition of this book and for complying with copyright laws by not
reproducing, scanning, or distributing any part of it in any form without permission.
You are supporting writers and allowing Penguin Random House to continue to
publish books for every reader.

BERKLEY is a registered trademark and BERKLEY PRIME CRIME and the B colophon
are trademarks of Penguin Random House LLC.

ISBN: 9780425280928

First Edition: January 2017

Printed in the United States of America
1   3   5   7   9   10   8   6   4   2

Cover art by Catherine Deeter
Cover design Sarah Oberrender
Book design by Tiffany Estreicher

ACKNOWLEDGMENTS

I'd like to thank Leis Pederson, the editor with whom this story started, and Katherine Pelz, the editor who brought it in and put it to bed. Thank you to Karen Kaminsky Klein who gave me the idea to combine bacon and popcorn and to stick it all together with caramel sauce, and thanks again to Barbara Bravo for her awesome caramel sauce recipe.

I have so many people that sustain me through the long journey of writing a book: my beautiful sisters, Marian and Diane; my writing sisters, Catriona McPherson, Spring Warren and Kris Calvin; my Sciroccos who cheer me on; my rock in the untidy tides of life, Andy Wallace; my children, Alex and Teddy, who make me proud every day.

I attempted to crowd-source these acknowledgments and was rewarded with many responses. Thank you to Becky Clark (I hate the haters), Boaty McBoatFace, Toad-stool McWhiskey, Donna Apidone (weather does matter), Lisa Trahan (that means you got thanked twice), Becky

Weinstein, Fergus Finnegan (purr on, my brother), Abby Fabian and Reese's Peanut Butter Cups.

Thank you also to the many people who've written to me since the publication of *Kernel of Truth*. Your kind words make it a pleasure to do this job.

One

I knocked on the hotel room door. No one answered. I glanced at my watch. Seven forty-five in the morning. I was right on time. The fact that I'd had to dump the hectic breakfast crowd on Susanna and Sam to be on time for this meeting didn't irritate me at all. Now that it appeared that the person who had insisted she could only make time to talk to me from seven forty-five to eight fifteen on Thursday morning wasn't answering her door, I didn't feel like the top of my head was about to explode like a can of dulce de leche left to simmer too long. No. Of course not.

I knocked again. I'd never really liked Melanie, not from the first moment Antoine Belanger hired her. Everyone thought it was about jealousy, but if it was, it wasn't because I was jealous of Melanie. I'd been fine with Antoine needing an assistant. I'd been fine when he hired a young and frankly quite good-looking woman. I'd even been fine when I'd realized that she looked like a younger, slightly prettier version of me, from her curly sandy-brown hair to her slightly-too-long feet. I'd gotten an odd vibe off Melanie. A vibe I recognized. A "you're in my way" vibe.

Well, I wasn't in her way anymore. Or I hadn't been until Antoine decided to come to Grand Lake and tape a segment on my popcorn shop for his television show.

I knocked a third time. Hard. This time, the door swung open with a quiet shushing sound as it scraped along the carpet. Melanie must not have latched it all the way. "Melanie?" I called through the open door. "It's Rebecca. I'm here for our meeting."

The meeting you called.

I wasn't even all that thrilled about the reason for the meeting. A few weeks before, my ex-husband, Antoine, had walked in on someone threatening to shoot me and had run the other way faster than you can burn garlic. While he kept explaining to me that he'd been running to get help, we both knew the truth. He was a big fat French chicken. He was also, however, a big fat French chicken with a seriously influential television show. A show that was watched by tens of thousands of people across the nation. A show that had launched Antoine's successful line of pasta sauces.

A show that could launch my little gourmet popcorn shop into the stratosphere.

To make up for leaving me to be gunned down in the lighthouse where my father proposed to my mother and where I received my first French kiss, Antoine had offered to feature my breakfast bars and popcorn fudge on his television show.

Antoine clearly somehow thought this might win me back, but I'd been done with him since before he'd left me staring down the very black cold tunnel of a gun. Now I was beyond done. So done you couldn't even stick a fork in me. The starstruck culinary school student who had run off with the man who taught her to make a béchamel sauce that could make gods weep existed no longer. In her place was a grown-ass woman who knew it was stupid to turn down free publicity even when it came from her ex-husband who was angling for something in return.

No one answered from inside the hotel room. I hesitated for a moment on the threshold and then walked into the hotel room, Sprocket at my side. Having my dog with me made me feel brave. Otherwise, I wasn't in the habit of marching into hotel rooms. "Melanie," I called again. "I'm here for the meeting."

It was a typical hotel room, maybe a little larger than most. It had a queen-sized bed, a desk, a dresser, a small couch. The bed was made. Clothes were strewn across the couch in the sitting area. Papers covered the desk. No Melanie, though. I turned in a slow circle. The bathroom door was ajar.

The first feeling of unease climbed up my spine. I ignored it. I watched way too many psychological thrillers. I was being dramatic. Apparently Sprocket had watched too many movies with me. He whined and then growled low in his throat. I knocked lightly on the bathroom door. It swung open, too. The bright lights reflecting off the white tile made me wince, but then my eyes adjusted. I took two big steps backward, not quite believing what I was seeing, not wanting to believe what I was seeing.

Melanie floated in the bathtub, sightless eyes staring at the ceiling. A big black blow-dryer plugged into the wall floated in the tub with her.

Apparently our meeting was going to be indefinitely postponed.

*   *   *

Sheriff Dan Cooper, my bestie and brother-in-law all rolled into one handsome broad-shouldered package, crouched down next to me where I sat slumped against the wall in the hallway. "You okay?" he asked.

I'd been drawing doodles with my finger in the industrial carpet, focusing on the warp and weave to try to get the image of Melanie out of my head. It wasn't working. I looked up at him and considered his question. "Define *okay.*"

He knocked his hat back a little on his head. "Are you going to barf or faint?" The words may have sounded harsh, but his tone was gentle. Dust motes swam behind his head like a halo. It made me want to sneeze.

I did a quick mental scan. "No, but I might have nightmares." I buried my nose in Sprocket's fur. Well, technically not fur. He's a poodle. He has hair.

"That's Sprocket's problem. Not mine." He patted my shoulder. "Do you think you can answer some questions?"

I nodded against Sprocket's shoulder. "Is there any chance that I could have some coffee while I do?" I felt ridiculously cold. Plus I'd sort of been counting on having coffee at the breakfast meeting that was now very clearly not going to happen. I was fairly certain that I'd remember more of what I'd seen with some caffeine in my system.

"Sure. We can go down to the coffee shop in the lobby." He rose up, blocking the light.

"Can we go to POPS? I meant real coffee." I wasn't sure what the Grand Lake Café used to make the fluid they sold as coffee—I suspected liquid from wringing out dirty rags—but I was fairly certain it had never come from a bean.

"I don't think this is the moment to be snobby about your coffee." Dan extended a hand down to help me up.

"I'm probably in shock. I can't think of a more important moment to be sure to have good coffee." I took his hand and let him heave me to my feet.

He gestured for me to walk in front of him down the hall. "Maybe they can make you some tea."

"I doubt it." Trust me. The number of restaurants in America that can make a decent cuppa are fewer than hen's teeth and hens have absolutely no teeth whatsoever. Well, except for that one mutant strain of chickens and I didn't count them. I walked anyway.

The hallway that had been deserted when I'd come out of Melanie's room to call 911 was now packed with people. Crime scene people, EMTs, deputies from the Sheriff's Department all crowded the narrow space. Dan and I threaded our way through the throng.

The Grand Lake Café was a typical hotel lobby coffee shop. Not quite a diner. Not quite a restaurant. Not quite anything, really, but a place where desperate travelers could at least get enough sustenance to maintain life. My footsteps balked as we crossed the threshold.

"Sorry, Bec. You're going to have to slum it. I can't leave here right now and I need to know what you saw." He shook his head. "Again."

We sat down in the café with Sprocket under the table. The waitress gave my dog a pointed look, but Dan smiled up at her. "He's kind of like a service dog at the moment," he said.

"As long as you're the one telling the Health Department that," she said with a shrug. Ah, to be young and cynical. I didn't recognize her. She looked maybe nineteen or twenty and like she might be pretty out of the horrid mustard-colored uniform she wore. It was weird to actually run into someone in Grand Lake that I didn't know somehow. Who knew? Maybe Haley had babysat for her back in the day and I just didn't recognize her.

Dan asked her to bring a cup of coffee for him and a pot of Earl Grey for me. Sure enough she showed up with a white mug full of a tannish, greasy-looking liquid for Dan and a do-it-yourself assembly kit of a tea bag, a mug and a pot of tepid water for me.

I sighed and poured the water over the tea bag. Aromatic oils were not released. I could tell. Dan took a sip of his coffee and grimaced.

"Told you so." The satisfaction of being right did little to make me feel better at the moment.

"I'll suffer in the line of duty," he said, dumping in enough cream and sugar to reclassify the coffee into the dessert category. "Now what were you doing in Melanie Fitzgerald's hotel room this early in the morning?"

I sighed, sipped at my weak tepid tea and explained about the meeting, about how we were going to go over the logistics, the shooting schedule, the cooking scenes in the kitchen, about how she'd insisted we meet this morning in her room. I picked at the edge of the table where the fake wood veneer was cracked and starting to peel.

Dan rubbed his face. "I knew there would be trouble the second you told me Antoine was coming to town with his crew."

Dan had never been exactly what I'd call an Antoine fan. First of all, Antoine tended to appeal to women more. They loved that hint of a French accent, the piercing blue eyes, the blond hair, the quick grin, the way he threw his head back when he laughed . . . basically all the reasons I fell in love with him. He had legions of female fans, many of a certain age. They called themselves the Belanger Bunnies. They had Facebook groups, Twitter hashtags, YouTube channels, Tumblrs, Pinterest boards. Well, everything. So Dan wasn't exactly Antoine's usual demographic or quite that up on social media. If you asked Dan to tweet he'd probably tell you he never did that in public.

Second, my marriage to Antoine had represented that moment when Dan decided I was never coming back to Grand Lake. At least, he thought I'd never come back. With my marriage to Antoine, Dan thought my life had taken a turn that set me firmly on a path that did not include little resort towns on Lake Erie.

Boy, had he been wrong about that! I had come running back full speed after my divorce. Somehow, though, Dan still harbored ill will toward my charismatic ex for stealing me away.

"I'm not sure you can blame Antoine for this one, Dan." Which was when it occurred to me to wonder who should be blamed. Who was responsible? Or if anyone was to blame at all. Maybe I was a little in shock. Maybe I really did need a decent cup of tea. Maybe it needed to have whiskey in it.

"We'll see. How well did you know Melanie?" Dan asked, taking his little notepad out of his breast pocket.

I shrugged. "She was Antoine's assistant for years, then he promoted her to executive producer. He relies on her for everything."

Dan arched a brow at me. "Everything?"

"Get your mind out of the gutter, Cooper. Seriously, do you think about my sister with that brain?" Men. Need I say more?

He grinned slightly wolfishly. "Actually I do, but that's beside the point. Was Melanie Antoine's lover?"

"I can't say what they are and aren't to each other now, but I don't think she was Antoine's lover when Antoine and I were married." I suspected it wasn't for lack of trying on her part, but that was another story. I also suspected that Melanie had had something to do with the last big fight Antoine and I had. She had been the assistant who packed up everything in our hotel room in Minneapolis while I was seeing a play at the Guthrie and had whisked Antoine off to a last-minute TV spot in Florida, leaving me behind without even a change of panties in Minnesota in February.

But I wasn't bitter. Not me. No siree bob.

"What do you know about her personal life?" Dan asked.

I leaned back and shut my eyes, but nothing much came to me. "Not a whole lot," I said, straightening up and looking at Dan. "I think there was a boyfriend in the picture back in the day, but that was over two years ago now. They could have broken up or gotten married. I wouldn't exactly be on the list of people Melanie would have notified about it. She wasn't wearing a ring, if that helps any." I blew out a big breath, hoping it would clean out the vision of Melanie's lifeless fingers floating in the tub.

"No. She wasn't." Dan chewed on the end of his pen. "Let's talk about the crime scene."

I took a big gulp of my tea. Luckily, it wasn't hot enough to burn. I didn't want to think too hard about the crime scene. It was bad enough as it was. The fact that it brought back memories of another time I had to describe a crime scene to Dan didn't help. The last time it had been my dear friend and mentor Coco Bittles who had lain dead at the center of the scene. I still saw her lifeless body slumped against her antique credenza as I fell asleep some nights.

I knew Dan had to do his job, though. I knew this was one of those times that I had to at least pretend to be a grown-up and suck it up. "Okay."

He touched my hand lightly and withdrew. He knew this was hard for me. He also knew too much sympathy might undo me. Damn, it was good to have friends, especially right after you found a dead body floating in a hotel room tub. "Tell me about when you first entered the room."

"The door swung open on its own when I knocked." I shut my eyes to try to picture it all. "The room was kind of a mess. She had clothes strewn across the couch and shoes all over the floor."

The bed had been made. I tried to picture the clothes on the couch. Dresses. Some jeans with a silky top. My head came up. "Dress-up clothes. Not everyday clothes. Like maybe she was getting ready for a date or something." A date that had never shown up. My hand flew to my mouth. "Do you think she was lying there in that tub dead all night?"

Dan's lips tightened. "I have to wait for the medical examiner to make that determination, Rebecca. She may have been, though."

Poor Melanie. Floating like that all night, waiting for someone to find her. The water getting cold around her. The light glaring down on her. I tried to choke back a sob and made a weird little whimpering sound instead.

"You okay?" Dan asked. "Do you need a break?"

I shook my head. It would be better to get this over with. Then maybe I wouldn't have to think about poor Melanie floating in the bathtub like an extra-poached egg no one needed for eggs Benedict. "What else do you want to know?"

"Did you see anyone in the hallway or the elevator as you were going up to her room?" His pen was poised over the notepad.

"No." I was sorry to disappoint him, but there didn't seem to be much point in making up sinister strangers hiding in stairwells.

"In the lobby?" He sounded hopeful.

I was about to shoot that down when I remembered something. "I saw a woman coming in here."

"Anyone you recognized? Someone from the show?" Dan arched a brow at me.

I thought for a second. "Not anyone I've met. She could have been someone else staying here at the hotel."

"Can you give me a basic description?" he asked.

"Younger than me. Shorter than me. Dark hair. Maybe Latina." I shrugged. "That's all I can remember."

"Would you recognize her if you saw her again?"

"Maybe."

"I'll get a list of who else is staying at the hotel and see if we can find out who she is just in case. Did you touch anything at the crime scene?" Dan asked, looking at me pointedly.

I'd known this question was coming. I'd known what I was—or more to the point, wasn't—supposed to do. After all, I'd been yelled at enough for straightening Coco's skirt after she died so the entire town wouldn't see her knickers. It couldn't be helped, though. Only a woman who did not have the milk of human kindness in her latte could have left Melanie like that, floating naked in the tub to be ogled and photographed and gossiped about. "I covered her with a towel." I said it really quietly in the hopes that Dan would let it go quietly.

I was disappointed. He slapped the table so hard our mugs jumped. Coffee and Earl Grey sloshed all over the fake wood and Sprocket yipped in surprise. "I knew it! The second I saw that towel I knew it. It's a potential crime scene, Rebecca. A. Crime. Scene. You're not supposed to touch anything. You know that."

"I wanted to grant her that much dignity. Lord knows she won't have much else." I grabbed some napkins to soak up the spills. "No woman could have left her uncovered."

"You said the same thing about Coco." His lips were set in a grim line.

I shrugged. "The circumstances were similar in a lot of ways."

He shook his head. "Did you touch anything else?" he asked.

"Nothing." I thought back through my trip through the hotel room. "Definitely nothing."

Dan made a note. "Did you notice anything else? Anything out of the ordinary? Anything that didn't seem quite right?"

Like it or not, every time I shut my eyes, the whole scene flooded back in high relief, every detail distinct and sharp. Melanie. The bathtub. The bathmat. The towels. The blow-dryer.

Wait. The blow-dryer. I sat up straight.

"What?" Dan asked. "What are you remembering?"

"That blow-dryer isn't Melanie's."

Dan leaned back in his chair and crossed his arms over his chest. "You don't know if she's married, but you know what kind of blow-dryer she uses?"

I ignored the blatant skepticism in his voice. "Melanie had curly hair like mine."

"So?"

"No self-respecting curly-haired woman would use a blow-dryer without a diffuser—if she used one at all—and Melanie respected herself plenty. Trust me. That was not her blow-dryer."

He shrugged. "So it was the hotel's."

Oh. I hadn't thought of that. Still . . . "Why was it plugged in, then? She wouldn't have used it."

"I don't know, Rebecca." He frowned. "Honestly, you know as much as I do."

"What do you think happened?"

Dan sighed. "I have no idea at this point, Rebecca." He leaned forward to look me right in the eye. "And if I did, I wouldn't tell you. You are a witness. In fact, you're barely that. You're the person who found the body. Nothing more. This has nothing to do with you and there is absolutely no reason for you to get involved in any way. Understood?" His eyes had gone laser-beam bright and a muscle twitched in his jawline.

I leaned back, slightly affronted. "I know. This isn't like what happened with Coco."

He leaned even farther forward. If this kept up, he'd be in my lap and then the gossips of Grand Lake would really have something to talk about. "There was no reason for you to get involved the way you did with what happened to Coco, either, Rebecca. You're a civilian. Not a detective. Not a police officer. You're a chef. Stick to the kitchen."

I'll admit it; that stung a bit. I got it. I had almost gotten myself killed, but I was also pretty certain that Coco's killer would never have been caught if I hadn't intervened.

Sometimes it takes a chef to sniff out what's rotten in a kitchen.

As I was about to leave the Grand Lake Café and go back to POPS to get a decent cup of coffee and make sure that Susanna and Sam hadn't burned the place to the ground dealing with the breakfast rush, Antoine whirled in.

When I say he whirled in, I don't mean he actually pir-
ouetted or something like that. It was more as if the air
whirled around him, like all the particles in his energy field
got excited and started pinging around faster and faster,
like the air started to hum. When he walked into a room,
people's heads immediately raised from what they were
doing. Most of the time, they didn't even know they were
doing it. It was like watching a magnet getting passed over
iron filings. He had that much charisma.

I hadn't really known what charisma was until I met
Antoine, and then I got a crash course. Sadly it took me
close to ten years to figure out that being attracted to someone wasn't the same as being in love with that person. I
didn't know if I'd ever been in love with Antoine. I hadn't,
however, been able to take my eyes off him if we were in
the same room.

I still couldn't.

"*Mon Dieu!*" He grabbed me by the shoulders and looked
me up and down. "Are you all right, Rebecca? Have you
been harmed?"

I shrank back. Just because I couldn't take my eyes off
him didn't mean I wanted his hands on me. "I'm fine. Melanie? Not so much."

He sank down into the booth with Dan and me. Sprocket
growled from beneath the table, but Antoine ignored him.
"Lucy phoned me. I could not believe what she was telling
me. Melanie is . . . no more?"

Dan had gone very still, but not a restful kind of still.
It was the stillness of a cat that had spotted a mouse, a lion
looking at a limping impala, Sprocket eying a stuffed animal left unattended by a child. "Where were you when
Lucy phoned you?"

"By your beautiful lake. Running." By nature of his

business, Antoine ate a lot. He especially ate a lot of things with butter and cream and cheese. He was pretty fanatical about exercise. Otherwise they'd have to lower him onto the set of his television show with a crane. He turned to me. "Thank you, by the way, for the brioche. Very thoughtful. You know how difficult these American breakfasts are for me."

"What brioche?" I asked.

"The brioche you left in front of my hotel room door, of course." He put his hand over mine.

I slipped my hand from underneath his. "I didn't bring you brioche."

"You are sure? It tasted very much like your recipe." He smiled. "Quite buttery."

Dan cocked his head a fraction to one side. Antoine didn't seem to notice. "Lucy phoned you to tell you that Melanie was dead and you took time to eat and to shower before you came to see what was going on?"

Antoine looked surprised. "Of course. I would not want to be offensive to anyone's senses and the brioche was just there. From what Lucy told me, there was nothing I could do for poor Melanie at this point anyway."

"That's true, I suppose." Dan rubbed his chin. "She was long gone."

Antoine's brow creased. "Long? Long gone? How long?"

Dan sighed and slid out of the booth. "I'll let the medical examiner make that call." He nodded to me and left.

Antoine sighed and turned to me. "Your *beau-frère*, he does not care for me."

"Nope," I said. "He surely doesn't. Never really has." There was no reason to sugarcoat it. Antoine didn't really care one way or the other. He was only stating a fact.

"I understand. I stole you away. He had to settle for

marrying your sister." He nodded as if putting a matter to rest.

I snorted. "Settle? For Haley?" Antoine's grip of reality was always a little loose. Dan no more settled for Haley than Marc Antony settled for Cleopatra.

Lucy, a production assistant for Antoine's show, tapped his shoulder. "I'm so sorry to interrupt, Antoine." Lucy was in her late twenties with hair I suspected would be mousey brown if it weren't highlighted to within an inch of its life. She had those narrow black-rimmed smart-girl glasses and a Bumpit in her hair. It was a look that was supposed to be casual but I suspected took a substantial amount of time to put together each morning. I wondered what time she had to get up to look like that by this time. She carried a little extra weight around her waist, hard to avoid when you work on a cooking show, but she had that healthy glow of youth. Plump and pretty.

"Hi, Lucy," I said.

She looked down at me. Her eyes narrowed and her nostrils flared. Then she shifted to turn her back to me as much as she could and didn't say hello back.

"What is it, Lucy?" Antoine asked, turning to look up at Lucy. It was an Antoine thing. Whatever was at the center of his attention was completely at the center of his attention. It was amazing. In the moment, you felt smart and chic and interesting. Not bad, right? I just hadn't been at the center of his attention often enough to keep me in my marriage.

"I know it's probably too soon, but the crew is wondering if we're going ahead with the shooting schedule today. We were supposed to be getting B roll for the show while Melanie made the rest of the shooting schedule." Lucy looked uncomfortable. I didn't blame her. One of her co-workers was dead. On the other hand, having the entire crew on location wasn't cheap. To have an entire day wasted . . .

Antoine took Lucy's hand. With another man, it would have been flirty. With Antoine, it wasn't. It was just . . . Antoine. "What do you think, Lucy? Would it be better for them to stay busy? Or to take a day to process what has befallen our Melanie? It is hard for all of us, isn't it?"

"I should have known something was wrong," Lucy said. "I should have known when she didn't call me to go over the shooting schedule. She almost always did that."

"You cannot blame yourself, dear. How could any of us have anticipated this?" Antoine said.

"I don't see how." Lucy pursed her lips. "I could ask the crew what they would prefer. See if there's some kind of consensus." A little color had risen in her cheeks.

"Excellent. Would you also perhaps attempt making the shooting schedule? We will still need one," Antoine asked.

Lucy flushed for real now. "Yes! Of course. I'd be honored."

Antoine nodded, let go of her hand and turned back to me.

Lucy stood for a second, as if suddenly not having the spotlight of Antoine's attention on her had disoriented her, like walking out of a dark theater on a sunlit day, like the sudden withdrawal of his attention caused vertigo. I'd walked that crazy weaving walk. I gave her a sad smile. She glared at me, then blinked a few times, pulled herself together and left to go find the crew.

"Whoa!" I said. "What eggshell fell into her meringue?"

Antoine shrugged. "My crew . . . they are very loyal to me."

I knew that. Antoine was demanding, but fair. He treated the crew with respect and they returned that with unswerving devotion. "And?"

"And things have not been so easy for me since you left." He rearranged the salt and pepper shakers on the table, not meeting my eye.

It took me a second to get his drift. "They blame me for that?"

"Who else are they going to blame?" he asked.

I bit back a host of replies, like maybe they should blame Antoine or even Melanie for some of it. It didn't matter and it wasn't an argument I wanted to have. Let the crew hate me. They'd be gone in a day or two and I'd never see them again. I changed topics. "So we're going to go ahead and shoot the segment on my popcorn breakfast bars and fudge?" I asked. It actually hadn't occurred to me to ask whether or not we were. *Cooking the Belanger Way* and POPS had been pretty low on my priority list since I found Melanie. Like they hadn't even made the top ten. Leave it to Antoine to edge his way to the top of my list again without even trying.

"Of course. It is show business and they say the show must go on regardless of whatever terrible accident has befallen Melanie." Antoine massaged his temples. This couldn't be easy for him regardless of how calm he was trying to be. He'd relied on Melanie for years. She'd been part of the *Cooking the Belanger Way* family, the only family Antoine really had.

I nodded. Of course, the shoot would go on. It was a tragic accident, but Antoine was right. His audience would still expect episodes of the show with, perhaps, one of those sad "In Memory Of" notices in white type against a black background with Melanie's dates of birth and death. That was the only thing that would really change for the viewing public.

Antoine took my hand like he'd taken Lucy's. I couldn't help it. I felt that pull, that sensation of being a flower that suddenly gets sunlight. "Will you be all right, darling? I know this must have been a shock. Especially coming so soon after the death of your beloved Coco."

The mention of Coco was like a little shot of ice water into my veins. Coco would not have approved of my holding hands with my ex-husband. I slipped my hand out of his. "I'll be fine."

"I will come by your apartment tonight to check on you," he announced. It was so Antoine. Why wait for an invitation when you can invite yourself? It never occurred to him that he wouldn't be welcome somewhere.

"No," I said. "No, you won't. It's not necessary."

He hesitated. For a moment, he looked unsure. It wasn't a look I'd seen on Antoine before. Too bad. It had humanized him a bit. "It may not be necessary for you, but I think it might be for me."

I stood up. "That would be your problem."

It was a good exit line and I took it. I was pretty sure anyone who saw me would think I meant it, too. And I did. Or I wanted to. It was hardly my fault that I kept wondering what Antoine meant by that the whole way home.

Two

I dropped my car back at the house. The sky was gray, but the weather report said it would clear up later. I figured I'd chance it and walk. If I didn't walk to work, I'd end up spending all my time indoors, either at POPS or at home. Maybe some fresh air would help me clear away the images of Melanie playing on an endless loop in my head. I snapped my hair back in a twist to keep it from blowing in my face as I walked down the driveway.

I lived in the granny apartment over the garage of the house I grew up in. My sister, Sheriff Dan and my adorable nephew, Evan, live in the house itself. I was almost down the driveway to the sidewalk with Sprocket when Haley popped her head out the door. "What's going on?"

"I'm going to work." It seemed fairly self-evident to me. I am a creature of habit. I go to work pretty much every day. I was okay with stating the obvious, though.

The rest of Haley—and there was quite a bit of the rest of her these days—followed her head out the door. "That's not what I mean and you know it. I heard your name mentioned when Dan was called in this morning."

I sighed. I was beginning to suspect that pregnancy had heightened all of Haley's senses. She had the hearing of a bat these days. I wouldn't be surprised if she could echolocate. "I had a breakfast meeting scheduled with Antoine's assistant. When I got there, she was . . . uh . . ."

"Dead? I'm pretty sure I heard she was dead." Haley rubbed her pregnant tummy. "What kind of dead?"

Was it another trick question? How many kinds of dead were there? "The kind where you stop breathing and your heart doesn't beat anymore."

"Rebecca," she said, a warning note in her voice. "Was it an accident? A suicide? A murder?"

Haley wasn't usually this nosey about stuff. Then again, the last time there was an unexpected death in Grand Lake things got pretty dicey for our family. "I don't think they know yet."

She rubbed her tummy harder. If she didn't stop soon, she was going to leave a shiny spot. "Do you think it'll be easy to figure out?"

I wasn't getting it. "Why?"

"Rebecca!" She gestured at her stomach. "This baby could come any day now. Any day. I need Dan available at the drop of a hat. You, too. You have to take care of Evan when I go into the hospital."

Ohhhhh. Now it made sense. She didn't care so much about Melanie as she did about how much Melanie's death was going to mess up her life. That made a lot more sense.

My sister was deep into nesting mode. I hadn't been around when Evan was imminent, but based on what Dan said, it was pretty much the same. Everything narrowed down into pinpoint focus. The nursery was ready. Diapers had been purchased. The freezer was stocked. But we were now veering into territory that my sister could not control and that was going to drive her certifiably batshit.

Our parents died in a car accident when I was sixteen and Haley was eighteen. I reacted by going totally out of control in the usual teenage girl kinds of ways. Some drinking. Some inappropriate boys. Some minor juvenile delinquency. At least until Coco Bittles realized I could cook and took me under her wing. Haley had gone the complete opposite direction. She'd stepped into adulthood and responsibility and never stopped. She lived in the land of order and control. While she loved being a mom (and who wouldn't with a sweet little cupcake of a boy like Evan), there were a lot of things out of her control, and that tended to make her a teensy-weensy bit craycray.

"I will be here," I assured her. "I have my cell phone charged and on me at all times. Text me a 911 and I will come running. Dan will be here, too. You know he will. There is nothing that is higher on his priority list than you, Evan and the Peanut." The Peanut has been our code name for my new niece or nephew ever since Haley brought home an ultrasound that looked a little like Mr. Peanut had taken up residence in her stomach. Sans monocle, thank goodness.

Haley's face crumpled a little. My sister was generally not weepy, but the end-of-pregnancy hormones were wreaking havoc with her tear ducts. "Promise?" Her voice sounded really tiny.

I bopped up the stairs to the porch with Sprocket at my heels. "Stick-a-needle-in-my-eye promise. Scarlett-O'Hara-swearing-to-the-sky-she'd-never-be-hungry-again promise. Inigo-Montoya-vowing-revenge promise." I wrapped my arms around her as best I could.

She snuffled into my hair. "I'm so glad you came back. I'm so glad you're home."

"Me, too, sis. Me, too. Sometimes I wish I'd never left." I released her and waved good-bye. This time she let me go.

Sprocket and I hurried along. I would have loved to make our usual detour up to the lighthouse on Lake Erie, but we were running way too late for that. A lot of people had expected me to avoid the area, what with the almost-being-killed-at-the-lighthouse thing. Even I hadn't been sure how I would react to walking by it on Sprocket's and my usual route. It, however, didn't seem to be the center of my concern. I won't lie and say that none of what happened there affected me. I've had some bad dreams. Dreams where I'm swallowed up by the end of a gun barrel. Dreams where Sprocket didn't pull through. Dreams where the lighthouse burns around me.

But they were only dreams. I may wake up gasping, but then Sprocket will lick my face and I calm right down again.

My cell phone buzzed in my pocket. "Good morning, Garrett," I sang into my cell.

"I can't believe you didn't call me." He didn't sound as pleased to talk with me as I was to talk to him. "You find a dead body and I hear about it from Pearl."

Grand Lake was a small town and news traveled faster than melted butter over a hot scone. Pearl was Garrett's secretary and was hooked up to the town's gossip pipeline like a Hummer to a gas pump. I winced. I probably should have called him. He seemed to feel kind of proprietary after saving my life. It was nice. I wasn't used to it, though. "Sorry. It all happened so fast and then Dan was questioning me and then Antoine . . ."

"Antoine? Antoine knew about this before I did?" It sounded like the words were coming out through gritted teeth.

Tactical error there. Garrett, like Dan, was also not my ex-husband's biggest fan. In fact, there didn't seem to be a lot of Antoine fans among the town's male population. The ladies were a different story. That didn't endear Antoine any more to the guys. "Garrett, it was his assistant who was dead. Of course he heard about it first."

There was a grunt on the other end of the line that I took as a lawyerly acknowledgment that he didn't have a good counterargument.

I turned the corner onto Main Street, onto the line of neat little shops, most in old bungalows that had been converted, one of which was POPS. "I'll make it up to you," I said. "I'm trying out some new recipes. Come by the shop for lunch. You can help me figure out what's working and what's not."

"What kind of recipes?" I heard a softening in his voice. I was honestly beginning to wonder if anyone had ever cooked for this man before in his life. I'd swayed a lot of people with food, but he was a total pushover. He was on the edge of forgiving, poised on the precipice of magnanimity just because of the offer of popcorn. "I don't want to give too many details, but I will tell you that bacon is involved."

"I'll be there at one." He hung up.

I tucked the phone back in my pocket with a smile. Who knew that pork products would be the key to solving all relationship problems?

I walked into my shop and found Susanna and Sam slumped in the little ice cream parlor chairs in the corner looking a little like they'd been kneaded and punched down. "How'd it go?"

Sam lifted his head from being pillowed on his arms. "How do you do that every morning? That's insane!"

"It's the new pumpkin-spice popcorn bars. The lines have been getting really long since I introduced those at the beginning of October." I'd wager I'd had close to a ten percent jump in business since I started selling them.

"People are super grumpy before they've had their coffee," Susanna said. "Like super, super grumpy."

"But then they brighten right up as soon as you caffeinate them, right?" As satisfying as drinking a cup of really well-made coffee was, it really didn't hold a candle to watching someone else drink a cup of coffee that you'd made really well yourself.

"Truth." Sam stood up and stretched, which meant his fingertips were practically brushing the ceiling. I'm pretty sure the boy grows an inch a week. Then he hitched up his jeans and said, "Come on, Suze. If we leave now, we'll be on time."

Susanna took off her apron and grabbed her backpack. "Ready." Then they were gone, Susanna's long dark ponytail swinging behind them like a flag.

The high school in Grand Lake had a late start on Thursdays, which was why my two helpers could be there that morning. It had gotten me through a lot of busy days, but the truth was I was going to need more permanent help for the morning rush. I had no idea where I was going to find that help, unfortunately.

Help or no, I figured I'd better get started in the kitchen or Garrett was never going to forgive me.

As usual, once I was in the kitchen I got lost. Lost in the sizzle and the steam, the scents and the tastes and the sounds and the sights. A few customers came in and out, wanting treats for their morning coffee breaks or mid-morning snacks for preschoolers. Mainly, however, the shop was quiet, letting me enjoy immersing myself into my own crazy kitchen world of popcorn.

That is, until a knock on the back door signaled the arrival of the owner of the shop next to mine. "Come in," I sang out. "I have treats."

Anastasia Bloom, owner of Blooms, the flower shop next to mine, walked in along with Faith Bates. Faith was Barbara Werner's niece. She'd moved to Grand Lake only a few weeks before, but she'd already become a regular at my back door with Annie for morning coffee break. Barbara was hoping to ease her way out of the antiques business and Faith was looking for a fresh start.

"Something smells amazing." Faith walked over to the counter to look over my shoulder.

"Bacon," I said as I heated up water for coffee. "Everyone loves bacon."

"What's it for?" Annie took her usual place at the long table in the center of my kitchen.

"I'm thinking of expanding into having some lunch offerings," I said over my shoulder as I measured grounds.

Annie raised one eyebrow. "You're going to need help."

"I know." I chewed on my lip. "I'm not sure where to even start, though."

"Hey, speaking of starting," Annie interrupted. "How did the meeting with Melanie go? When is the taping going to start? Is Antoine going to be here in the shop?" She sounded a little too interested in Antoine's schedule. A lot of the women in town had been a little too interested in his schedule. Annie surprised me, though. She had a silver fox of her own these days. What really surprised me, though, was that she didn't know exactly how the meeting had gone. Or not gone.

I looked at her closely. Then I looked over at Faith, whose face was equally bland. Were they bluffing? Or had they seriously not heard? "The meeting did not go well."

Annie snorted. "Figures. That woman has been jealous of you since she laid eyes on you. Is she trying to sabotage the segment?"

Faith shook her head. "Allowing your ex-husband back in your life is a mistake, if you ask me." Faith had recently gone through a fairly acrimonious divorce and her opinion of ex-husbands was pretty low. Her opinion of present husbands wasn't much higher. Actually, to be honest, she was kind of anti-man at the moment.

I looked back at Annie. She was a damn good actress. She'd had me and pretty much the entire town convinced that she hated the very air that our illustrious mayor Allen Thompson breathed. Turned out they were having a steamy affair right under everyone's noses. I hadn't had a clue. In fact, I'd been convinced that Allen was lurking around behind our stores for reasons that were a lot more sinister than booty calls. I'd accidentally outed them when I smacked him over the head with a flowerpot while they were in flagrante delicto on Annie's potting table. "You really don't know?" I asked.

"Know what? I've had my nose stuck in the flowers for the Elks Lodge Supper Dance all morning." She looked over at Faith. "Did you hear anything?"

She shook her head. "I dropped the girls at school and went to the shop. I've been photographing items for Auntie Barbara's eBay shop. I had music on. I didn't hear anything."

I looked back and forth between the two of them. "I didn't have the meeting with Melanie. She's dead."

In retrospect that may not have been the best way to

tell someone about an unexpected death. Annie reared back in her chair, which caught on a crack in the wood floor and tipped over backward, landing with her legs sticking up in the air. Faith dropped her coffee mug, which fell onto the floor and cracked.

I raced to Annie and leaned over her. "Are you all right?"

She blinked up at me, her clear blue eyes even brighter than usual. "What happened?"

"You fell over backward." How hard had she hit her head?

"I know that. How did Melanie die?" She reached her hands up to me to have me help her up.

I straddled her and tried to pull her up into a sitting position. It wasn't working. "I don't know. I think she may have electrocuted herself. She was in the bathtub and there was a blow-dryer in the tub . . ."

"That shouldn't work." Annie started to wiggle her way backward on her back.

Faith crouched behind Annie and tried to tug her free. "Don't they have some kind of safety thing built in? The weird plug thing."

I didn't know. I have a poor relationship with blow-dryers. Point one at me and I erupt into frizz. You don't even have to turn it on. "Maybe it malfunctioned."

Faith tsked. "Even so, people should know better than to have electrical appliances near the tub. Was she dim?"

"No," I said. "Actually very sharp. Maybe she knew about the plug thing and thought it would be safe." That didn't explain why she would have someone else's blow-dryer there and plugged in, though, and I was still convinced it wasn't hers.

Annie wiggled herself off the chair so she could sit up. We had managed to get her into a sitting position again when Dan walked in. He took one look at the three of us on the floor with me crouched over Annie and Faith with her arms around Annie's waist and said, "I don't want to know."

After sending Annie and Faith off with some still-too-hot-to-eat bacon popcorn, I poured Dan a cup of coffee. He took a sip and set it down. He didn't add any cream or sugar.

"There's something about the three of you together that makes me think of Shakespeare's witches," he said.

"I can see that. I'm totally planning a new Eye of Newt Popcorn." I sat down across from him with my own cup of coffee.

He took another sip.

"Really? That's it? No sigh of relief?" I prodded. I thought there'd at least be a smile when drinking my coffee after the weird brown liquid at the café.

He took out his notepad. "You make a lovely cup of coffee, Rebecca. You know that. I need to know a few more things about what you saw this morning."

"I can't think of anything I noticed that I didn't tell you about." I got up and started wiping down my already clean counters. I certainly didn't want to mentally take myself back to that hotel bathroom.

"Humor me a second." He took another sip of coffee. "I need to know more about the blow-dryer."

I stopped scrubbing and turned to look at him. "The blow-dryer? Beyond that it didn't have a diffuser? Why?"

"It wasn't the hotel's blow-dryer. At least it wasn't the one that came with her room. That one was still in its bag stowed underneath the sink." He leaned back in his chair.

"Well, it wasn't hers." I shrugged.

He didn't respond to that. "Did you notice anything else about it? Anything else . . . girly that I might not know?"

Ah. Poor man. Dan had never owned a blow-dryer in his life and Haley's hair was like mine, too curly to suffer that kind of treatment. "Sorry. I don't have anything else."

"Someone altered that blow-dryer, Rebecca. Someone removed the GFCI protection," he said.

That must have been what Annie had been talking about, about why a blow-dryer wouldn't—or shouldn't—electrocute someone. "Do they all have that?"

"Since about 1991. There used to be electrocutions from blow-dryers all the time. Then the Consumer Product Safety Commission mandated that all units have GFCI protection. You should be able to throw a blow-dryer into a tub while it's on and have it shut itself off harmlessly. Unless someone messes with it and removes that GFCI protection," he explained.

"Why would someone do that?" I was pretty sure I didn't want to hear the answer.

"The one reason to do that is to use it to electrocute someone," Dan said, bringing the front legs of his chair down with a thump. "It doesn't make the blow-dryer more effective or lighter or . . . well, anything that I can figure out."

I stared at him. "Who would do something like that?"

"I think Melanie might have done it herself." Dan shook his head. "I think it may have been suicide."

"Wait. She went out and bought a blow-dryer just to electrocute herself with it?" There had to be better ways.

"Looks like she might have done exactly that. You were right about her having one with a diffuser. It was in her suitcase. So she must have bought this one for this purpose." Dan rubbed at his face. I refilled his coffee cup.

"Do you know why?" My life had pretty much disintegrated a couple of years ago. I'd been down. Way down. But suicide? How far down did you have to be to decide that was your best path?

"We've only started to look, but I can tell you she was in a massive amount of debt. Tens of thousands of dollars and the creditors were closing in," Dan said. "We ran a preliminary background check and found that. I'm not sure what more we'll find as we dig a little further."

Antoine might not pay great, but he didn't pay subsistence wages, either. "That surprises me."

"It might not if you'd taken a closer look at her lifestyle. The girl liked to spend." He pushed his coffee mug at me for a refill.

I'd sort of known that. When I'd still been around Melanie on a regular basis, I'd noticed more than once that she always had top-of-the-line items. Kate Spade purses. Louboutin shoes. The newest phones. Late-model cars. She'd made me feel a little shabby sometimes. Still, debt was a reason to declare bankruptcy, not kill yourself. Besides . . . "Her hotel room didn't look like someone who was getting ready to commit suicide. Her hotel room looked like someone who was getting ready for a date." I poured the last little bit of coffee into my own mug and sat down across from him.

"That's not uncommon, Rebecca, especially with women. They want to be found looking good." He turned his mug around and around in his hands.

"But she wasn't found looking good, Dan. She was naked. In the bathtub. I mean, next to being found on the toilet, I'm not sure I can think of a way most women would want less to be found. I mean, it wasn't even a bubble bath!" No woman with a shred of vanity in her would have wanted to be found like that.

He looked up, surprised. "Bubble bath? Why would that make a difference?"

"You know, all those frothy bubbles strategically placed. I can see being okay being found like that. But naked? With no makeup? All pruney and shriveled from the water? No." I shook my head. "Absolutely not."

"I'll take it under advisement." He shoved a computer printout of a photo across the table to me. "Is this the woman you saw in the café this morning before you went up to Melanie's room?"

The woman had dark hair like the one I'd seen, but it definitely wasn't her. She did look somehow familiar, but I wasn't sure why. I pushed the paper back. "No. Not her."

"You're sure?" he asked, sliding the paper a little bit toward me again.

"I'm sure. I may have seen this woman before, but it wasn't the lady in the café. Who is she?"

"Just the only other dark-haired woman who was staying at the hotel besides Antoine's crew. We tried her room. No answer." Dan slid the paper over to the corner of the table. "Probably just someone passing through."

"So whoever I saw came into the hotel just to go to the café?" I couldn't imagine the desperation that would take.

"Possibly." He stood up. "Thanks for the coffee, Rebecca. See you at home tonight?"

I nodded. "I'll be there. Haley's about two seconds from a full freak-out, you know."

He grimaced. "I'm aware."

He was almost out the door when one more thing occurred

to me. "Hey, Dan. If it was suicide, why do you think she left the door to the hotel room unlocked?"

Shyly, I pushed the plate toward Garrett. "I made it just for you."

He snorted. "I'm well aware that you were making this anyway and all I am is your guinea pig."

"A super cute guinea pig. A guinea pig whose opinion I care about." I pushed the plate a little closer to him. I wasn't lying. He was totally supercute. Dark-haired, dark-eyed, broad-shouldered. It was a nice package. I'd liked him pretty well before he saved my life. Risking his own well-being to make sure of mine hadn't exactly lowered him in my estimation. The fact that he was the one who rushed toward the gun while the man who'd sworn undying love and devotion to me had run the opposite way was not lost on me, either. I felt confident I wasn't repeating the same mistakes. Garrett was like the anti-Antoine.

He picked up one cluster and took a healthy bite, then nearly choked. "Too sweet."

I frowned. I'll admit it. I have a sweet tooth. Sometimes it skews what I think tastes right. I took a bite. Ewww. No. I must have gotten the proportions wrong. It wasn't a mistake I would usually make, but today hadn't been a usual day. Apparently finding dead bodies threw me off my game. "Sorry. I don't think I'm at my best today."

He picked the bacon from it. "As peace offerings go, it leaves a little to be desired."

"I'll try again tomorrow." I swept up the failed experiment and put it in the trash.

"Will you try not to stumble across any dead bodies tomorrow, too?" he asked.

I thought about it as I came back to the table and sat down. "I will certainly do my best."

"And if you do, could you shoot me a text or something so I don't hear about it from my secretary?" There was hurt in his voice. I'd put it there. That didn't feel so fabulous.

"It'll be on the top of my post-body-finding to-do list from now on," I promised. I gave myself a little mental kick. Antoine had mainly cared about my activities as they related to him. Having someone around who just cared was taking some adjustment.

He reached out and took my hand. "Seriously, are you okay?"

I sighed. "It's not like before. It's not like seeing Coco. I didn't know Melanie that well and what I did know of her I didn't particularly like. It's not like I wished her dead or anything, but it's also not the punch in the gut that Coco's death was."

He nodded. "I can see that. But?"

"But what?"

He reached out and caressed my cheek. I found myself leaning into the touch. "I can see the caveat on your face, Rebecca. It's not the same as Coco, but . . ."

I pulled away and covered my eyes. "But it's still awful." My voice cracked a bit. I doubted I'd ever be able to erase the vision of Melanie, naked and vulnerable in her bathtub, face turned to the ceiling, hair blossoming around her like that painting of Ophelia.

Ophelia. Ophelia committed suicide. Maybe Dan was right. Maybe Melanie did kill herself. Who was I to question the methods of someone so deeply in despair that she would choose to end her own life? Maybe I'd decide that throwing an electrical appliance into the tub with me would be the best way out. Maybe I would buy one just for that purpose. I could see maybe not wanting to mess up your real blow-dryer in case you changed your mind. Maybe that's what had happened. Maybe something happened while she was getting ready for her date or whatever it was that pushed her over an edge on which she already tottered. I hadn't walked in her shoes. Not the Louboutins and not the sorrowful ones, either.

"Hey," he said, pulling my hand away from my face. "It's okay. It's normal. In fact, it would be kind of abnormal not to be upset. How about I take you to the movies tonight to take your mind off it?"

I shook my head. "Haley would kill me. I'm not allowed to be anywhere that requires me to turn off my cell phone until after she gives birth to the Peanut."

He chuckled. "She is getting a little panicky about all the arrangements. Dan jumps about ten feet every time his cell phone buzzes."

"You should see the house! I don't think I've ever seen it gleam like that. There's not a surface that hasn't been scrubbed and polished. I'm afraid if I stand still in there she'll go after me with lemon Pledge and a rag."

"Fine. How about I pick up some takeout and a DVD?" he offered.

I loved that he understood my priorities. "That'll be great, but no takeout. I'll cook. It'll be my makeup for that mess." I pointed to the garbage can and the sad remains of the bacon popcorn.

"Let me know if you change your mind." He stood up and kissed the top of my head then left.

I cleaned up the kitchen and started cutting up blocks of Coco Pop Fudge for the afternoon rush that usually started around two. I made more coffee as well. POPS was quickly turning into a place for people to chase away those mid-afternoon drowsies. That was fine with me. It was, however, getting to be a little relentless between the morning rush and the afternoon rush. Annie was right. If I really was going to start adding lunch, I needed more help than Susanna and Sam could give me with their school and sports schedules.

I needed to move forward, but suddenly a wave of exhaustion washed over me. I sat down at the table and ate a chunk of fudge. Sugar would probably help.

It did. A little. It also made me think. Coco Pop Fudge would never have existed if my life hadn't fallen apart. If my marriage hadn't fallen apart, I wouldn't have moved back to Grand Lake and I wouldn't have spent hours in the kitchen with Coco trying to find a way to collaborate. If Coco hadn't died, I wouldn't have ended up making Coco Pop Fudge my own. Some bad things happened to bring that fudge into existence. Yet, it still tasted sweet.

Sprocket whined. I washed my hands and got him one of his own treats. No chocolate for him.

I went back to boxing up the fudge and brewing fresh coffee for my afternoon crowd. So bad things had happened to create this fudge, but then it had saved my store. Things had been bleak, but never bleak enough to make me want to take my own life. I'd found Coco Pop Fudge before I sank that low. I boxed up another block of fudge and wished that Melanie could have found her Coco Pop Fudge. Then maybe I wouldn't have found her in the bathtub of her hotel room.

Three

On the way home, Sprocket and I made our usual stop at the lighthouse on the edge of Lake Erie. Or we tried to. As we came up Marina Road, I saw a knot of people clustered around the edge of the pier. "Our spot's getting popular," I said to Sprocket.

He harrumphed in reply.

Then I saw why it was so popular. Antoine and his crew were filming. Apparently the crew had decided they would rather stay busy than take the day off to mourn Melanie. I knew they wanted to shoot parts of the town. It was always part of Antoine's shows. Wherever they went, they tried to give as much local color as possible. It was almost as much a travelogue as it was a cooking show. You couldn't do much better than the lighthouse made out of melted-down cannons from the Civil War, with its original Fresnel light, for iconic images of Grand Lake. Given Antoine's history with it, however, I was surprised. I slipped into the edge of the crowd to watch.

My presence didn't go unnoticed. It started with a couple of elbow nudges and glances from Sophia Kelley and Katherine Newman, who then tapped Malcolm Taylor on the shoulder and whispered something in his ear. Malcolm chuckled and bumped Janis Carpenter with his shoulder. She turned, looked at me and giggled. I pretended not to see any of it.

The cameraman—I thought his name was Jason—was checking the light on Antoine's face as he stood far enough from the lighthouse so that it would show up in the shot. The fading light of the day played over the whitewashed walls. There was enough wind to whip the waves up a little but not so much as to muss Antoine's hair. It was going to be a beautiful shot. I had a little twinge of pleasure from thinking that the segment that featured POPS would be gorgeous. That couldn't hurt anything. Then Antoine opened his mouth.

"It was at this very spot that I found a crazed person threatening Rebecca Anderson, owner of POPS, with a gun. I was able to make my escape and summon the authorities before harm was done to her," he said, looking earnestly into the camera. "I am grateful every day that I was able to stop that tragedy from unfolding."

I gasped. Was he seriously going to rewrite history to that extent? He didn't stop tragedy from unfolding. Garrett did. Plus, it was at least a little bit tragic. Sprocket had taken a bullet. He still limped a bit because of it. And the crazed person? That person was locked up. Kind of tragic, wasn't it? Not to mention losing Coco.

"Good take, Antoine," Jason said lowering his camera. "Where to now?"

I pushed my way through the crowd. "Antoine, what are you doing?"

He turned to me, a smile breaking out on his face. "Rebecca, we are getting some film of this beautiful Grand Lake landmark."

"I can see that. I also heard what you said. You need to cut that part." I stalked straight to him, Sprocket growling at my heels.

Antoine looked surprised. "Why?"

I threw my hands in the air. "Because it's not true."

"What part of it is not true? You were threatened by a crazy person with a gun. I summoned authorities. All true." He took a step toward me. We were nearly nose to nose.

Sprocket growled a little louder. I wanted to growl, too. "You didn't save my life," I said. "You ran away."

"Ran for help. Ran away. I think you are splitting the hairs." Antoine set his hand on my shoulder.

I shrugged him off. "I think you are deliberately misleading people to make yourself the hero of the story. You were not the hero." I turned to the crew and the crowd. "He was not the hero."

Lucy marched over to where we were standing. "You need to go, Rebecca. You're disrupting the shoot. We only have the light for a few more minutes."

"The light? You're worried about the light? How about worrying about the truth?" I whirled on her.

"I don't have to worry about the truth, Rebecca. Antoine explained the whole story to us. Nothing he's said is untrue. We double-checked the facts. He was the one who called the police." Lucy stood with her feet braced and her hands on her hips.

"Yes, but he wasn't the one who threw himself at an armed person who had already killed once." I drew myself up.

Lucy pressed her lips together. "What the situation required was sound and rational thinking. I'd say summoning the authorities showed exactly the kind of quick mental work that really helps in an emergency situation."

I opened my mouth and closed it again. It would be a waste of time arguing with Lucy. Her loyalty was absolute and it belonged to Antoine. I turned back to Antoine. "We're not done discussing this, Antoine."

"We can talk about it tonight," he agreed.

"No. We can't." Sprocket and I pushed our way back through the crowd. For a second, I thought I saw the woman from the coffee shop that morning in the mob. I stopped and tried to push my way to her, but people shifted and I lost sight of her. Or maybe I'd never seen her at all. It was hard to tell with so many people milling around. I elbowed my way back to the edge of the group and went home feeling cranky and tired.

My ex certainly knew how to overachieve. Antoine had done what an unbalanced person with a gun hadn't been able to do. He'd taken my happy spot and turned it sour.

I got back to my apartment and immediately started making risotto. Risotto required attention. You needed to stay with it, stirring, adding liquid a little at a time and helping the rice absorb it. It will reward you back with bursts of flavor on the midpoint of your tongue and a warm sensation in your tummy. In the meantime, it made me focus on watching the rice turn golden in the olive oil rather than strangling Antoine.

Garrett showed up and settled himself at the breakfast bar in my little kitchen. Sprocket got up from his bed in the corner and laid his chin on Garrett's thigh. Garrett gave him an under-chin scratch and said, "You didn't have to cook. I could have picked something up."

"From where?" The options for takeout in Grand Lake were exceedingly limited.

"The diner," he answered without hesitation. Perhaps like a man who ate too much takeout from the diner. No wonder the promise of bacon made him forgive my transgressions.

I considered. The diner did make a fine grilled cheese and there's no way to get fries the way I like them without an industrial fryer, but by the time Garrett got them here, they'd be soggy and cold. Blechh. Not interested. "I like cooking." It soothed me. Some people drank. Some people exercised. Some people gambled or shopped. I cooked. "And this is simple stuff."

"Yeah. It looks real simple." Garrett shook his head.

I looked around at the chopped onions and garlic, the knobs of butter, and the mound of freshly grated Parmesan on the kitchen counter. "Looks can be deceiving."

"Can I help?" he asked. Then, after I shook my head, he asked, "How about I open a bottle of wine?"

"That would be lovely." There are all kinds of ways to help in a kitchen, after all. Plus, I'd need the wine for the risotto in a few minutes. I opened a cabinet to get a bowl.

"How long has that been creaking like that?" Garrett asked, pointing at the cabinet door.

"Long enough that I don't know what you're talking about." I returned my attention to the risotto.

He retrieved my toolbox from the closet and started doing something to my cabinet door hinges. After a minute, he opened and closed it. The door was silent.

"How'd you learn to do that?" I asked.

"After my stint as a waiter while I was in college, I did some carpentry." He poured two glasses of wine.

"There's an awful lot I don't know about you, Garrett Mills." I pointed at him with my wooden spoon.

"I like to be a man of mystery." He raised his glass to me and blew me a kiss. "Now keep cooking. That stuff smells good. Plus you owe me for feeding me whatever that stuff was this afternoon."

I was enjoying that lovely floaty sensation I get after the second sip or so, when someone knocked at the door. "I swear, if that's Haley checking on my Peanut Day readiness . . ." I said as I answered the door, not sure exactly what I'd do to my pregnant sister if it really was her. Make fat jokes? Pretend to forget Evan's name? Pinch her really hard on the butt?

It didn't matter. It wasn't Haley. It was Antoine. With a bottle of wine and a bouquet of flowers. As if he was showing up for a date.

I'm pretty sure both Garrett and Sprocket growled. "What are you doing here?" I asked.

"I told you I would stop by to check on you." He held out the wine and flowers and sniffed the air. "You're making risotto. I knew you were upset. You always make risotto when you're upset."

It made me want to growl that he knew me that well. "I told you it wasn't necessary. I'm fine."

He shrugged. "Just because something is not necessary does not mean it shouldn't be done. Fresh Parmesan on top of your risotto is not necessary, but you were planning on putting it in, were you not?"

Garrett walked over to stand behind me. "Your presence is not only unnecessary, but unwelcome."

Uh-oh. I shifted to stay between them. The last time the two of them tangled, Antoine ended up with two black eyes and I had to bail Garrett out of jail.

Antoine rolled his eyes. "The small-town lawyer? Still, *chérie*?" he asked me, ignoring Garrett.

"Still," I said. "Good night. Go comfort your crew. They're probably all still shaken up about Melanie."

As if on cue, Antoine's phone rang. "Yes, Brooke." He shoved the flowers and wine at me as if I was a servant and turned away. "No. I don't think that would work." He stopped and listened again. "Please explain to Lucy that . . ." He broke off and listened again. "Yes. Fine. I am on my way." He hung up the phone. "I am sorry, darling. I must go. You were correct. The staff, they do not know how to operate without Melanie. The smallest thing throws them into chaos. I must oversee them." He turned to go.

"Wait," I called after him, holding out the wine and the flowers.

He shook his head. "Keep them. Enjoy them. Maybe think a kind thought about me as you do." Then he trudged back down the steps, looking more than a little dejected.

I shut the door and turned around, flowers and wine still in my hands.

"What are you going to do with those?" Garrett asked. Were his shoulders always so close to his ears?

I looked at the wine bottle and then the flowers. It was a nice bottle from a little winery not too far from L'Oiseau Gris. It wasn't cheap and I wasn't sure you could even get a bottle of it in stores around here. It was also not my favorite. Too much French oak in their barrels for my taste. It was, however, one of Antoine's favorites. The flowers were lovely as well. I wondered if he got them from Annie. I wasn't sure where else to get a bouquet like this one in

Grand Lake. "I'll take the flowers to Barbara tomorrow. She likes bouquets in her store. Not sure about the wine, though. Maybe regift it to someone?"

Garrett's shoulders relaxed a little. "I'll put the flowers in water while you finish cooking."

But as I walked past him, he grabbed me around the waist and pulled me to him. Then he kissed me.

It was the first time I ever burned risotto.

The next morning at POPS, I printed out a Help Wanted sign from the Internet. Seriously, was there anything a person couldn't find with the right search engine? I was taping it up on the window of POPS when Eric Gladstone came in. Eric was a firefighter and emergency medical technician. We'd met when Barbara got bashed on the head a month or so ago and then met again when I was knocked on the noggin by the same person. I'd brought him some Coco Pop Fudge as a thank-you and since then he'd become one of my regulars. He worked a twenty-four-hour shift and usually came in as I was opening before his shift started at seven in the morning and then a little after I opened the next day when he got off at seven that morning.

He must have been going on duty because it was only quarter to seven when his face popped up in the glass of POPS's door.

"You're hiring?" he asked through the glass.

"I hope so," I said, opening the door so he could walk in.

"Full-time?" he asked.

I headed for the kitchen to get his coffee. "Not yet. Part-time for now. Maybe fifteen or twenty hours a week."

"Counter only or would the person help in the kitchen?" He trailed after me.

"Eric?" I asked. "Are you thinking about moonlighting here at POPS?"

He blushed. "No. Not me. A friend. I know someone who's looking for a part-time gig who also happens to be amazing in the kitchen." He blushed a little harder.

"A grown-up or a kid?" I asked. I needed someone who could be in the shop during regular hours, not just after school and weekends.

"Grown-up," he confirmed.

"Tell your friend to come by. Make sure he or she mentions your name. Now, do you want the usual?" I started pulling out to-go cups.

"Times two," he said. I packaged up four white-chocolate cranberry breakfast bars and two large coffees. By the time I'd taken his money and sent him out the door, the morning rush was on and I didn't have time to wonder what had made Eric blush to the roots of his handsome crew-cutted head.

Around ten, Dan stopped in for coffee. "Have I finally converted you into being a coffee snob?" I asked, pulling out a chair at the kitchen table.

He shook his head and sat down. "If I only drank good coffee, I'd spend three-quarters of my life with a caffeine headache."

"So what brings you here?" It wasn't like he never stopped by, but usually during working hours Dan was . . . working, not hanging out with me drinking coffee and eating whatever breakfast bars came out too deformed to sell.

"Oh, just wanted to see how you were doing." He cocked

his head and looked at me. "You know, after finding Melanie."

Ah. Checking up on me. "I'm fine." I was, but I didn't want to dwell on it. Sometimes a person was better off not thinking too much. "How's the investigation going?"

"Everything we're finding points to suicide, Rebecca. Everything." Dan picked at his breakfast bar.

"What kind of everything? So her finances were a mess. Everybody's finances are a mess at some point or another." It didn't seem like enough to me.

"That boyfriend you remembered from a couple of years ago? Well, he left her about six months ago. It's part of why she's swimming in debt. She couldn't make the payments on her condo without him." He turned his mug in circles on the table. Something was bothering him. He only did that when something was gnawing at him. "Of course, her reaction to that seemed to be buying an awful lot of purses over the Internet. Seriously, why do those things cost so much?"

"Workmanship and snobbery," I said, although I wasn't sure I always understood why, either. "Okay. Disappointment in love and money. That's not a good combination." Still, didn't everyone end up in a place like that at some point? It was part of the whole adulting thing. I wasn't saying it didn't suck, but it was on the list with paying taxes and regular flossing. If you were a grown-up you pushed through those things.

"Her cat died, too." He stopped rotating the mug and took another sip.

That got me. I'd be devastated if something happened to Sprocket. I had been beside myself when he was shot. I didn't have to imagine it. Hideous. "Oh. That's hard." I reached down and patted his head.

"Yeah. The cat—Freckles—was seventeen years old and after the boyfriend left, the cat stopped eating." He shook his head. "Like maybe he liked the boyfriend better than her. That's got to hurt."

"How do you know that?" I stood up to get the coffee to refill his mug.

He shifted in his chair. "Facebook and Twitter. It didn't take Huerta long to dig up all that."

"Huerta's cyberstalking Melanie?" Sometimes I wondered if there was anything Huerta couldn't do. Or wouldn't do if Dan asked him.

"It's not stalking when the police do it, Rebecca. Then it's investigating and is considered good form." He smiled and there was my old friend. The boy who put a worm in my chocolate milk. My partner in crime through a million junior high and high school adventures.

"So she's in debt, her boyfriend left her, and her cat died." I winced as I sat down. "It sounds like a country song."

"Pretty close. Her car broke down, too. I think it would have had to be a truck to be a really good country song."

It still bothered me, though. Something still didn't feel right. "Did she leave any kind of note?"

"No, but that's not uncommon," he said.

"The door and the clothes still bug me. Why lay all those outfits out and then not wear any of them? And why wasn't the door fully closed?" I couldn't come up with a scenario where I would do any of those things, but then again, I wasn't Melanie.

"There could be an easy explanation. Maybe she left the door a little ajar so it would be easy for someone to get in and find her. Maybe she thought about dressing herself up, but decided that it was too much effort. You know how

it is when you're down. Everything feels like it's too much."
There was a note in his voice I hadn't heard before.

I gave Dan a look. "When have you ever been depressed?"
Dan was always a ship sailing through calm waters. He'd
been that for me through my childhood and now he was
that stable ship for my sister and my nephew. I'd never seen
his boat rock, but maybe I hadn't been looking. There were
those years I was away and, embarrassingly, those years
when I was too involved with looking at myself to notice
much about anyone else.

"No one's up and happy all the time, Bec. Even if I were
perpetually cheerful, I could still have empathy for depressed
people and listen to what they say," he said, not looking up
at me.

That shut me up for a second. I put my hand on his
shoulder. "If you were depressed and I wasn't there for
you, I'm sorry." I doubled my resolve to be there for Dan
and Haley and Evan from now on.

He patted my hand. "I'm fine, Bec. Just fine."

"How's Antoine's crew taking it?" I asked.

"Not well. There's a lot of chaos. I guess Melanie ran
a pretty tight ship and no one else seems to know how to
steer it. Brooke and Lucy? They're bickering like an old
married couple. Your guy isn't really helping, either." Dan
said *your guy* like a person might say *your diseased worm
with leprosy.*

"My guy? You mean Antoine? I'm pretty sure the divorce
papers definitively prove that he is no longer my guy." I
felt defensive. He wasn't my guy, but the only reason he
was here was because of me. The only reason this whole
mess was on Dan's plate, rocking his usually stable ship,
was because of me.

Dan pressed his lips together. "You're right. I'm sorry. Still, he's kind of a mess."

That surprised me a little. Mess and Antoine didn't exactly go together. He didn't seem in too bad a shape the night before. "What kind of a mess?"

"I think he might have been drinking, for one. Then he keeps crying." Dan didn't look at me as he explained.

"Antoine?" The crying I understood. Antoine's passions lived pretty near the surface. Drinking during the day? That really wasn't his style.

"Yes, Antoine. He keeps asking if there were signs he should have seen or if he could have done something to prevent it," Dan said, leaning back and scratching his chest. "It's like he feels responsible and that makes me suspicious."

"I can see him feeling guilty. If someone you spent every day with killed herself, you'd feel a little responsible. Maybe you should cut him a little slack." I probably would be asking those same questions if I were in Dan's shoes, but I was pretty sure he was on the wrong track.

Dan nodded. "You're right. Maybe you're right about me cutting him slack, too." He shrugged. "We still have a few more things to check out before we close the case, but I'm pretty sure I know how this is going to go."

"What kind of things?" I asked.

"Mainly details. There are a few things bothering me still, like why there aren't any fingerprints on the blow-dryer."

That seemed like a no-brainer to me. "It was in the tub with her, under water."

"Yeah, but there should still be a few partials at least on the plastic and definitely one or two on the inside where she had to alter it. So far it's completely clean. That seems a little weird to me."

It did to me, too. "Thanks for letting me know." I shook my head. So sad. I might not have liked Melanie much, but I certainly would never have wanted her to be in a place that seemed so without hope that she would take her own life.

"Thanks for keeping your nose out of it." He shifted in his chair and turned his coffee cup around a few times. "Although speaking of Antoine, Haley wants to know if that was him showing up at your place last night."

My eyes widened. "Haley sent you to check up on me?" That explained the mid-morning coffee klatch.

"Not exactly. If she'd wanted me to check up on you, she would have sent me over to your place last night." He still hadn't met my eye.

Dan had a great cop face. He could do that thing they all seem to do with keeping their faces totally blank. With most people, it meant he could keep a lot to himself. It didn't work with me and he knew it. I could tell when he wasn't saying something and that's all I needed to know to get me to start digging. "She wanted you to do it last night, didn't she?"

He slumped. "Yeah. I told her it was overstepping."

I whistled. "How'd she take that?" I didn't imagine that she'd taken it well.

He snorted. "I got a ten-minute lecture on the importance of family and then a five-minute follow-up on your role in our birth plan."

"And you still didn't come over?" That had taken some serious spine.

He laughed. "Antoine had left by that time. I was just relieved I wasn't going to have to arrest Garrett for assault again." His face turned serious. "Try not to tweak her too much, Rebecca. She's really on edge."

"I'm not trying to tweak her. In fact, the only reason I was home instead of at the movies was so I wouldn't have to turn off my cell phone. Just in case," I protested.

He smiled. "I'll tell her that. Maybe it will calm her down a little if she knows you're taking this seriously."

"As seriously as a grease fire, and that's about as serious as I get."

Once Susanna arrived in the afternoon, I grabbed the flowers Antoine had given me to take them over to Barbara's. A dark-haired woman left the antique shop when I was still about a half a block away, started toward me then pivoted and took off walking in the opposite direction. For a moment, I thought it was the Café Lady again, but that was crazy, right? Besides, what did it matter if it was? Melanie had committed suicide. Inside the store, Faith had set up a table to one side and was getting ready to photograph a silver tea set. She had the camera on a tripod and a white sweep on the table. I waited until she'd squeezed off a few photos and was frowning at the digital display.

"Would flowers help?" I asked, holding out the bouquet.

She looked them over without taking them from me. "They're nice, but I'm not putting out for a measly bouquet."

"Wouldn't have expected it." I looked around for something to use as a vase.

"As long as we're clear." She started packing up items. "Where'd they come from?"

"Antoine brought them by my apartment last night." I selected a cut crystal vase and put the bouquet in it.

She whistled. "To make up for that fight you two had over by the lighthouse?"

I blinked. "How did you know about that?"

"Rebecca, you had about a quarter of the town as an audience." She stowed her camera behind the counter.

I cringed. "Do you think someone's told Garrett?"

"If Pearl hasn't, Megan probably did at lunchtime." She rearranged the flowers in the vase. "Auntie Barbara will love these. Good idea. Make sure he knows you won't even keep flowers from him, that you don't want a damn thing he's selling."

"But I kind of do. This spot on his TV show could set me up with enough business to keep the shop afloat for the next few years." I was starting to wonder if it was actually going to be worth it. Maybe Faith was right. Maybe I should tell Antoine to pack his stuff up and leave right now.

She glanced at her watch. "I gotta bounce. The girls will be done with soccer in a few minutes. Talk to you tomorrow?"

"Sure." I started to leave then remembered the dark-haired woman. "Hey, was there a customer in here right before I got here?"

Faith looked up from digging through her bag for her keys. "Yeah. Why?"

I shrugged. "She looked familiar. I was wondering who she was."

"I thought she was trying to shoplift something. She kept scurrying around near the window and . . . skulking."

"Skulking?" I wasn't sure what skulking looked like.

"I don't know how else to describe it. She skulked. Plus with that trench coat . . . it was weird." Faith picked up her purse.

She had a point. Does anyone really wear trench coats outside of New York City? "So what did you do?"

"I accused her of putting a paperweight in her pocket." Faith blushed.

"Had she?" I asked.

"No. But when she emptied her pockets, she started crying."

"Whoa! Seriously?"

Faith shifted her feet. "Yes. Seriously. Something about everything going wrong and her husband and I'm not sure what else. It got garbled."

"Then what?"

"I gave her some tissues, told her to dump the bastard's sorry ass, and she left."

A jilted woman. It probably wasn't even the woman I'd seen in the coffee shop or the one I'd seen by the lighthouse when Antoine was creating his own personal mythology. I was losing my mind, seeing conspiracies around every corner.

We said good-bye and I went back to POPS and the safety of my own kitchen. I did feel safe there. Safe and happy and content. I'd worked hard to make it that way. Maybe it could be my new happy place now that Antoine had ruined the lighthouse for me.

Later that afternoon, the chime on the door tinkled. I continued working on my new lunch item plans. Susanna could handle any customers that came in. Then I heard her call my name. I wiped my hand on a dishcloth and poked my head out of the kitchen into the main shop area.

A man filled the shop. I was used to Sam taking up a goodly amount of space. This man took up more. I didn't think he was taller than Sam, but he was definitely broader through the shoulders although just as narrow through the hips. He had that whole classic V-shape thing going on for miles. Then perhaps a few kilometers past that.

And his skin. Oh, my. My own skin tone tended more toward marzipan, perhaps with a touch of honey in the summer. By midwinter it would be way more toward mayonnaise. To be honest, most of Grand Lake trended that way. Oh, sure. Susanna and Huerta were more caramel-toned. Reverend Lee was more golden. This man, however, was deep into the chocolate ranges and he was fricking gorgeous.

"Can I help you?" I asked.

"Are you Rebecca?" His voice was deeper than deep, like bottom-of-the-ocean deep.

I resisted the urge to flip my hair. "I am."

He stuck out his hand and smiled. "I'm Dario. I'm Eric Gladstone's friend. He said you were looking for some part-time help."

"Come on back to the kitchen. Let's talk." I indicated the way with a tilt of my head.

"Coffee?" I offered as we got settled.

He looked over at my setup and said, "How about I make you a cup of coffee? It can be part of my interview process."

I hesitated. I didn't like to admit it, but I knew one of the big barriers to me getting some extra help was that I might have had the teensiest, tiniest bit of control issues in the kitchen. Elsewhere in my life? Have at it. Change my hair. Do my makeup. Tell me where to invest what little money I have. I would smile and barely notice. But touch my whisk and suddenly I'd be all tensed up. When you started messing with my coffee grinder and my French press? Hooey, baby. My head might pop open.

I knew, though, that I'd have to get over some of that control problem if I was to get some truly helpful help. Letting him make me coffee would be like a therapy session along with the interview. What small business owner doesn't take every opportunity to multitask? "Go right ahead."

I sat down and tried not to twitch. I will admit that a little tic started in my left eye when he didn't measure the grounds, but it actually looked about right when he started pouring the water in. He set a timer, then turned and leaned back against the counter and crossed his arms over his chest. He had on a cotton V-neck T-shirt and jeans and somehow made it look like something from a fashion magazine.

"So . . ." I started.

He held one finger up to his lips to hush me. "Wait for it." He walked over to the refrigerator, pulled out the cream, found the pitcher, poured it into the pitcher and set it on the table. The timer went off. He poured a cup for each of us into thick white china mugs, then sat down across from me.

I poured in a little cream and took a sip. My eyebrows went up.

He laughed, which was a wonderful sound. Rich and rumbling. "Eric says you make the second-best cup of coffee in Grand Lake."

I smiled. "I think I do. This is excellent. What's your training?" I sat back, waiting to hear about a culinary institute or cooking school of some kind.

"Standing at my grand-mère's elbow from the time I

was two until I joined the military at eighteen." He smiled back.

"Eric did tell you this is only part-time, right?" This man seemed way too together and way too skilled to need a part-time job at my little popcorn shop in my little Podunk town.

He nodded and drank his coffee. "He also said you might be able to be somewhat flexible."

"Within reason." I tried to figure out how to ask all the questions I had and finally said, "What's your story?"

He retrieved a folder from his messenger bag, took out a piece of paper and slid it across the table to me. A résumé.

Everything started to make more sense. "You're a photographer?"

"At least, I want to be. It's not the easiest profession to break into." He leaned back in his chair and crossed his legs. "Or to make enough money in to cover all the bills. I need a little something steady coming in while I get my business off the ground."

This could be perfect. There really was only one way to know, though, and it wasn't by looking at a piece of paper. "When can you start?"

"Tomorrow?"

I stuck my hand out. "I'll have the paperwork ready for you by six thirty."

Before we could say good-bye, however, my phone buzzed. It was the sheriff's office. My first thought was that Dan was calling to tell me that we were at T minus zero. Haley was in labor. It was go time! The Peanut was on the horizon!

"Hello!" My voice sounded breathless.

"Hello, my lovely." Not Dan. Antoine.

"Why are you calling me from the sheriff's office?" I didn't bother keeping the disappointment out of my voice.

He sighed. "I have only the one phone call. The only person I could think to call was you."

"Wait. One phone call?" I really didn't want that to mean what I thought it meant.

"Yes. I have been arrested, Rebecca." He sighed. "The one phone call isn't only on television, apparently."

"What are the charges?"

"Murder."

"How about starting now?" I asked Dario.

"I'm on it." He grabbed an apron from behind the door and tied it around his waist. I ran out without even bothering to put the fudge away.

Four

I marched into Dan's office, not bothering to stop at the front desk. Vera trailed after me, protesting that I needed to check in. "What the heck, Dan? I know you don't like Antoine, but arresting him for murder? This is ridiculous."

"This has nothing to do with whether or not I like Antoine. If I arrested everyone I didn't like our jail cells would be packed." Dan leaned back in his chair, waving Vera away with one hand.

It wasn't strictly true. Dan had an annoying tendency to try to see the good in everyone. I actually think it made him a better peace officer than most. It seemed to let him accept people's flaws without letting those flaws obscure the whole picture. Antoine might have been the exception to that rule. Well, him and Truman Schneider, the dad who had to be forcibly removed from one of the Grand Lake High football games for trash-talking. "Then what does it have to do with?"

"Evidence, Rebecca. Cold, hard evidence." He crossed his arms over his chest.

I sat down hard, feeling like I'd been punched in the gut. "What kind of evidence? I thought you said everything pointed to suicide."

"It did originally. But then we dug deeper into her finances and it looks like Melanie was stealing from Antoine. She had access to all his accounts. I told you she was in debt. It looks like she was helping herself to some of Antoine's money to ease her way out of that." He leaned forward again. "She wasn't too subtle about it, either. Huerta tracked it back pretty fast."

The ball of anxiety in my stomach loosened a bit. That proved nothing. "First of all, how do you know Antoine even knew?" Antoine was terrible with money. As long as there was enough of it to do what he wanted to do when he wanted to do it, he couldn't have cared less. He didn't see the point of balancing a checkbook or making a budget or anything else. His pride wasn't caught up in it nor was his passion.

"Well, to start with, we have a very angry message on her voice mail from Mr. Belanger," Dan said.

Angry Antoine? Oh, yeah. I'd seen that before. The flip side of the coin of his joyous passion was his sudden descents into fury. I couldn't believe it was about money, though. "And he said that he knew she was stealing from him?"

Dan nodded. "You don't have to take my word for it. I'll play it for you."

"Do it." I folded my arms over my chest, mirroring his body language. Dan had misinterpreted whatever Antoine had said. I was sure of it.

He took the phone out of the desk, punched some numbers and hit the speaker button. Antoine's voice came out of the phone, tinny and faraway, but still definitely Antoine's voice. "You little thief. I know it was you. Prepare yourself. Prepare a defense if you have any. I am on my way."

Sprocket had started to growl the second he heard Antoine's voice. I patted his head. "It's okay, boy." He barked in reply, like maybe he thought I was lying. I thought maybe I was, too. The ball of worry had returned big-time. "When did he send that?"

"Around seven o'clock the night Melanie died." Dan put the phone back in his desk drawer. "Actually, if it hadn't been for everything you said about it not looking like Melanie committed suicide, I don't know if I would have dug deep enough to find all the evidence we have against him."

Great. So I was responsible for Antoine getting arrested. The phone message sounded bad, but I still couldn't believe that Antoine would kill anyone ever, especially not over money. "Can I see him?"

"Rebecca." Dan looked pained. "Do you think that's a good idea?"

I absolutely did not think it was a good idea. I thought it was a terrible idea. I thought any sane ex-wife would be happy to let the man who had broken her heart rot in jail whether or not he was guilty of the accusations leveled against him and whether or not she felt she had any responsibility in getting him arrested. I knew many sad and tragic stories started with "I thought it was a good idea at the time." All my sad and tragic stories started with "I knew it was a bad idea, but I did it anyway." Fingers crossed that this was going to be one more Antoine story that I would tell to acquaintances later over too many martinis for big laughs. I said, "I don't think that's relevant. I need to see him."

"It's your funeral," Dan said. He got up and summoned Officer Huerta.

Glenn Huerta is pretty much the definition of tall, dark and handsome. Coal-black hair, soulful brown eyes, flashing white teeth, shoulders like the linebacker he was back in high school. He flashed his dazzling Chiclet smile at me. "Hey, Rebecca. How's it going, girl?"

It was impossible not to smile back. "Well, you know, I hired someone to help out at POPS and you've arrested my ex-husband for murder, so it's kind of an up-and-down day."

"I hear you. Come on, I'll take you to see Antoine." He beckoned me out the door. "Is Sprocket going to behave himself in there?"

I glanced down at my dog. There were only two people he had ever acted aggressively toward. Since the first had been a killer, I felt that he'd shown better judgment than most people on that one. The other, unfortunately, was Antoine. Every time he heard his voice, he'd start to growl. A horrible thought hit me. What if Sprocket was some kind of early murderer detection system? What if he'd known all along that Antoine was a killer and had been trying to warn me to stay away?

Then I remembered that Sprocket had recently tried to eat a dirty sock and decided he simply wasn't that smart. He still didn't like Antoine, though. "Maybe he could hang out with you while I talk to Antoine?"

"Sure thing." Huerta took Sprocket's leash from me and opened a door. Antoine was sitting at a metal table inside the room and was chained to a large hook in the center of it. A wave of déjà vu passed over me. The last man I'd seen chained to that table had been innocent. Jasper. I'd nearly helped convict him, too. The only reason I wasn't still racked with guilt over it was because I'd also been the one to clear his name. And got him to bathe more regularly. And frankly, he was still kind of a pain in the ass, so every once in a while I wondered if I'd really done anyone any favors by clearing him.

Antoine tried to rise from his seat, but the chains around his wrists stopped him, half stooped over the table. "You came. Oh, *chérie*. I cannot tell you what a relief it is to see you, *mon coeur, mon vie*."

Sprocket growled.

Huerta looped the leash a couple of more times around his meaty forearm. "I'll be back in five minutes. Dan says that's all you get."

I went in and Huerta closed the door behind us. I sat because I knew Antoine would not until I did. He would stand there half bent over the table until either whatever lady was in the room had sat down or hell froze over. You pick. "Are you okay?" I asked.

He shrugged. No one can shrug quite like the French. Say what you will about their habit of surrendering to the Germans or their casual attitude toward marital infidelity, no one can touch their gestures of insouciance. "I am afraid I am in a bit of a tight spot."

I snorted. "No joke."

Antoine frowned. He wasn't crazy about me doing things like snorting. He liked me to at least pretend to be ladylike. "First of all, you must know, I did not do it. I did not hurt Melanie."

"Dan played me a pretty nasty little voice mail you left her." I watched his eyes.

"I admit. I was angry with her. Very angry." He leaned back in his chair as much as the chain would allow him. I tried to figure out how he managed to get an orange jumpsuit that fit him so well. Seriously, it looked tailored. "But I did not harm her."

"When did you find out about the money, then?" Antoine's temper was ferocious, but it burned out as fast as it blew up. He must have figured it out moments before he made the phone call to Melanie.

Antoine drew back a bit. "Money? They think I killed her because she was stealing money?"

"I heard the message, Antoine. You called her a thief." Apparently Dan hadn't been too forthcoming on why they were arresting him.

"Ah, yes, the message. I was going to fire her and tell her that she would be forever ruined in this industry. I would have her blackballed from one side of the globe to another." The color was rising in Antoine's cheeks. "I would make sure she would never work as even the lowest line cook at the greasiest diner in Detroit, Michigan. I would . . ."

I held up my hand to stop him. "Kill her? Is that what you were going to say? That you would kill her?"

Antoine deflated. "No, Rebecca, no. I was as angry as I have ever been in my life, but I swear those words never crossed my lips because that thought never crossed my mind."

"Did you go see her, Antoine?" I asked.

He nodded again, this time looking miserable. "I went to her hotel room. I knocked, but no one answered."

"Can you prove that?" I asked.

"I'm sure someone heard me knocking. I was angry. I was perhaps a bit louder than I should have been." He looked down at his hands, his shoulders hunched.

I snorted again. That would probably be an understatement. Antoine's very good at projecting his voice. When he wants to be loud, he can be very, very loud.

Instead of frowning at my unladylike noises, though, Antoine's face crumpled. "Do you know what breaks my heart the most, Rebecca?" He took my hand from across the table. "Maybe I could have helped. Maybe I could have stopped whatever happened. If she committed suicide like your Sheriff Dan thought at first, maybe I could have stopped her."

I patted his hand. "There are a whole lot of maybes floating around right now, Antoine. The one thing that isn't even the slightest bit of a maybe is that you need a good lawyer and you need one now."

It was a good thing I knew where to find one.

Garrett stared at me from across his desk, completely unmoving. It was as if he had turned into a statue. "You cannot be serious."

I had come directly from the jail to his office. "I'm dead serious."

"I will not represent your ex-husband in his murder trial. That's just crazy." He still hadn't moved. It was as if I'd stunned him into immobility.

"You have to, Garrett. He's innocent. He looks guilty, but he's not. He needs someone who can really represent him. Someone smart. Someone good." I left out the part where it was sort of my fault that Antoine had been arrested in the first place and that I maybe kind of owed him.

"There are lots of lawyers in . . ." His words drifted off. He was about to say there were lots of lawyers to choose from, but there weren't in Grand Lake. There was Garrett and there was Phillip Meyer. I wouldn't trust Meyer to get me out of a traffic ticket, but Garrett had experience as a defense attorney. He knew how this all worked.

"Think about it. You'd be representing an innocent man. How often does a defense attorney get to do that?" I tried to make it sound as enticing as bacon.

Garrett gave me a withering look. "Don't play that game with me, Rebecca."

I held my hands up in front of me. "I'm not playing a game. Someone's life is truly at stake here."

Garrett picked up a pencil and began tapping it rapidly against his desk blotter. It was a relief to have him finally move. Sprocket thumped his tail in the same rhythm. Garrett stopped tapping. Sprocket stopped thumping. "I don't like him," Garrett said. "I don't like him one bit."

The first time Antoine and Garrett had met there was a fistfight. I'd pretty much gathered they didn't like each other. I also didn't think it should be relevant.

"Is that a reason to let an innocent man be railroaded on a murder charge?" I asked. "How many of your clients back in Cleveland did you actually like?"

Garrett raised his eyebrows. "A surprising number. Just because a person is a felon doesn't mean he or she isn't good company."

"Okay. So how many of them were innocent?" I pressed.

Garrett went stony still. I don't know what scab I'd picked at, but apparently it was one that bled pretty easily. "Innocence or guilt doesn't matter, Rebecca. Everyone is entitled to a defense. Everyone. The job of a defense attorney is to provide one."

Ha! He'd made my argument for me. "Then why won't you provide one for Antoine?"

Garrett took a deep breath and blew it out. "When do you think Antoine is going to stop trying to get you back?"

Now it was my turn to look uncomfortable. "I don't know. Maybe tomorrow. Maybe never. I don't know why he's so fired up to get me back in the first place."

"How hard do you think I'll fight to get my rival for your affections out of jail, where he can pursue with everything he can bring to bear? The wealth. The fame. The travel."

I blinked. "He's not your rival." There had been an unfortunate incident when Antoine was trying to get me to return to him where he had gone down on his knees in front of the whole town and it had looked like I'd accepted his proposal. I hadn't. It was all a big misunderstanding, but unfortunately it left Garrett looking at Antoine like he was an actual rival for my affections.

"Really? Could have fooled me." Garrett pushed back in his chair.

"I am not going back to Antoine. Not now. Not in a week. Not in a month. Not in a year." I leaned forward. "When you were both at my apartment, who stayed and who left? We didn't even drink his wine."

"I still don't think I should represent him." Garrett's shoulders relaxed. "He really should have someone who's going to give him the best possible defense and it simply isn't me, Rebecca."

He had a point about that. "Fine. Then who do you suggest?"

He wrote a name, a phone number and an address down on a piece of paper and handed it over to me. "This is the contact info for Cynthia Harlen. She's good. Very good. Tell her I sent you, otherwise you might not be able to get an appointment."

"She's in Cleveland?" I made sure I could read his handwriting and then folded the paper and tucked it into my jeans pocket.

"Yeah, but she'll make the drive for a case like this. Trust me." He hesitated. "You do realize the press is going to be all over this, right? Famous chef arrested for homicide? It makes good copy."

I hadn't considered that. "How long do you think I have before they get wind of it?"

He glanced at his watch. "Given that they'll all have to fly into Cleveland or Toledo, rent cars, drive here . . . I'd say you have until about seven tonight."

I ran back into the shop. "Everything going okay?" I called to Susanna and Dario as I hurried past them.

I got thumbs-up from both of them. It took me a second to realize what was different, but then it hit me that someone had turned some music on. It was some kind of oldies station. Dario and Susanna spun back and forth behind the counter, boxing fudge, ringing up customers, keeping the line moving as if they were doing a dance they'd choreographed for weeks. Half the people in the shop were bopping their heads. The other half was tapping toes.

Everyone was smiling.

For a second I wanted to cry. I wanted to be bopping behind the counter with smiling people. I wanted to be handing out sweet fudge. I did not want to be rushing around town trying to find someone to get my ex-husband out of jail. What's more, it's where I was supposed to be. I'd put in the hours. I'd sweated, scrimped, saved and swallowed my pride. Enough with the adulting! I deserved a break.

I wasn't getting one, though. I pulled myself together and went into the office to call the lawyer Garrett recommended. The sooner I got a lawyer for Antoine, the sooner I could get back to my real life: the one I'd made for myself here in Grand Lake, the one where I got to dance around behind the counter while selling popcorn and fudge, the one I deserved. "May I speak to Cynthia Harlen?"

"Ms. Harlen is not available at the moment. May I take a message?" the very smooth voice told me.

Figured. If she was as good as Garrett said, she probably wasn't sitting around waiting for clients to call. "My name is Rebecca Anderson. I'm calling on behalf of someone who has been accused of a serious crime. Garrett Mills suggested I call."

There was a sharp intake of breath, then a choking noise. "Garrett sent you?"

"Yes," I said. "Are you okay?"

"Yes, of course." She coughed again. "Just a moment."

Vivaldi suddenly blasted into my ear. I set the cell phone down and put it on speaker, figuring I'd be waiting a while. I wasn't. In less than a minute, a smooth contralto voice said, "This is Cynthia Harlen. How may I help you?"

I laid the basics out for her as succinctly as I could. "Would you consider representing Antoine? He didn't do this, but I know it looks bad for him. Garrett says you're the best in the area."

Cynthia chuckled. It was an earthy sound, like it came right up from her belly. I already liked her. I'd bet she was a good eater. I loved a good eater. "Garrett would know," she said. "I'd like to meet with Mr. Belanger before I commit, but I'm very interested. Tell me again, you're Mr. Belanger's ex-wife?"

I knew this would be hard to explain. "Yes. Ex-wife. That doesn't mean I want him to go to jail for something he didn't do, though."

"Of course not." There was that chuckle again. "And Garrett Mills recommended me. Is there a reason that Mr. Mills doesn't want to take the case himself?"

I felt heat rise to my face. "Uh, conflict of interest is the best way to put it, I suppose." I could explain more later if she actually took the case, not that it probably mattered in the least.

"Okay, then. I need to cancel some appointments here, but I should be able to be in Grand Lake by . . ." There was a pause as she did some quick calculations. "Four thirty. Would you check with the sheriff to make sure I can see Mr. Belanger as soon as I get there?"

"Of course." We hung up. I dialed Dan. "I've found a lawyer for Antoine."

"Probably a smart choice. He needs one. That's who he should have contacted with his one phone call. Seriously, who calls their ex-wife when they've been arrested? Who'd you get? Phillip Meyer? Russ?" Dan sounded relieved.

"No. I went with someone from Cleveland that Garrett recommended. Cynthia Harlen. She said she'll be here by about four thirty and wanted to make sure she'd be able to see Antoine then." I could literally feel my heart rate start to slow down as I said the words. A good lawyer. She would clear this up in no time. Then Antoine could shoot the segment on my shop and get out of Grand Lake before the door hit him in the ass on his way out of town.

There was a choking noise on the other end of the phone. "Cynthia? Harlen? Garrett recommended her?"

"Are you okay? And yes, Garrett recommended her."

My heart rate started to pick back up. The receptionist at Harlen's office had sounded like she was choking, too. What was up with that?

"Okeydokey, then. No problems at all. I'll make sure the guards know to let her in. And I'm fine. Something . . . uh . . . went down the wrong pipe."

There seemed to be a lot of that going around.

I heard a car door slam. Then another. Then two more. I looked out the window of the shop. A crowd was gathering on the sidewalk in front. I walked out onto the porch to see what was going on.

Big mistake.

I heard someone yell, "Is that her?"

Then about a thousand flashes went off in my eyes. Okay. That might be a slight exaggeration, but it definitely felt like a thousand flashes. I flung my arm up to shield my eyes and staggered backward. Before I could register much more, I felt a hard hand on my upper arm and I was being dragged back into the shop. "Are you okay?" Dario asked.

I felt a little dazed. "I think so."

He was pulling down blinds as I tried to get the spots to clear from my eyes. "Your lawyer buddy was wrong. The press got here a little faster than he anticipated."

I peered around one of the mini-blinds to see a van with a big antenna on top parked at the curb. A woman in a suit stopped people on the sidewalk and shoved a ginormous microphone in their faces.

Two more vans were across the street. Thin people with enormous heads were standing in front of cameras with microphones, gesturing to my shop.

I called Dan again.

"There are a bunch of people with cameras and microphones in front of my store," I reported.

"Excellent powers of observation, Rebecca. Is the sky also blue?" he asked.

"Bluish. Can you make them go away? They're blocking the way into my shop. Plus they almost blinded me with their flashes. Isn't that illegal somehow?" I could still see spots when I closed my eyes.

"Are they physically keeping people from walking into your store, Rebecca?" He sounded tired.

"No." I had to say no because Janet Barry had picked that moment to walk into the shop and Dan could probably hear the tinkle of the little bells that announced a customer.

"Call me when they do. I have enough on my hands trying to deal with the ones here," he said.

"There are more reporters at the jail?" How many of them had shown up in Grand Lake?

"Yes, Rebecca, there are. You're not the center of this show. Antoine is. You're just B roll for them."

That stung a bit. Both the parts about being B roll and the part where he implied I always thought I was the center of the show. I knew I wasn't. I never was when Antoine was around. That, in fact, might have been one of the things I liked about having been married to him. It's a little easier to operate on the sidelines than it is in the center of the field with everyone watching. "Okay. I get it. I'll call if they're more than a nuisance."

"See you tonight?" he asked, sounding relieved.

"Wouldn't miss it."

Dario walked back in from the kitchen. "Doesn't look like they figured out that there's a back alley yet. It's probably only a matter of time, though."

My cell phone and the store phone started ringing simultaneously. I didn't recognize the number of the caller ID. "Hello?"

"May I speak to Rebecca Anderson?"

"This is she."

"Hello, Ms. Anderson, this is Anna Day with CNN. Do you have any comment on your ex-husband's arrest?"

"Nope. No comment at all." I hung up.

Dario had answered the store phone. "No comment," he said, hanging it up, too.

They both started ringing again. "Let the voice mail get it," I said, gesturing with my chin to the store phone. I turned the ringer off on my cell.

Dario smiled at me and said, "Well, at least it's not dull."

Five

Friday-night dinner at my sister's had become something of a ritual. I was usually exhausted when I got home. Friday afternoons are my busiest time. There are the special orders for events and people planning movie nights. Then there are the drop-ins who realized that the weekend was here and wanted something to bring to whatever dinner or party they'd been invited to. Plus, of course, my regulars who needed their mid-afternoon coffee and fudge break. Even with the reporters outside, we had a steady stream of customers coming into POPS all afternoon.

I set aside some fudge and some popcorn balls to take as my contribution for dinner. Haley knows how busy I get on Fridays and doesn't expect anything more. I finally finished up and shut everything down. "Ready, Sprocket?"

He stood up from where he'd been napping on his dog bed in the corner and shook himself out. I took it as a yes. I snapped the leash on him, shut off the lights. A quick peek out the front windows revealed the news vans still on my sidewalk. That was not a gauntlet I wanted to face. We went to the back door. No news vans. No people with microphones. Just Jasper.

Jasper was the person who I almost managed to get charged with Coco's murder, but then managed to clear. Since then, he'd taken to showering, shaving and wearing clean clothes on a daily basis. It was a definite improvement. He still did not have a job, however.

"Hey, Rebecca," he said. "Any leftover popcorn?"

"Just a little bit of the chili cheese," I said. "Want me to get it?"

He shook his head. "Not my favorite. Too spicy." He made a face.

I considered saying something about beggars and choosers, but decided against it. "Sorry." I stepped outside, shut the door and locked it.

"Quite a zoo out front," he said, falling into step beside me as I walked down the alley.

"That's one way to describe it." It felt more like a wolf pack waiting to tear into sweet soft caribou news meat to me.

When we got to the end of the alley, he said, "Want me to run a little interference for you? Walk out front while you go the other way?"

"Thank you, Jasper. That would be really nice."

He shrugged. "I kind of owe you one."

We split up. I could hear the people yelling questions at him from a block away.

Sunset was coming earlier and earlier. It was going to be my first winter back in Ohio after years of California sunshine. I wasn't looking one hundred percent forward to it, but I was enjoying fall. Sprocket and I were running a tiny bit late so we didn't linger on the shore of Lake Erie. A stiff wind blew off the lake and it stung my nose and eyelids. Sprocket sneezed. Still, it was worth it to watch the last rays of the sun dance over the waves, sparkling and winking against the gray of the sky.

We turned around and headed back to the house. It was cold enough that no one was sitting out on front porches anymore. I have to admit it was kind of a relief. One of the things I hadn't considered when I decided to open POPS was the unrelenting amount of small talk I would have to make.

I am, by nature, a friendly person. I like people. Not everyone, but in general, I think people are okay. That didn't mean I wanted to discuss the weather with every single blessed one on the planet Earth, though. It was one more reason I'd needed to hire someone to help out. If one more person asked me if I thought it was going to rain, it was entirely possible that I was going to leap over the counter, grab that person by the throat and shake him or her silly while screaming at them to check the weather app on their phone.

I suspected that wouldn't be good for business.

I got home in time to help Evan with his bath—another Friday night ritual—and read him a story. I came downstairs with him on my hip, already molding into my body as sleep started to take over. "Something smells delicious."

Haley smiled from over by the stove. "Thanks. It's chili. I made a double batch so I could freeze some to have after the baby comes."

I wasn't surprised. She'd made a double batch of pretty much everything she'd cooked for the last two weeks. I was beginning to wonder if she had a magic freezer with no bottom that she could continue to stock endlessly and never run out of room. "Excellent. You guys won't have to worry about meals for weeks."

"But you'll still be here to help, right?" Her voice rose a little on the last word into something that sounded almost like a squeak.

"Of course I will." I wasn't sure exactly how many times I would have to reassure Haley of that, but I would do whatever it took.

"This thing with Antoine won't stop you from being here?" Now her chin wobbled a little bit.

"Absolutely not." He'd been my priority when Evan was born. Not this time.

"Okay, then," she said, rubbing her belly and wincing.

"What was that?" I asked. That wasn't a normal face. Was that the face of my sister going into labor? "Is it go time?"

She laughed. "No. It's only Braxton Hicks contractions. It means things are tuning up and getting ready, but it's not go time yet."

"Is that normal?" I didn't know who Braxton or Hicks were, but I wasn't crazy about the faces they were causing my sister to make.

"Absolutely. I had Braxton Hicks for three weeks before I went into labor with Evan." She winced again.

I hadn't known that. I hadn't been here. I'd been in Italy with Antoine. I hadn't come back even for Evan's birth. Something I felt deeply ashamed of now. I could have held him when he was only minutes old. I could have been a part of his entire life instead of skating in with my hair on fire when he was two. I could have—should have—been there to help my sister when she brought her first child home. Instead, I'd sent flowers and arranged for Olive Hicks to come clean the house once a week for three months. I'd thrown money at it when I should have thrown my heart and my arms and my back into it. I couldn't change that now, but I could be sure to be here when the Peanut was born. Nothing was going to keep me from doing that.

Haley reached for Evan. "Come on, champ. Let's go find Daddy so he can tuck you in."

"Daddy," Evan repeated in a snuffly sleepy voice.

"Right here, my man." Dan came in off the porch and held out his arms. Haley passed Evan over, but for a second all three of them were part of one big embrace. Four of them, I guessed, since Haley's tummy was part of the group hug. My heart did a little dance move in my chest. Something between a clutch and a leap.

I loved my life. I loved the shop. I loved my apartment over the garage. That didn't mean I didn't see the value in Haley's life, though. Oh, I knew it wasn't all sweet-smelling toddlers and group hugs in a warm kitchen. I knew there were dirty diapers and late nights and teething and tantrums.

I also knew that sometimes when Sprocket and I walked into my apartment over the garage, it felt very empty.

Garrett arrived about ten minutes later and we all sat down to eat. Of course, the conversation turned to Antoine's arrest.

"Antoine hired Cynthia Harlen to represent him?" Haley squinted her eyes at Garrett. To my immense relief, she didn't choke. I wasn't sure how to Heimlich a pregnant woman. "Are you going to be okay seeing her around town all the time?"

I set my glass of wine down. "Why wouldn't Garrett

be okay with seeing Cynthia Harlen? He's the one who recommended her."

Now Haley's eyes went wide. "You did?"

Garrett didn't meet her gaze. "She's good. Antoine's going to need somebody good whether he's guilty or innocent."

"He's innocent," I said at the same time that Haley sputtered, "Yes, but . . ."

"But what?" I demanded. "Did she beat you in court or something? What kind of history do you have with her?"

"She was my, uh, partner." Garrett had become extremely engrossed in the embroidery on the tablecloth.

Haley snorted. "So that's what the kids are calling it these days."

I stared at Garrett until he looked up. "Cynthia and I had a small private practice together for a while. We also lived together for a couple of years." He said the words quickly, like ripping a bandage off, like he was getting it over with, like maybe if he said them fast enough I wouldn't notice.

"Like roommates or like . . ." I didn't really want to say *lovers*, but that's what I was thinking.

"Not like roommates," he confirmed. Apparently he didn't want to use that other *L* word, either. He'd gone all still again.

"Wait a second. You're telling me that you referred me to your ex-girlfriend to represent my ex-husband?" I wasn't sure what, but something sounded terribly wrong with this situation.

"I knew it was weird. That's why I didn't tell you. I'd hoped you wouldn't find out. Cynthia and I are ancient history." He sighed. "I sincerely think she's an amazing lawyer who will do a great job for Antoine. I think a case like this is exactly what she needs to break into the big time, too. Really, it's a win-win, Rebecca. Now we can gracefully bow out." He took another sip of his wine.

"You mean act like this has nothing to do with us?" It had been exactly what I was thinking. I think I actually licked my lips in anticipation.

He nodded. "Yep. Because it actually doesn't." He leaned toward me over the table.

"I found the body, Garrett," I pointed out, leaning back and gesturing toward him with my fork.

"So you're a minor witness for the prosecution. Then it's peace out for you, baby." He made the safe motion as if I'd slid into first rather than found my ex-husband's assistant's body floating in a tub.

"For the prosecution? I don't want to be part of the team that convicts Antoine." Maybe I hadn't heard him right.

"I know, but that's how it works. The prosecution is the one that lays out all that information. How the body was found. When it was found. Like it or not, you're batting for the other side." He took another bite of chili.

"Then I'll be a switch-hitter. I'll bat for the other side." I set my spoon down.

"That's not what a switch-hitter is," Dan said.

I threw my hands in the air. "I will be whatever a person would be who's called by the prosecution, but is actually on the side of the defense."

Garrett sighed. "I know exactly what that's called."

"What?" I asked.

"It's called trouble."

And that's when Dan's phone rang. He frowned at it and then answered. After listening for a few seconds, he handed it across the table. "It's for you," he said.

"Ms. Anderson? It's Cynthia Harlen," said that sweet contralto voice on the phone. "I tried to reach you on your cell phone, but it kept going to voice mail and that appears to be full."

"Sorry. I turned it off when the press started calling. I forgot to turn it back on." I scooted back from the table and went into the kitchen, but not before I heard Dan say, "Speak of the devil . . ." Why did I have a feeling that there was a whole lot more to the Cynthia/Garrett story than a breakup?

"Has the press been bothering you?" she asked.

"They showed up in front of my store right before closing. Then my phone started ringing." And ringing and ringing.

"Did you speak to anyone?" Cynthia's voice became sharp.

"Beyond to say no comment, no."

"Excellent. Let me handle that. You might want to change your voice mail to ask the media to call my office number. Believe it or not, this is good news. Antoine is already a beloved media presence. We'll make sure to stoke those flames." She paused. "We do have a little bit of a problem, though, Rebecca. Antoine refuses to sign the papers hiring me unless you're present."

"He what?" I didn't actually need her to repeat herself. I'd heard and understood exactly what she'd said. She repeated it anyway.

"Could you come down to the jail for a little bit? I don't want him to say too much more to me without it being covered by attorney-client privilege."

I peeked through the swinging door into the dining room. No one at that table was going to be happy if I announced I was leaving in the middle of Friday-night dinner to do something for Antoine. On the other hand, I doubted I'd be able to look at myself in the mirror if I didn't.

I knew I was being manipulated. I wasn't stupid. Or at least not that stupid. I knew Antoine was trying everything he could to keep me in his life.

I also knew that he was probably terrified. Who wouldn't be?

"I'll be there in fifteen minutes," I told Cynthia Harlen, and then went in to face the shit storm that was about to erupt at my sister's table.

I left the warmth of family dinner behind me in more ways than one. I had not been mistaken in thinking that everyone would be pissed at me if I left to help Antoine. Haley had looked at me and said, "No. Just no."

"I'm not asking for your permission, Leelee. I'm not in high school anymore." I felt like I was, but we all knew I wasn't.

She'd scowled, rubbed her belly and said, "Well, you have pretty much the same lack of judgment you did back then."

I'd turned to Garrett. "It's your ex-girlfriend who's asking me to go down there."

It apparently wasn't the correct argument. "You're setting a bad precedent," was all he'd said. I could tell he was angry, but he'd offered to keep Sprocket and helped me with my coat. So how angry could he actually be?

On the other hand, Dan had said nothing. He'd just kept eating chili as if I wasn't even in the room. It scared me a little.

Outside it had gotten cool. I walked fast to stay warm.

The moon was half full, but I could see the outline of the rest of it in the clear sky. The stars winked over the black abyss of the lake. It was a night for hayrides and bonfires, not ex-husbands and ex-girlfriends and murder charges.

I walked up to the jail not really sure how I felt. Worried? Yes. Antoine was in some serious trouble. Irritated? Definitely. With Antoine for dragging me over here and with Garrett for being jealous and with my sister for being focused only on the coming baby. Guilty? A little bit. Somehow there wasn't a way to deal with the situation that didn't leave me disappointing or hurting someone I cared about. I wasn't crazy about the combination. They weren't great tastes and they definitely didn't taste great together.

Vera Bailey at the front desk was expecting me this time. Vera and I had gone to high school with each other. Actually, she'd been in Haley's year, two years ahead of me. She hadn't aged quite as well, though. She'd thickened in the middle and the cop uniform didn't do much to downplay it. Her light brown hair was pulled back so tight in its bun that I could see the pink of her scalp through some of it. "Hey, Rebecca. How's it going?" she asked as she signed me in.

"Pretty good except for this mess." I handed over my cell phone and keys.

"Looks like your shop is taking off," she observed.

"So far so good." I slid my belt out of its loops and put it in the bin. I wasn't sure how I felt about being this used to the routine of visiting people in jail.

"Dan brought in some of that Coco Pop Fudge. Good stuff." She patted her hips. "Definitely not figure friendly, though. I don't suppose much in that shop of yours is, though."

I froze a second. A bit of a brainstorm flitted through

my head. I was missing out on an important demographic. "You know what, Vera? I'm going to see what I can do about that."

She smiled. "You are?"

"Yeah. It would be a great idea to have some popcorn snacks that were a little more diet friendly. Thanks for the idea."

She drew herself up a little taller. "You're welcome. Come on this way. Mr. Belanger and his fancy lawyer lady are waiting for you."

Cynthia Harlen was not what I expected. I didn't think I'd been creating mental pictures of her in my mind, but apparently I had. First of all, she was bigger than I expected. She was easily as tall as me, but where I was kind of a straight line from shoulders to hips, she was all curves. I mean all curves. Even in her conservative lawyer lady suit that looked like it cost more than my utility bill for the year, she could only be described as a bombshell. Her hair was pulled back into some kind of bun on the back of her head, but I could tell it was probably thick. It was definitely shiny and smooth and a beautiful russet color. Then there were her skin and eyes. Beautiful smooth, porcelain, poreless skin with these huge, luminous, hazel-green eyes shining out.

Garrett had gone from this to me? What on earth had he been thinking? Or maybe I was the one who should be thinking. Was I his rebound girl? Because if he was used to a Cadillac like this, I wasn't sure what he was doing with my beat-up Honda Civic ass.

"You must be Rebecca." She put out her hand. Her voice was low, throaty. Sexy as hell. I was about ready to ask her out.

"And you're Cynthia?"

She smiled. "One and the same. Shall we get started, then?"

"Yes," Antoine said. "Now we can get started."

Cynthia slid a stack of papers toward me. "This is my standard contract for representation. Understand that the amount listed is only a retainer. My fees could end up being much higher depending on what kind of investigative help or expert witnesses we need as the case continues."

The number listed on the paper made my eyebrows shoot up, but I knew Antoine had the money. Besides, how can you put a price on personal freedom? "Is this okay with you, Antoine?" I asked.

He nodded. "It is fine."

I glanced through a few more pages, but there were an awful lot of *therefore*s and *werewithal*s. I'd never been great with legalese. Antoine, however, was usually able to decipher it. "Did you read this?" I asked him.

"Of course."

"And it's okay with you?"

"It seems reasonable considering the work we are asking Mademoiselle Harlen to do," he said.

I slammed the pen down on the table in front of him. "Then sign it, Antoine. Stop playing games."

He looked over at Cynthia and did one of his one-shouldered wildly Gallic shrugs. Then he picked up the pen and signed the contract.

Cynthia smiled and took the pages from him. "To be completely honest, Rebecca, getting you over here was partly my idea."

I looked back and forth between them. "Really? Why?" I wasn't sure I wanted my ex-husband and my boyfriend's ex-girlfriend/high-powered lawyer colluding against me.

She shrugged and pulled away from the wall she'd been leaning against. "I wanted to see you two together and I wanted to talk to you about finding the body."

"Couldn't we have done that tomorrow or the next day?" Like not when I was having a family dinner?

"I didn't want you to have time to prepare, to put on a game face, as it were. I wanted a more unvarnished sense of you." She was watching me like I was a zoo animal.

"Do you have one now?" I knew my face was probably red. It was quite possible steam might have been coming out of my ears. I don't like a lot of games, not even Monopoly. I especially didn't like head games. Maybe I was getting a sense of why Garrett and Cynthia had broken up.

She smiled. It was a slow, lazy thing that spread across her face. "I do. And I think I like it. Now, as long as you're here. Let's sit down. I'd like to hear your account of finding the body firsthand."

That smile took some of the steam out of my kettle. I took her through the sequence: Melanie setting up the meeting, me showing up, not getting an answer, walking in, finding her. Cynthia typed her notes into a tablet.

"So the door wasn't fully closed?" she asked.

"I guess not. It swung open."

"But not the first time you knocked? Or the second?"

"No. The third time." I hadn't touched the knob. It must have been partly latched, like maybe whoever had closed it had been in a hurry and hadn't made sure it closed properly.

She jotted more notes down. "And she had clothing laid out on the bed. What kind of clothing?"

"You know when you're trying to decide what to wear and you lay out things across the bed to compare them?" I asked. We all do it.

She nodded, a quirk of a smile at the corner of her full lips. "I do."

"It looked like that. Kind of chaotic, but chaos with a purpose." And the purpose hadn't been electrocuting herself in the tub.

"Based on those clothes, what kind of thing would you think she was planning on doing that evening?" Cynthia asked.

I closed my eyes and saw again the ruffled top with the distressed jeans and high-heeled wedges, the short skirt with the long-sleeved top and flats, the little black dress. I already knew my answer, but my memory confirmed it. "It looked like she was going out on a date. She wanted to look good, but like she wasn't trying too hard. Does that make sense?"

She snorted. "Totally."

I smiled. Damn it. I liked her. I wasn't sure I liked that I liked her, though. "It makes sense with the bath, too. You know, soak off the day's dirt and tension so you can go out relaxed and fresh?"

"Absolutely." She leaned in. "So what bothered you about the scene?"

"The blow-dryer bugged me. I knew right away it couldn't be hers." I leaned in, too.

Her eyebrows went up. "Why not?"

"No diffuser. Melanie's hair was like mine. Curly. Using a blow-dryer on it without a diffuser would have turned it into a huge mass of frizz."

Cynthia sighed. "A nice problem to have. Mine's as straight as spaghetti no matter what I do."

"Trust me, curly isn't all it's cracked up to be. I feel like it has a life of its own some days." I'd spent years trying to tame my hair and now just let it have its own way. I'm not that proud. I can admit defeat.

"At least it has life!" she exclaimed.

Antoine cleared his throat and we both glanced over at him, then back at each other. "Sorry. Got off track there," Cynthia said. "So you knew right away the blow-dryer wasn't hers. Did you notice anything else about it? Anything about the cord?" she asked.

I hadn't. If it had been tampered with, I hadn't noticed it. "No. Sorry. That escaped me completely."

She tapped another note into the tablet. "Can you think of anyone who might have been able to do the kind of rewiring necessary to remove the GFCI protection?"

"Anyone on Antoine's crew would have known how to do it. It's a TV show that travels. Everyone has to know how to make everything electrical and digital work. I probably could have figured out how to do it given an hour and the Internet." I'd occasionally been pressed into service backstage at the show when Antoine and I were married.

She stopped typing. "Would Antoine have known how to do it?"

"I did not touch that blow-dryer," he cried, full of indignation.

She reached across the table and put her hand on his. "I know, Antoine. I have to know whether you could have done it so I can build a defense about how you didn't do it."

He settled back down.

"He could have done it in his sleep," I said, with a glance over at him. He knew it was true. It wouldn't help to lie.

Cynthia nodded and made a *hmmm*ing noise as she

typed. "Now, tell me why someone might think you would want to hurt Melanie."

Antoine suddenly became extremely engrossed in examining his fingernails. They were immaculate. They always were. Cynthia sighed and looked over at me.

I couldn't believe he was leaving the dirty work to me. "She was stealing from him."

"Money, then." She nodded. She cocked her head to one side and asked, "Is there proof of that?"

I looked over at Antoine. He shrugged. Cynthia sighed. "Antoine, I can't help if you won't talk to me. Did you have proof that she was stealing your money?"

"It will be in the accounts," was all he said.

Cynthia made that *hmmm*ing noise and tapped more notes into her tablet. "So where were you two nights ago?"

"We arrived in town at around two. We went immediately to Rebecca's shop to see what we were working with." He smiled at me. "You have done a beautiful job, darling. Truly it is like an exquisite little jewel box. It will look magnificent on television."

Cynthia looked over at me, beautifully sculpted eyebrows slightly arched. "I own a popcorn shop here in Grand Lake. Antoine was going to feature my breakfast bars and popcorn fudge on his show," I explained.

She nodded and typed a little more. "Okay. You went to Rebecca's shop. Then what?"

"The crew was hungry. We went to the diner down the street," he said.

"Melanie was with you?" Cynthia asked.

"Of course," Antoine said. "I would be lost without her. She is an excellent assistant."

"Except for the part where she was stealing from you," Cynthia said, almost like it was an afterthought.

"Yes, well, but I did not know that then. Then she was still the person who knew all the plans and schedules and what papers needed to be signed and when." Antoine rubbed at his forehead with his thumb and forefinger. "Then she was still the best assistant I have ever had."

"What happened after the diner?" she asked.

Antoine snorted. "Besides indigestion?" He turned back to me. "*Chérie*, that diner is horrific. Have you thought about opening a restaurant here? There would be no competition."

"Your schedule, Antoine?" Cynthia interrupted.

He sighed. "We checked into the hotel. Everyone was tired. We all went to our rooms."

"You all stayed at the same hotel." It was a statement more than a question.

"There is not much to choose from here in Grand Lake. Many bed-and-breakfast establishments along the lake, but that is not really appropriate for a group such as ours." I couldn't imagine the havoc Antoine's entire crew would wreak on the average B&B. All the equipment. All the tramping in and out at strange hours. "The Grand Lake Inn was really our only option."

"What happened after you checked into the hotel?" Cynthia prompted, still typing.

"I checked e-mail, then social media. That is when I saw it." Antoine let his head fall forward.

Cynthia stopped typing and looked up. "Saw what?"

Antoine hesitated. "I saw what led me to believe Melanie was stealing from me."

"So you called Melanie to confront her? Around what time was that?" Cynthia asked.

Antoine ran his hand down his face in an effort to calm himself. I knew that gesture. He was near his breaking point. I knew I could help. The calmer he was, the easier it would be for him to answer Cynthia's questions; the faster he answered the questions, the sooner I could be out of here and home; the sooner I was home, the less angry everyone there would be with me. I got up, went behind Antoine and rubbed his neck. His shoulders relaxed beneath my hands. Cynthia shot me a look. I shrugged. It probably wasn't as expressive as one of Antoine's shrugs, but she seemed to get the point.

"You could check my cell phone. The police have it. Probably around nine thirty," Antoine said.

"Do they have a time of death for Melanie?" I asked.

Cynthia shook her head. "Not that I know of. Or at least not yet. I imagine the body being immersed in water is going to complicate making those determinations."

"How long after you called did you go to her room?" she asked.

"Right away." His shoulders tensed a bit again. "I was upset. I did not want to sit in my room and stew while I waited for her to answer my call."

"You knocked and no one answered?" Cynthia set the tablet down to really focus on Antoine.

Antoine nodded. "Then knocked again. Then perhaps called to her through the door."

"Loudly? Loudly enough for other people to hear?" she asked.

He nodded again and sank down in his seat a bit. "I believe it would have been hard for people not to hear."

"And when she didn't answer?" she pressed.

His hands flew up in the air a bit. "I returned to my room. What else could I do?"

"You didn't enter her room." Cynthia leaned forward to look Antoine directly in the eyes.

"Of course not!" He stiffened again.

"The door was locked?" she asked.

"Yes," Antoine confirmed.

"Did you try the door? Will your fingerprints be on the knob?" The questions were coming faster now.

Antoine didn't reply.

"Antoine, it will be better if I hear it from you than get blindsided by it during the trial. Did you touch the door-knob?" Her voice had gotten louder.

He nodded.

"Were you in her room earlier?" she asked.

He nodded again. "I helped to carry some of the equip-ment to her room when we unloaded the van. The entire crew's fingerprints will be in there."

She picked the tablet back up. "After you went to her room and knocked, what did you do?"

"What could I do? I went back to my room, took a sleeping pill, and went to bed," he said.

Cynthia's head shot up. "Sleeping pill? Do you take them often?"

"I travel a great deal. Time zones change. It's difficult to sleep. I use them often, but not all the time." Antoine shrugged.

Something else bothered me about the scene at the hotel. "If someone messed with a blow-dryer for the express purpose of murdering someone, they would have to know that there'd be an opportunity to use it. How would they know that Melanie would even take a bath?"

"Because she always did," Antoine said. "It was one of her road rituals. She would take a bath when we were done for the day. She said it helped her relax."

"Who would have known about that?" Cynthia asked.

"The entire crew. Possibly the hotel staff. She always

made a point of asking if her room had a tub. There is a desk clerk in New Orleans whose ears are probably still blistered from Melanie's diatribe after being promised a tub and not getting one." Antoine smiled and chuckled a bit. "She had such spirit."

Cynthia snapped her tablet shut. "Well, we do have our work cut out for us here. Basically, Antoine, you have means, motive and opportunity. I can see why the sheriff arrested you. I think there are more than enough holes in their evidence for us to exploit, though, as well as a few other angles we might be able to use."

"That is good, yes?" He leaned forward.

"Very good. Now try to get some rest. I'll be in touch on Monday." She rapped on the door to the room. Vera showed up and ushered us both out. We retrieved our cell phones and other items. When I started to say something, Cynthia shook her head and pointed at Vera. I took the hint and waited until we were out on the steps to talk. A small knot of people stood at the bottom of the steps. "The press?" she asked, straightening her skirt and tucking an errant lock of hair behind her ear.

No lights. No camera. I squinted. Lucy. Brooke. Jason. It was Antoine's crew. "The press must have headed home for the night," I said.

She shrugged. "I'll give a press conference in the next few days."

"What do you think? Do you think you can help?" I asked.

"Absolutely. I see all kinds of room for creating reasonable doubt. It should be more than enough. If nothing else, I might be able to argue diminished capacity with the sleeping pills." She blew out a breath and squared her shoulders. "It's actually going to be kind of fun."

My shoulders dropped with relief. It wasn't my idea of a good time, but I'd learned a long time ago that someone who enjoys her job puts a whole lot more of herself into it. "That's good. That's very good."

"To really cinch it, however, I'd love to come up with an alternative explanation of the crime. Someone else who could have done it. Juries eat that up like frozen custard on a hot summer day," she said. "Any ideas?"

I hadn't had time to consider that. Dan had gone from insisting it was suicide to insisting it was Antoine too fast for me to wonder too much. "I'll see if I can find anything out."

She cocked her head to one side. "You two don't seem like a normal divorced couple. Some of the divorced couples I know would likely plant the evidence to get their exes arrested. Even if they weren't that vindictive, they certainly wouldn't be giving each other shoulder rubs in jail cells."

"Antoine's not an ordinary guy," I said.

"I have a feeling you're not an ordinary woman, either." She took a few steps down and then turned. "So is the rest of your family as friendly with Antoine as you are?"

I laughed. "Not exactly."

"Oh?"

"They never really got to know him when we were married. We were always traveling or busy at L'Oiseau Gris. Then we split up. So you can see how they wouldn't be close with him." I wasn't entirely sure that Dan and Haley would have liked Antoine any better if they had gotten to know him, but it was a convenient excuse.

"Oh, I definitely see. I was just curious. Your relationship with him seems good."

I shrugged. "He's not a bad guy. He didn't beat me or

cheat on me. It just wasn't the right relationship for me. Or
it wasn't anymore." It actually would have been a lot easier
to leave him if he had been a bad guy. If someone cheats on
you, or hits you, or gambles away your mortgage payments,
or snorts cocaine, or drinks until he blacks out, everyone
understands why you have to leave. When it becomes clear
that you'll never truly be happy if you don't leave, everyone
looks at you with that vaguely quizzical look sort of like
how Sprocket looks when he's eating peanut butter.

"Mmmm." She looked thoughtful and then smiled. We
walked down the stairs and into the arms of Antoine's
crew. Talk about out of the frying pan. I braced myself for
the storm of invective and took evasive action, trying to
walk to the side and onto the sidewalk without walking
through them. Brooke moved in front of me. "What did
you do? Why has Antoine been arrested?"

I thought about pushing past her, letting her comments
roll off my back, but I was a little sick of Antoine's crew's
attitude. I wasn't the enemy here. I looked down at Brooke.
"Antoine's been arrested because he had the means, motive
and opportunity to murder Melanie."

Lucy gasped. Brooke stared at me openmouthed.

"I found a lawyer for him and arranged for them to
meet." I gestured toward Cynthia. "This is Cynthia Harlen."

I pushed through them to the sidewalk.

"Wait," Brooke called. "How is he? Is he okay?"

I stopped. "So you're speaking to me now?"

She had the decency to blush. "Yes. I am. We all are.
What can we do? How can we help?"

Lucy stepped up next to her. "We'll do anything. Anything at all."

I looked from one to the next. Their loyalty said more

positive things about Antoine than anything else I knew. Forget his celebrated restaurant, his successful television show, his booming product lines. His people felt this loyal to him. Loyal enough to treat me like vermin when they thought I'd hurt him. Loyal enough to swallow their anger if they thought it could help him.

"I don't suppose any of you saw him that night after you got back to the hotel," Cynthia asked.

Looks were exchanged. Lucy shook her head. "We were all pretty exhausted. I went to my room and crashed. I didn't come out until the next morning."

"You mean when I saw you in the café?" I asked, remembering the way she'd turned her back on me.

"I guess." She looked down at the ground, clearly embarrassed.

Whatever. The rest of the group nodded and made agreement sounds. Nobody had seen Antoine after their return to the hotel. Nobody had seen Melanie, either. Nobody had even seen one another.

I would have been suspicious. These people were young and healthy. One could reasonably assume that they'd be interested in partying on the road, but I'd gone on the road with Antoine a few times. I knew how exhausting and long those days could be, especially for the crew. The amount of equipment that had to be shifted, the arrangements that needed to be made and double-checked, the personnel that had to be tracked. It was a huge job.

"So we can't help, then?" Lucy asked.

Cynthia shrugged. "Only if you know of someone else who might want to hurt Melanie."

The group fell silent. I looked around, but no one met my eyes. Whatever anyone knew, no one was telling. "Call me if you think of anything," Cynthia said.

Cynthia and I started down the sidewalk toward where she'd parked her car. I heard a sharp bark and turned. It was Garrett with Sprocket. "Wait up, will you?"

"What are you doing here?" I asked.

He shrugged. "I thought I'd walk you home." He handed over Sprocket's leash.

I was about to make a smart-ass comment about it being Grand Lake and it not exactly being a high-crime area, but then remembered that a woman associated with my ex-husband was dead and we didn't know why or how. "Thanks."

He turned to Cynthia. "Nice to see you again, Cynthia." He stuck out his hand.

Instead of taking his hand and shaking it, though, Cynthia stepped forward and straightened the knot in Garrett's tie. "Thank you, Counselor. That means a lot coming from you. I was surprised you recommended me. I know you haven't always been a fan of my work."

"That's not true, Cynthia. I just operate a little more within the boundaries than you do. It doesn't mean I didn't admire your . . . moxie." He tried to take a step back, but Cynthia still had hold of his tie.

She laughed that deep throaty laugh, her head tilted back a little. I stared at Garrett staring at the white column of her throat. "Moxie? Who says words like that?" She let go of his tie with one hand for long enough to hold it up traffic-cop style. "Never mind. I know. You use words like that. This little town might be the perfect place for you."

"It's okay," he said.

Okay? It was okay? I bent over and pretended to straighten Sprocket's collar and got a good look at my food-stained jeans. I looked over at Cynthia in her beautifully cut suit, the pencil skirt hugging her in all the right places. Everything about her was in place. Everything about her was in order. Stray hairs didn't escape and curl wildly around her head. She wasn't smudged with flour or sugar or chocolate. What the hell was Garrett doing with me?

Garrett took a step back, forcing Cynthia to let go of his tie or strangle him. "Is this your car?"

She nodded and got into a sleek Mercedes sedan. "See you around," she said through the window, and then drove away.

"How'd it go?" Garrett asked, head bowed slightly against the night breeze as we started to walk.

"Antoine's crew is speaking to me again." I wasn't entirely sure it was good news, but it was nice not to be a pariah.

"I noticed. It's part of why I waited a block away. I didn't really want to talk to them."

"Part of why? Is the other part Cynthia?" Our hands brushed as we walked.

He took hold of mine and intertwined our fingers. "Possibly."

I tamped down the twinge of jealousy that spiked up in my chest. "Wanna talk about it?"

"No. Right now I want to hold hands and walk." He gave my hand a squeeze.

It sounded good to me, too.

Six

When we got to the end of the driveway, we could see Dan sitting on the front porch with two beers and a blanket. Garrett kissed me on the forehead and said, "Talk to you tomorrow?"

I nodded and made my way to where Dan was sitting. I wrapped the blanket around my shoulders, sat down and took one of the beers. "How'd you know when I'd get here?" I asked. I would have suspected Garrett, but I hadn't seen him text or call.

"I had Vera give me a heads-up." He bumped me with his shoulder. He might as well have held up a neon sign announcing he forgave me.

"That feels weirdly stalkerish. You and Huerta are getting a little creepy." I bumped him back.

"Live with it." He shrugged. "How'd it go?"

"Fine." I took a long sip of the beer and sighed.

"Was it worth pissing all of us off?" he asked, his tone even.

"If it keeps Antoine from being convicted it was." I didn't look at him. It wasn't the answer he wanted, but it was the truth. "He didn't do it."

"Rebecca, he had everything. Motive, means, opportunity. All of it." He shifted a little away from me on the step.

That sounded unhappily close to what Cynthia had said. It didn't matter, though. "He's not a murderer, Dan. A raging narcissist? Probably. A bit of an egomaniac? Also probably. I don't think he'd kill anyone because of it."

"You're always cutting him too much slack." He shot me a look from the corner of his eye.

I pointed at him with my beer bottle. "You've never cut him any."

"I never felt like he deserved it." He tapped my·bottle with his as if we were toasting.

I couldn't totally blame Dan. He'd only seen one side of Antoine and only heard about one side of him from me. Ex-wives really aren't the greatest publicity people. "You should see how upset his crew is, Dan. He's got to deserve something or that many people wouldn't be that loyal to him. They'd do anything for him."

He settled back down next to me. "So you met Cynthia," he said, changing the topic. "What did you think?"

I sighed. "I think she's smart and focused and gorgeous. I also think there's a whole hell of a lot more to the story of her and Garrett than I know."

"Probably." Dan drank some more beer.

That was not much of an answer. "Care to elaborate?"

He stood up. "Nope. It's Garrett's story to tell, not mine." He reached down a hand and helped me to my feet.

"You know, that doesn't make me feel like there's nothing for me to know." I brushed off the seat of my jeans.

"It wasn't supposed to." He took my beer bottle from me. "Go to bed, Rebecca. It's late."

I was about to argue, but then realized how exhausted I was. "Good night, Dan." Sprocket and I went to our apartment. I let myself in. This was one of the times the apartment felt empty. I hoped it wouldn't stay that way.

My morning rush on Saturday tends to start and end a little later than the weekday rush, but I still get quite a few people coming through for coffee and breakfast bars. Usually. It didn't quite work that way with the news vans parked in front of my shop. It probably didn't help that we were keeping the blinds down at the front of the shop. We barely looked open. A few courageous souls braved the sea of cameras and microphones to get their coffee and breakfast bars. I figured the same would be true in the afternoon. People had to have their fudge. I had at least five advance orders. That was worth staying open for, right?

Susanna had a lacrosse game, so Dario came to help—not that there was much to help with. Janet Barry, my most regular regular, backed her way into the shop with her double stroller at about two. "Whew," she said. "It's getting bad out there."

Dario hurried around the counter to hold the door open for her. Joey—Janet's two-year-old— said, "Hi, Dawio."

Dario reached down and fist-bumped Joey. "What are they up to out there?"

"They're asking people if they met that poor murdered girl or Antoine or . . ." Her words trailed off.

"Or?" I asked.

She squatted down to wipe some drool from Jack's face.

He must have been teething again. "Or if we know you and what you're like."

"What did you tell them?" I asked, crossing my arms over my chest as if I could protect my heart that way.

"I told them I've known you since third grade and that you make a heck of a popcorn bar." She straightened Jack in his stroller seat.

I didn't expect it, but hot tears pricked behind my eyes. "Thanks, Janet." I hadn't always felt like my hometown had my back. In fact, I'd pretty much never felt like my hometown had my back. It was nice to know that at least one person outside of my family thought well enough of me to say it to the news media.

She turned to me and smiled. "No problem. Now what else does a girl have to do to get some caramel cashew popcorn around here?"

Dario dished up a small bag.

"It's on the house," I said when he went to ring it up.

Janet looked around the empty shop. "I'm not sure you can afford to be giving stuff away, Rebecca."

"I'm not sure I have a better way to say thank you." I managed to say it without my voice wobbling, but only just.

She waved her hand at me as if she could wave away the compliment. "I'll be going, then."

Dario went to hold the door open for her as she maneuvered the stroller out. In unison, they both said, "Uh-oh."

"What kind of uh-oh?" I asked.

Neither of them answered. Dario clapped his hand over his eyes.

I walked to the window to peek outside at the street through the blinds. A new group had joined the throng in front of the shop. This group wore blue shirts. I couldn't actually make out the logo embroidered on the breast pocket, but I didn't need to. I knew what it was as soon as I saw that Mediterranean blue. It was BB. It stood for Belanger Bunnies. Antoine's supporters. They had arrived in Grand Lake and a group of around twelve of them stood across the street holding signs with my face on them, but with devil horns and goatees added with thick black ink.

"Rebecca is the root," they chanted. "The root of all evil. Rebecca is the root. The root of all evil."

"Oh, come on," I said.

We all jumped when a sharp knock sounded on the back door. "I'll see who it is," Dario said. "You stay here and stay out of sight."

Janet waved. "Good luck, Rebecca. Let me know if I can help."

Dario came back in with Lucy and Jason.

"Hi," Lucy said, a little breathless. "We thought we'd come in this way to avoid the media out front."

"Good thinking, but what are you doing here?" I asked Lucy. Then I asked her again. Then I nudged her. Then I turned to see what she was staring at. It was Dario. He was certainly stare-worthy. "Stop drooling," I whispered in her ear.

She startled. "We wanted to shoot some footage of you working in the store." She turned to Jason. "Get some footage of the people who come through the store."

"Lucy, do you really think the segment is still going to run?" I didn't mention that Antoine's whole show could be canceled as soon as the network figured out he'd been arrested for murder and certainly would be canceled if it actually went to trial.

"Sure. I talked to the boss this morning. He said you lined him up with an awesome lawyer and he'll be out in

no time. The only thing this little episode will do is get
him more publicity. The show will be more popular than
ever. I mean, look outside at all the media and the Bunnies." Lucy spoke quickly. Maybe too quickly. Almost as
if she was trying to convince herself as much as me. "It's
going to be fine. Just fine."

I blinked as if that would make the picture before me
come clear. It didn't. "I'm really glad that Antoine has a
lot of faith in Cynthia, but don't you feel this is a little
premature?" And a little weird.

"I know it probably seems that way, but the crew is all
here. Because of Antoine's . . . situation, we'll probably
have to put the episode together faster than usual. We
might as well get all the film we can without him. It will
make it all simpler in the end." She smiled. "Let's get
started, shall we?"

It was one of those weird situations where the person's
logic flowed seamlessly, but somehow their original
premise—in this case, that Antoine was going to be out
of jail any second—seemed flawed. I never knew how to
argue in those situations and decided it would be easier
not to at this moment. I might as well let them do their jobs
while I did mine, assuming I could keep mine with no
customers coming into the store.

Flashes started going off like strobe lights at the front of
the store. I turned to see what had gotten the camera people
out there all excited and saw Brooke talking to Yolanda
Barnett of WCLV News in Cleveland. I cracked the door
open so we could hear. "We are all confident that Antoine
will be released very soon. He is, of course, completely
innocent and the entire situation is simply a travesty."

"What do you know about the evidence against Mr.
Belanger?" Yolanda asked.

"I doubt there's any evidence against him. He didn't do it. It's really that simple." Brooke nodded her head for emphasis.

"Is that why you've decided to go ahead and film here at his ex-wife's popcorn shop?" Yolanda gestured to POPS and the camera panned in our direction.

"It's quite expensive to have a crew on the road," Brooke said, adjusting her glasses. "We decided to make sure we got whatever film we could so we'd be ready to finish the segment when Antoine is released."

"She's making it sound like it was her and Antoine who decided to film today," Lucy said. "The nerve!"

"Wasn't it?" I asked.

"Of course not. I was the one who went to the jail this morning. I was the one who spoke to him. I can't believe she's taking credit on television for my decisions." Lucy stamped her foot. "I was Melanie's assistant. Not her. I was the one who was always at her beck and call. I was the one who always had to fetch and carry for her."

"We are as committed as Antoine to making sure our show continues to run smoothly even without our executive producer, although we, of course, mourn her passing. We feel we're honoring her by making sure the show does go on. Melanie would have wanted it that way." Brooke bowed her head for a second.

Lucy gasped. "As if Brooke would know what Melanie wanted! She was so scared of Melanie she'd barely ask her for her coffee order. Melanie relied on me. She talked to me."

"Let it go, Lucy," Jason said from behind her. "It doesn't matter who gets credit. It just matters that we get the work done."

Lucy shot him the kind of side eye that would make a

lesser man wilt. If he noticed, he didn't let it slow him down. He stood up from where he was crouching over a piece of equipment in a case. "Mind if I mike you up?"

Somehow it sounded dirty coming out of his mouth. I'd bet a lot of things sounded dirty coming out of this guy's mouth. It was that kind of mouth. Full and sensual without being in any way feminine. His thick black hair was cut short, but you could still see the flecks of gray in it. What was it about those little flecks that made a guy irresistible? Was it the promise of experience? Or was that just me? None of it was hurt by his broad shoulders and square jaw. He really belonged in front of the camera instead of behind it. "Sure," I said. "Mike away."

He laughed and something inside me quivered. I shivered a little as his broad blunt fingers brushed against my collarbone when he affixed the small microphone to my blouse. "Tell me what you had for breakfast," he commanded.

"Black coffee and a cranberry white-chocolate popcorn breakfast bar," I blurted.

He checked the gauges on his equipment and winked at me. "Perfect."

Brooke came in through the front door of the shop.

"What was that about?" Lucy demanded.

"I was doing a little PR work, making sure they knew that Antoine is absolutely not guilty." Brooke started rummaging through one of the equipment cases.

Lucy loomed over her, arms crossed tightly over her chest. "Who elected you to do that?"

Brooke looked up at her. "No one, I guess. It needed to be done so I did it."

"I don't think it's appropriate for you to decide to go

talk to the press without consulting Antoine." She gestured to herself and Jason. "Or the rest of the crew."

"Antoine's not here to consult, in case you haven't noticed." Brooke didn't even look up at her.

Lucy flushed bright red. "I did notice. That's why I visited him in jail this morning. I know what he wants us to do and not do. I'm the one who gets to say when we talk to the press."

Brooke straightened up. The two women were much too close, both of them leaning in toward each other. "I don't recall anyone making you my boss."

Lucy glared and opened her mouth, but before anything else came out, Jason interrupted. "A little help here?" He gestured around the shop and then to all the equipment.

Lucy and Brooke both backed away from each other. Next Brooke was holding a light gauge by my face and taking readings. "A little hot in here, but I think we can compensate." She patted my shoulder. "Just pretend like we're not even here. Do your thing."

I didn't have a lot of choice. Suddenly, a large group of people pushed through the door to the shop. At first I thought it was the media taking the next step and actually coming in. Then I thought maybe it was the Belanger Bunnies coming to physically attack me and I shrank back behind the counter. Then I realized that Faith was at the head of the line with her two daughters.

"We just finished soccer and the girls need a snack." She marched up to the counter. Behind her were Olive Hicks, Aaron Woodingham and Carson Jenkins. Mayor Allen Thompson held the door open for everyone.

"I haven't had coffee yet," Carson said from the back of the line. "Well, not good coffee."

I pushed through the crowd to take a look out the door. Janet Barry was running interference between the media people and the townspeople, using her double stroller alternately like a battering ram and a bunker. Angelina Choi had joined her with her umbrella stroller. Teri Daniels ran down the street with her jogging stroller in front of her. It was like a wall of strollers.

The line was getting longer, and while Dario was magnificent in so many ways, he couldn't do it all. I did my thing and the next hour slid by with me hardly noticing the cameras and microphones, except for when Jason stepped backward, tripped on a chair and almost took out one of my few tables.

When the customers finally were served and chatted with about the weather, I made a fresh pot of coffee for the crew and we all sat down. "Did you get what you needed?" I asked Lucy.

She nodded. "If it's not everything, it will be easy to shoot around it. Honestly, we'll be able to shoot Antoine's part in an afternoon, I think. As soon as he's out of that jail cell, we can be on our way."

"You're pretty sure Antoine didn't do it," I said.

She laughed. "You are, too. You're the one who got him the fancy lawyer lady, aren't you?"

True enough. "Who do you think might have done it?"

Lucy went very still. "I'd rather not speculate."

Something about her tone made me look at her a little more closely. "What does that mean?"

"Look. Melanie wasn't the easiest person to get along with. I'm not saying that that makes her a target for murder, but it does mean that there are probably a lot of people who are not all that sorry to see her gone." She twirled a strand of her hair around her index finger.

I looked around my shop and saw Melanie's co-workers less than seventy-two hours after her death, enjoying coffee and snacks, chatting and laughing. No one seemed particularly broken up. I'd been more upset than they seemed to be. "Do you think someone from the show could have done it?" I whispered.

Lucy shook her head. "Don't be ridiculous. If any of these people didn't want to work with Melanie, all they had to do was get a different job. We're not the only cooking show out there, you know."

I did know. I also knew that Antoine's show was one of the most prestigious and most profitable and came with some fun travel opportunities. Not all their shoots were in small towns in northern Ohio. I looked around at them again. No one seemed to be mourning, but no one seemed to be crushed by guilt, either. I'd seen what that looked like. It wasn't pretty.

"I still can't believe Melanie would steal from Antoine like that, though." Lucy sat down.

I turned to look at her. "Wait a second. You were the one who said no one liked her."

"Yeah, no one liked her, but no one doubted her loyalty to Antoine. I thought she'd bleed Belanger Blue if you pricked her. Although . . ." Her words trailed off.

"Although what?" I asked.

Lucy shrugged. "She hadn't been at the top of her game lately. She'd been . . . slipping. Forgetting little things. Mixing things up."

That didn't jibe at all with what Antoine had said. "I thought Antoine relied on her absolutely."

"He did." She leaned in. "I'd been covering for her a lot. I figured it was a phase. You know, with the breakup and everything. Plus, it gave me a chance to see a little more of her job. You know, in case there was ever a chance to step up, I'd already have the experience. I'd been consulting with her almost every night." She made a face. "Sometimes even while she took her evening bath."

The group made their way out of the shop through the kitchen. Lucy looked around the kitchen. She got a funny look on her face when she saw the photo of the woman that Dan had thought might be my dark-haired lady. "Why do you have a photo of Marie Parsons?"

"You know that woman?"

She nodded. "You do, too."

"She looked familiar, but I couldn't place her."

"Really? I suppose she was just revving up into higher levels of crazy when you left."

It suddenly came to me. "You mean Antoine's stalker?"

I'd mainly known about Marie from news accounts. No wonder she'd seemed familiar. I'd been gone before things got out of hand. She'd started out as another one of the Belanger Bunnies. She'd show up at tapings of *Cooking the Belanger Way*. She'd be at book signings of Antoine's cookbooks. She'd eat at L'Oiseau Gris. Well, not often. It wasn't a cheap restaurant to eat at and it wasn't particularly easy to get reservations.

Then things got a little weird. She started making special little items for Antoine. A special scrapbook of the launch of his salad dressings. A painting of him in his kitchen done from a photograph we weren't sure how she'd taken. Sweet, but a little over the line. Then she started dropping them off at our house in Napa. That's when Antoine started getting nervous.

After I left, she escalated. A lot. It was as if she thought she could move right into my spot next to Antoine. Like literally move right in. She actually showed up at the house with a U-Haul full of her stuff.

What followed was a series of restraining orders that she would then violate and I believe finally some jail time.

"Yeah," Lucy said. "That's totally her. We've all been shown her photo dozens of times so we remember to watch out for her. She was released from jail a few months ago."

"But there's still a restraining order in place, right? She's not supposed to be anywhere near Antoine." I turned the photo around to look at it again myself.

"If she obeyed restraining orders, she wouldn't have done the jail time, Rebecca." She picked up the photo. "It still doesn't explain why you have her photo here."

"Dan brought it over to see if she was the dark-haired woman I'd seen the morning I found Melanie. She was the only dark-haired woman staying at the hotel who wasn't part of your crew." Could this woman have something to do with Melanie's death? It wouldn't be the first time a stalker had turned violent.

"She was at the hotel?" Lucy's eyes went wide.

"That's what Dan said." I chewed my lip.

Lucy grabbed my hand. "Where is she now?"

"Dan said he tried to find her, but she wasn't in her room. I'll call him right away."

The crew slipped out the back door to shoot some more scenic backdrops for the show. I had a feeling that if this particular episode ever aired there were going to be a lot of scenic backdrops with voice-overs from Antoine. After they left, I slipped out the back to take out the morning's garbage before calling Dan and, frankly, to clear my head for a second. There was a little too much hustle and bustle going on for my new small-town tastes. I came out onto the porch.

A woman stood with her back to me. I froze for a second, not sure what to do. What was she doing back here? "Can I help you?" I asked in my best "I don't want to help and never will" voice.

She whirled around. It was the woman I'd seen going into the café and by the lighthouse when Antoine was filming and maybe coming out of Barbara's shop.

"No," she said, backing away like I might take a swing at her with my giant Hefty bag. "Just leaving. Sorry to bother you."

"What are you doing back here?" I stepped toward her. Maybe I would take a swing at her with my Hefty bag. "Who are you?"

She turned and scurried down the alley.

"Wait. What's your name?" I called after her.

She didn't turn. I dropped my Hefty bag and started walking after her. She glanced over her shoulder and took off running.

After retrieving my garbage and depositing it in the Dumpster, I went back inside. Dario was taking off his apron. "Okay if I take off, Rebecca?"

"Absolutely. Thank you so much. You haven't even been here a week and you're already saving my life multiple times over."

He laughed. "I sold some food to people and made some coffee. Lifesaving is his bag." He nodded his head out toward the front of the shop.

I peeked out. Eric stood in the middle of the room, looking around as if he'd never seen the shop before. "Hey, Eric."

"Hi, Rebecca. How's Dario doing?" he asked.

"He's magnificent." In oh so many ways.

He chuckled. "I've heard him described that way before."

Dario slipped out from behind me. "Oh, you," he said and walked up to Eric and kissed him. On the lips.

Ah, that was why Eric had blushed when he described Dario as his friend. He was an extra-friendly friend.

I said good-bye to Eric and Dario and called Dan. "That picture you showed me earlier? The one of the dark-haired woman who was at the hotel?"

"Yes."

"Well, Lucy just saw it in my kitchen and said that it was Antoine's stalker, Marie Parsons."

"That's not the name she was registered under. The ID she gave Derek said her name was . . ." I heard paper rustling. "Mandy Pope."

"Lucy was really certain it was her."

"I'll see if I can find her."

"Oh, also, I saw the mystery woman again."

Seven

For a second, I wasn't sure Dan had heard what I'd said because he didn't say anything. "The woman I saw at the café the morning I found Melanie was lurking behind my shop."

"Lurking? What does lurking look like?" He yawned.

"It looks like someone who might have been hiding underneath my back porch." That seemed like bona fide lurking to me.

"Are we talking about a woman or a stray cat here?" Dan asked.

"Dan, why aren't you taking this seriously? This is the third time I've seen this woman." I was beginning to think he really didn't want to examine any other possibilities besides Antoine. "She was skulking in Barbara's shop, too. Faith thought she was a shoplifter."

"Lurking and skulking?"

"Yes. Lurking and skulking. What are you going to do about it?"

I heard what sounded like a pen tapping on a desk over the phone. Finally he spoke. "Here's why I'm not taking your reports of strange women lurking or skulking in the area seriously. First of all, you're the only person who saw this woman at the hotel. Julie at the café doesn't remember anyone coming in who wasn't with the television crew."

"She was busy. Maybe she didn't notice. Maybe . . ." I could have spun a dozen reasons Julie might not remember a woman coming through, but Dan interrupted me.

"Maybe pigs flew by the window and distracted her, Bec. I don't know. I'm supposed to gather evidence, not speculate. I just know she doesn't remember seeing this woman you report being in the area. Second, I'm guessing Cynthia told you one of the best defenses for Antoine was to find someone else to blame for the crime."

That knocked the top off my meringue. "That's beside the point." My face felt hot. Was he implying what I thought he was implying?

"No. It's not. I know Cynthia and I know her tactics. I also know how persuasive she can be. And now here you are delivering two suspicious people to me. I don't think it's a coincidence." He was speaking slowly and clearly, a sure sign he was getting ticked off.

Which was fine, because I was already ticked off. "It's not a tactic. That woman was here. She was at the café. She was at the lighthouse when Antoine was filming there, too." I couldn't believe he wasn't taking my word for it. "You're the one who gave me the picture of the woman who went to jail for stalking Antoine and said she was at the hotel the night Melanie was killed."

"Do you think there might be tape of your lurker at the lighthouse? That the crew might have caught her on tape?" He sounded a little more interested.

My answer wasn't going to encourage that, though. "Probably not. They keep the camera focused on Antoine for the most part. I mean, he's why people tune in after all. You could ask Jason. Maybe he panned over the crowd for some reason."

"I'll ask," he said, but it didn't sound like it would be at the top of his priority list. "I'll see what I can do to track down Marie Parsons, too."

The news vans were still in front of the store when it was time to close up. So were the Belanger Bunnies with their signs. Seriously, what had I ever done to them? Whatever it was that they thought I'd done, I didn't have the energy or the heart to confront them about it today. I snapped Sprocket's leash on and we snuck out the back door into the alley.

Jasper was waiting for the leftovers. He wasn't always here when I left, but he generally came by. I thought he'd eventually get sick of popcorn leftovers, but it hadn't happened yet. Then it occurred to me that with the amount of time he spent in the back alleys of Grand Lake looking for handouts and leftovers, he might have seen my mystery lady.

"Hey, have you happened to see a dark-haired woman hanging around here?" I asked.

"Nope." He took the bag of popcorn from me. "Looking for a one-armed man, are you?"

"What?" I didn't think I'd mentioned numbers of limbs at all.

"You know. Like that old TV show. *The Fugitive*. The guy always says there's a one-armed man who actually did the crime."

"Did he do it? In the show?" I asked.

"Come to think of it, he did." Jasper scratched the back of his head. "I'll keep an eye out for her."

When we reached the end of the alley, Jasper turned to stay with me as I took the back route home. "Isn't your place the other direction?" I asked.

He looked a little uncomfortable. "Yeah, but those Belanger Bunny ladies? They really kind of hate you."

"Really? What was your first clue? Their chants about me being the root of all evil? Or was it the posters with my face inside a red circle with a slash through it?" The Belanger Bunnies had a way of making their opinions known.

"Both, to be honest."

"Do you know why?" I asked. I really couldn't come up with something I'd done to make them hate me so much.

"Something about deserting Antoine. Leaving him heartbroken." He shrugged. "Anyway, I thought I'd walk you home. Make sure you got there okay." He shoved his free hand into his pocket.

I stopped. "Jasper, that is really sweet." I wasn't sure I'd ever heard of Jasper doing anything that altruistic before.

He shrugged. "I kind of owe you. With that whole making-sure-I-didn't-get-charged-with-murder thing."

I may have also been part of why he'd been arrested in the first place, but I decided not to bring that up, and he walked me to the house.

"Thanks, Jasper."

"No problem. See you tomorrow." Then he turned and walked away, bag of leftover popcorn tucked beneath his arm.

* * *

Sundays I sleep in. I still open the shop, but not until the afternoon. The problem is that since I get up every other morning at five, sleeping in tends to mean seven. I like the extra sleep, but it doesn't feel as decadent as I'd like it to.

I sat up slowly in bed so as not to knock my head against the slanted ceiling. Sprocket lifted his head from where he slept in his bed and gave me a harrumph. "I hear you, boy," I said. "I'll be up in a minute."

It was more like fifteen minutes, but I figured that Sprocket couldn't tell time so he'd never know I lied to him. By seven thirty, I was in the kitchen with the radio switched on, making scrambled eggs. I'd considered poached, but it brought back too many memories of Melanie in her tub.

I was grooving to "Body and Soul" when the announcer cut in. "We bring you breaking news from Grand Lake."

I turned the heat off under the eggs. We had breaking news? I cringed. It had to be about Antoine.

"Antoine Belanger's attorney is about to make a statement."

I ran over to the television and snapped it on. Sure enough, on channel thirty-seven Cynthia was climbing the steps in front of the Sheriff's Department to stand in front of a veritable forest of microphones.

"Thank you for coming out today," she said, smiling to the reporters. "I wanted to make a brief statement on behalf of Monsieur Belanger."

She unfolded some papers and smoothed them in front of her on the podium. "Monsieur Belanger would like all of you to know that he is not guilty of the heinous crime of which he has been accused. The death of Melanie Fitzgerald was tragic. She was an integral part of his team for many years and was a trusted part of the *Cooking the Belanger Way* family. She will be missed. He is, however, in no way responsible for her passing."

Cynthia took off her reading glasses and looked out at the camera. "Monsieur Belanger was here in Grand Lake to feature his ex-wife's shop on his very popular television show. This kind of generosity is typical of him. A mention from Monsieur Belanger can make or break a restaurant or a product. He chooses to help people who he deems worthy no matter what his personal relationship is with them. Unfortunately, there are some who do not understand that sort of kindness. Ms. Anderson's relatives, such as Sheriff Dan Cooper, have always harbored ill will toward Monsieur Belanger and have used this opportunity to persecute him."

I gasped and sat down on the couch. Sprocket nudged my hand with his nose and I scratched his ears. Cynthia had just accused Dan of arresting Antoine because he didn't like him. On television. In front of God and everybody.

"Monsieur Belanger will be pleading not guilty tomorrow at his hearing. It is our first step in proving that he is completely innocent and is being framed by a malicious and vindictive law enforcement official." She folded up her papers and said, "That's all for now. No questions." She strode away from the podium.

I bet Dan wished he picked up my strange lurking woman now or had found Marie Parsons.

I went back over the conversation I'd had with Cynthia on the steps of the Sheriff's Department. Had I said anything about Dan in particular? Had I mentioned who my family was? I was still sitting on the couch with the spatula in my hand when the pounding on my door started.

I knew it was Dan. Of course it was Dan. Who else could it be but Dan?

I opened the door.

It was Dan.

"What the hell did that piece of French filth say to his lawyer about me?" he demanded.

"I'm not sure it was Antoine," I said. "I'm afraid it might have been me."

In the end, Dan decided it wasn't my fault. He even conceded it wasn't Antoine's fault. After all, Cynthia knew exactly who Dan was because of his long friendship with Garrett. It wouldn't have taken Sherlock Holmes to figure out that I was Dan's sister-in-law as well as being Antoine's ex-wife. He wasn't happy about it, but he wasn't calling Antoine names by the time he left. Even better, he wasn't calling me names.

I called Garrett. "Did you see Cynthia's press conference?" I asked.

"I did."

I waited for him to say something more, but he didn't. "Did you know she was going to do that?"

He sighed. "No. I'm not really surprised, though."

"You're not?"

"One of the reasons I suggested you contact Cynthia is because she will do anything—and I do mean anything—to defend her client. She will use the media to create sympathy for Antoine. She will point fingers. She will do everything she can to muddy the situation until it's not really clear why anyone would have ever suspected Antoine in the first place. If there's someone out there who can get him out of that jail cell smelling like a rose, it's Cynthia." He didn't sound like he totally admired that quality.

I knew that was good, but I still felt uncomfortable. "Did she have to do that at the expense of Dan's reputation?"

"Until Dan hands over a retainer to her, he is simply another tool to be used in the service of clearing her client. She's that single-minded."

"I don't think he likes her anymore," I said. "He was a little angry."

Garrett made a funny noise. "He never liked her. Don't let him try to tell you any different."

It made me feel kind of good that Dan had never liked Cynthia. "What didn't he like about her?"

"I'm not going there, Rebecca. Ask Dan if you really want to know."

"He said the same thing about talking to you about her. What did you guys do? Take some kind of blood oath?" Boys. They were so frustrating sometimes.

"Sort of. Think of it as our own personal code."

"Fine. See you later?"

"You bet."

Maybe I could use bacon to get the information out of him.

By Monday morning, the television news people had figured out what time POPS opened in the morning and were stacked two deep out front by the time I opened the doors. They had also figured out where they needed to go to get decent coffee. They might be vultures, but they weren't stupid. The second the doors opened, they rushed in, demanding coffee, popcorn bars and comments on the feud between Dan and Antoine. Yolanda Barnett took her large coffee and breakfast bar and shoved a microphone in Dario's face. "Do you have any comment on Sheriff Cooper's persecution of celebuchef Antoine Belanger?"

Dario pointed to the counter and said, "Half-and-half and sugar is over there." Then he turned to the next customer who ordered the same thing and asked if it was true that Antoine had been sleeping with Melanie. It went like that for about five minutes and then Dario looked at me and said, "I can make this stop. Permission to set a few ground rules?"

"Permission granted."

In one smooth move, he leapt on top of the counter. If he loomed before, he was now mega-looming. I was surprised he hadn't hit his head on the ceiling. "Listen up, people."

Cameras went off. Microphones turned toward him. "From now on, only one member from each news team is allowed inside the shop at a time."

"Wait. What?" Rick Day from the *Chicago Examiner* asked.

Dario pointed a finger at him. "I'm not finished. If that one person wants to fill orders for his or her team, that's fine, but the second a question is asked that is not related to the food we are serving you, that person will be banned. For life."

Someone gasped. Someone else said, "Hey, that's not . . ."

Dario whirled. "There will be no arguing with those rules. Arguing with POPS staff about the rules will result in you being ejected from the shop."

"For life?" someone asked.

Dario nodded. "For life." There was silence. Dario looked over the crowd. "I suggest all of you who have not been served yet go outside, choose a representative, give that person your order and send that one person back in. Make sure it's someone who doesn't ask a lot of questions."

No one moved.

"Or go get your morning coffee from the diner." He crossed his arms over his chest and his biceps bulged.

Two reporters got stuck in the door trying to go out at the same time.

Antoine's hearing was scheduled for eleven o'clock. I left Dario at the shop as soon as the morning rush was over and began my walk over to the courthouse. Normally, I felt a little jolt of pleasure every time I walked out of POPS onto Main Street in Grand Lake. It was so perfectly small-town picturesque, especially on a crisp fall day, yellow-orange leaves silhouetted against a crisp blue sky with little wisps of clouds floating around like marshmallows melting in hot chocolate.

Today, not so much. Virtually everyone who had been in front of my shop that morning was gone. I had a feeling they were already at the courthouse. They'd left behind what large groups of people always leave behind. Flattened grass, trash, the detritus of human life. I went back into the shop and grabbed a garbage bag. As I walked, I picked up the discarded wrappers and cans and cups.

"Who assigned you community service?" Faith asked as I passed her antique shop.

"My conscience?" I suggested. After all, none of these

people would have been massing on Main Street if it weren't for me and my cuckoo ex and his thieving assistant.

"Those things are overrated if you ask me." Faith leaned against the doorframe of the shop.

I shrugged. "I feel a little guilty about the mess." I gestured at the litter on the street. "I don't want all the other shop owners to be pissed at me."

She waved her hand as if to clear it away. "They should all be thanking you. Everyone's business has doubled since the press arrived. We've got people in here doing early Christmas shopping. The diner can't make the grilled cheese sandwiches and hamburgers fast enough. It's all good."

"Thanks. That makes me feel a little better."

"Besides, if anyone's to blame it's that ex-husband of yours."

"It's not exactly his fault he was arrested for murdering his assistant when he didn't do it."

She shrugged. "So you say. Have fun at the hearing." She went back inside.

I walked the rest of the way to the courthouse. I was right. Everyone was there. The press. The Bunnies. Half the town. What was worse, they were intermingling. I overheard one of the Bunnies talking to Yolanda Barnett. "You know she was suspected of killing that nice little old lady here just a few months ago," the Bunny said. "She was even brought in for questioning. Twice."

"Wasn't someone else charged with that killing?" Yolanda asked.

The Bunny shrugged. "Eventually, but everyone here in her own hometown thought she could have done it. Tells you something about a person, doesn't it?" She pursed her lips.

Mayor Thompson strode up next to the Bunny. "Excuse me, but not everyone here in Grand Lake considered Rebecca a viable suspect. Many of us knew she was innocent from the start. We are proud to have her return to Grand Lake and think her shop is an excellent addition to our Main Street thoroughfare."

I blinked. I guessed Mayor Thompson totally forgave me for hitting him over the head with a flowerpot. Good to know.

I didn't wait to hear more even if it was giving me a big case of the warm fuzzies deep inside. I headed for the front steps. I would have much rather stayed at POPS and made the fudge for the afternoon rush, but Cynthia had been adamant that I must be by Antoine's side when he came in front of the judge.

I opened the door to walk into the courtroom and immediately backed away and shut it again. The room echoed with noise. The oak of the door pulsed under my hand when I touched it. I looked over at Deputy Stephens, who stood next to the door, hands clasped behind his back, staring straight ahead, his head so low it seemed to rest on his thick shoulders. Stephens was one of the beefier of Grand Lake's deputies. Between the imposing muscles and the shaved head, not many people wanted to mess with him.

"How long has it been like this?" I asked, pointing at the door.

"They started showing up at nine," he said. "Just been getting louder and louder since then."

"Is it at capacity yet?" There had to be rules about how many people were allowed in the courtroom.

He unclasped his hands and looked at the round clicker he held. "We can take three more people after you." He shot me a look. "You are going in, aren't you? Please don't make me reset the clicker, Rebecca. Dan'll kill me if I screw up the numbers on this one."

I really didn't want to go in. I hadn't wanted to go at all, but Cynthia had made it clear that my attendance was mandatory. "We need to have a show of support for Antoine. The crew will be there in the front two rows with you as well," she'd said.

"I'm going in. I just need to brace myself." I shut my eyes and took a couple of deep breaths. First I thought about the lighthouse and the lake and the way the light played across them in different seasons, but then I remembered Antoine standing in front of the lighthouse claiming to have saved me from a killer and I felt my blood pressure rise. Instead I thought about my kitchen at POPS. I imagined the blue walls and the big wooden table. I listened for the sound of caramel sauce bubbling on the stove and smelled the aroma of coffee brewing. I focused on the way Coco Pop Fudge melted on my tongue. Then I opened my eyes and smiled at Raymond.

"Went to your happy place, did you?" He smiled. "Mine's a beach."

"Kitchen for me," I said.

"Makes sense." Then he blew out a deep breath and went back to staring straight ahead, probably mentally picturing warm sand and blue water.

I pulled the door open again and walked in with my head held high. I sailed down to the front row and sat down next to Lucy. Next to her was Brooke, with Jason on the other side of her.

Cynthia was over at the table for the prosecution chatting with the assistant district attorney. "What is she doing?" I whispered to Lucy.

"Honestly? I think she's engaging in some kind of psychological warfare. That woman's a little scary." Lucy shivered.

"I think scary's what Antoine needs right now. By the way, where is he?" I looked around the courtroom.

"They haven't brought him in yet," Brooke said.

He was probably changing into the clothing that I brought for him. He'd given me his hotel room key and I'd gone through his things to pick out his courtroom clothing. Cynthia had said to go sophisticated, but not snobby. I had ended up picking out a blue sweater that brought out his eyes, a pair of gray slacks and a pair of shoes that were shined to a high gloss.

I knew the second he walked in. I felt the change in the air. I saw the women reporters sit up taller. A few of them licked their lips. I turned around. I had maybe done a little too good of a job picking out his clothes. The sweater and slacks hung a little loose on him, but otherwise he looked like the picture of French sophistication and elegance. The bailiff led him to the table and he sat.

Lucy leaned forward and put her hand on his shoulder. He patted it and she began to cry.

"Lucy, are you all right?" Antoine reached into his pocket and frowned. I knew immediately what I'd forgotten. A handkerchief. Antoine always carried one. He shot me a look.

I scrounged some tissues from my purse and handed them to Lucy.

"Thanks," she said between sniffles. "It's just . . . it's been so many days since I've seen you. I'm so relieved you're all right."

"Calm yourself. It will all be fine." Antoine patted her hand and then turned to me and rolled his eyes.

Back in the day, I'd respond to an eye roll from Antoine by intervening somehow, creating a buffer between him and whoever was irritating him. I wasn't intervening this time. She was his crew and he was on his own. I didn't have time to tell him that because Judge Romero walked into the courtroom at that moment. All the sudden it was *All rise* and all that. Then Judge Romero took the bench.

He was an imposing man. Tall and broad-shouldered, but with a little extra weight on him as well. The mark of a man who enjoyed what was set before him at the table. Not gluttonous. Just appreciative. He had thick black hair, a well-trimmed beard and expressive bushy eyebrows. He took a moment and looked around the courtroom.

"I'd like to make some things clear before we get started," he said. "I will not tolerate disruption in my courtroom. I have a zero-tolerance policy. That means one outburst, you're out. One flash goes off, you're out. One cell phone rings." He paused and looked around the room like someone might be stupid enough to answer him. No one was. "That's right. You're out."

He shifted in his seat and looked down at Antoine. "One last thing I'd like to say before we get started. Monsieur Belanger, I am a great admirer of your books, your show and your products. We use your vinaigrette all the time in our house. Exquisite. That does not mean, however, that you will be receiving special treatment in this courtroom. As much as it would pain me to lock up the man who taught me to emulsify a mayonnaise, I will do it if that is what the law dictates. Understood?"

"*Oui*, Your Honor," Antoine said.

I started to giggle, but Romero glared at me and I settled down. Antoine knew exactly when to start speaking French and when to stick exclusively to English. It was another weapon in his arsenal that he used to subtly manipulate people into doing exactly what he wanted them to do. Judge Romero was the first official I'd heard him speak to in French since this whole debacle had begun. It was a subtle appeal to the man's snobbery and had been deftly done.

Romero banged his gavel twice and Cynthia and Ron Ramsey, assistant district attorney, leapt to their feet. Ron was, well, a white guy. A middle-aged white guy in a suit with a tie. He was a little on the thin side. I didn't think he was a good eater. "Are you ready, Counselors?"

In unison, they said, "Yes, Your Honor."

"Excellent." Judge Romero cocked his head to one side. "And how do you plead, Monsieur Belanger?"

Cynthia said, "Monsieur Belanger pleads not guilty, Your Honor." Her voice was silky smooth. "In fact, we have before you a motion to dismiss. There is no concrete evidence linking Monsieur Belanger to the crime and there are a number of promising leads the police have not followed up on. He should never have been arrested in the first place."

"And yet," Romero said, "here we are."

"Yes. We are here, but you could change all that, Judge." Cynthia smiled. "You could dismiss this disaster of a case."

Judge Romero looked through some papers on his desk that I assumed were the motion Cynthia mentioned. Then he looked up and said, "No."

"Your Honor," she began.

"No," he repeated. "Do not irritate me this early in the proceedings."

Cynthia quieted.

He nodded. "Now as to bail . . ."

Ramsey leapt in. "Judge Romero, Mr. Belanger has substantial funds and property in other countries. He is nearly the definition of a flight risk. Given the seriousness of the crime of which he's accused—"

Romero waved his hand to cut him off. "I know. I know. I expected these arguments." He rubbed his chin. "I'm afraid I cannot release your client on bail, Ms. Harlen. Mr. Ramsey is correct. He is a flight risk. He shall be held in custody until the time of his trial. Care to set a date for that, Counselors?"

There was an extended negotiation on dates and times, with Antoine's trial date being set for two months from now. Antoine gasped when he heard the date. Cynthia dropped one hand to his shoulder and he stilled. "That will be fine, Your Honor."

Judge Romero rapped his gavel twice and stood. The bailiff made all of us stand. Then the judge left the room.

"That's it?" I asked Cynthia. "That's the whole thing?"

"It was a preliminary hearing. What did you expect?" She packed papers and folders back into her briefcase.

"I don't know. A reason for you to want us all there, I guess." It hardly seemed worth it.

"Oh, you thought that was for the judge." She smiled. "That was for them." She gestured toward the mass of reporters and cameras and microphones.

I stared at her. "For the press? You wanted us here as a photo op?"

"Of course. You think this case is going to be tried in a courtroom? Don't be naïve, Rebecca. This case is being tried in the court of public opinion and we are winning. I want to keep it that way." She flashed a brilliant smile at one of the photographers.

I cringed. I wasn't so impressed with the court of public opinion. It had had me in its spotlight not too long ago and it had thought I was guilty. I didn't trust public opinion's judgment one bit.

Eight

That afternoon, Sprocket and I drove into Cleveland to pick up supplies. Grand Lake is great, but there's
no one who can get me the quantities of butter I need at a
price I can pay without choking, so once a month or so I
drive in to shop at the big warehouse store. With all the
increased business at POPS, I needed to make the trip
earlier than I'd intended. Plus, sometimes it's good to get
out of town. The constant buzz from the reporters in front
of the store and the chanting from the Belanger Bunnies
had all started to get to me.

I clicked on the local talk radio station as I came into
range and listened to a local poet read and talk about the
book launch party she would be having at a bookstore that
weekend. I wondered if she needed a caterer. It was a good
poem. It would be even better with popcorn. The segment
ended and the host announced she would be going to com-
mercial, but to stay tuned because celebrity chef Sunny
Coronado would be on next.

I almost drove my Jeep off the road. Sunny was here? In Ohio? How many tirades had I listened to about Sunny Coronado? How many plates had been flung against the wall as his name was spit into the air? Sunny Coronado was Antoine's nemesis. I know it sounds ridiculous to say that someone has a nemesis. Somehow it conjures up pictures of well-muscled men and women in spandex suits with stuff blowing up around them. Trust me, if Antoine could have blown up Sunny Coronado's kitchen and gotten away with it, that man's Viking would have been blown to smithereens years ago.

I listened to the interview as I drove the rest of the way. Sunny was starting a new line of spice mixes. There would be a Mexican-themed mix, a French-themed mix, and an Italian one to start. The radio host asked, "Will you be doing an English-themed mix?"

Sunny laughed and said, "No need. Just boil whatever you're cooking until it's dead."

You really can't go wrong with a joke about the Brits' cooking or their teeth.

This was one of the reasons Antoine hated Sunny as much as he did. Sunny made people smile. Antoine tended to make people swoon. It's also a good reaction, but not the same reaction. Antoine wanted all the reactions, all to himself.

Sunny was, in many ways, Antoine's total opposite. Short and round where Antoine was tall and lean. Sunny always seemed to be a little bit sweaty and doughy. Antoine was quintessentially cool and calm.

One would think that Sunny would be the jealous one. One would expect that Sunny would be the one wishing he were more like Antoine rather than the other way around.

POP GOES THE MURDER   137

One would be wrong.

Sunny exuded a certain joie de vivre, an unconditional embrace of everything that life had to offer. Antoine was all about discernment and taste. Sunny's messy haphazard approach in the kitchen, on his television show, in his cookbooks drove him crazy.

Now Sunny was branching into creating products like Antoine had. That was going to go over like a cake with a burned bottom. One more thing was bothering me. What the heck was Sunny Coronado doing in Ohio of all places?

When I got back to Grand Lake, I dropped off my butter at the shop and went over to the jail. Huerta took me back to see Antoine. The weight he'd lost was even more apparent in his orange jumpsuit than it had been in the courtroom. "Have you been eating?"

"I wish I could." He sounded morose.

Antoine was not one of those people who stopped eating during times of stress. Of course, I didn't think I'd ever seen him under this much stress. The fate of a television show might seem like big stakes, but it's nothing compared to fighting to keep yourself out of jail for life. "You need to relax and eat. Have you tried yoga? Deep breathing? Visualization?"

"I do not need to relax, Rebecca. I need something edible. Do you know what they served me for lunch today?" He shuddered.

I shook my head. I didn't know, but I had a bad feeling.

"Bologna! Bologna sandwich! On white bread. With that horrid orange cheese your country claims so proudly. It tasted as if they had left the plastic wrapping on! And whatever that substance was that they said was mayonnaise." For a second I thought Antoine might actually be sick talking about Miracle Whip.

"I'll bring you something." The words were out of my mouth before I thought about what I was saying.

He reached across the table to take my hand. "Oh, would you? Nothing elaborate. But maybe a slice of that fabulous quiche you used to make? The one with the leeks?"

I knew which one. "Of course."

"And perhaps a salad with a nice vinaigrette." He rubbed his thumb over the back of my hand.

I steeled myself against the little shivers his touch was sending through me. I didn't want to feel those, but after ten years of marriage he knew all too well how to cause them. "Sure." I pulled my hand out from his.

"Can one get a decent baguette here?" he asked, looking thoughtful.

Can one get a decent baguette anywhere outside of France? Honestly, not really, according to Antoine. "Sadly, no. There are some good breads, but no baguettes that you would like."

He sighed. "I suppose no cheese, either."

"No. There's some good cheese. That I can bring." There was even some decent Brie coming out of Millersburg.

"And yet nothing to eat it on. *Dommage*." He shook his head.

I knew where this was going and I wasn't going to rise to the bait. I was not baking bread for my imprisoned ex-husband. There were lines. "No," I said. "You can eat cheese on a cracker or not at all."

He made the same face he'd made about the Miracle Whip. "Not at all, then."

"Do you need anything else? Some books?" I asked.

He shook his head. "No. The magazines, the shaving cream and the deck of cards you dropped off earlier should suffice for a time."

"What magazines and cards?"

"Someone left them at the front desk in a box with my name on it. The desk sergeant brought them to me after they'd been examined. You didn't bring them?" He frowned.

"No. I didn't." I shrugged. "Probably one of the Bunnies."

He nodded. "Of course. That makes sense."

"By the way, did you know that Sunny Coronado is in Cleveland getting ready to launch a new line of spice mixes?"

"Sunny Coronado is here? In Ohio?" Antoine sat up so abruptly his chains jangled.

"Uh, yeah. That's what I just said." Jail time had taken away Antoine's appetite. Had it taken away his hearing, too? "He's launching a new line of spice mixes."

"Rebecca," he said, reaching across the table as best he could to take my hands. "You need to find out what Sunny is doing here. It is very important."

"Why?"

"Please. Just believe me. He should not be here. Something is not right." He looked down at his hands. "If I were Sunny, I would be anywhere but near here at this moment."

"Antoine, what's going on?"

He shook his head. "No. Never mind. Forget I said anything. Please, just bring me some of that lovely quiche before they kill every taste bud I have in my mouth."

I didn't push him any further, but the idea of asking me to pretend that he hadn't said anything was as ridiculous as asking his ex-wife to bake bread for him.

* * *

It wasn't hard to find information about Sunny on the computer. I checked his travel schedule. The trip to Cleveland seemed out of place. Dario walked in as I was looking. He leaned over my shoulder. "Is that Sunny Coronado?"

"Sure is." I wasn't surprised that Dario recognized him. Sunny was almost as famous as Antoine. Almost, but not quite. Until this new venture into spice mixes, he hadn't had any product lines. So no giant cardboard cutouts in the grocery stores, no commercials on television, no advertisements in magazines or newspapers or on websites or blogs. This move could be the step that put giant cardboard cutouts of him in grocery stores all over the country and his name on the lips of every even vaguely foodie-type in the country.

"Aren't he and your ex kind of like the East Coast/West Coast feud of the cooking world?" Dario sat on the edge of my desk, head cocked to one side.

"Basically. Sunny's in Cleveland right now. It seems like a weird coincidence." Or perhaps no coincidence at all.

"Mmhmm." Dario straightened. "No one likes weird coincidences once the popo get involved, now do they? You think this has something to do with your man?"

"First of all, Antoine is not my man." I really was getting tired of explaining that. I was wondering if I should start carrying my divorce papers around with me. "Second, do you think that's crazy?"

Dario looked off into space for a second. "Yeah. I do, but I think any murder is probably pretty crazy. What do you think his connection with the chick who got offed might be?"

I sighed. "Does it sound even crazier to say that I have no idea? I mentioned Sunny being here to Antoine and he reacted in a really strange way and then wouldn't explain."

"It's no crazier than anything else I've heard around here. Did you know that Joyce Lawrence rigged the voting on what color to make the school basketball uniform because that color blue made her son's eyes pop more?"

"Really?" I was momentarily distracted by the mental picture of Joyce sneaking ballot boxes around.

"Hand to God," Dario said, raising his right one. "See you tomorrow?"

"You bet. Thank you so much for your help. You've been amazing."

"Just you wait, Rebecca. I've got a few more tricks up my sleeves for you." He blew me a kiss and left.

As if the man ever wore sleeves on a shirt. It would be a crime to cover up those particular guns, but still . . .

At about six thirty I was heading out the back door with bags of garbage for the Dumpster in the alleyway. I bounced down the stairs with my load of refuse and nearly bounced up to the roof when a voice behind me said, "Can we talk, Rebecca?"

I squealed and whirled around. Lucy. Lucy was lurking by my back stairs.

"Lucy! You darn near made me wet my pants. What the hell are you doing?" What was it with women lurking by my back stairs? Was I suddenly in a Gordon Lightfoot song?

"I was, uh, hoping we could talk." She glanced up and down the alley. "In private."

I walked the rest of the way to the Dumpster, got rid of

my garbage, brushed off my hands and turned back to her. "Do you want to come in?"

She nodded.

I walked up the stairs and gestured for her to come into my kitchen. I hadn't forgotten the way Lucy and the rest of the crew had turned their backs on me when they first arrived in Grand Lake. I got it. Really, I did. It still stung, though. I shut the door behind us and leaned against it. "What's up?"

"There are some items missing from Melanie's room," she blurted.

I froze. "What kind of items?"

She pulled a pad of paper out of her purse and read from it. "Two of our smaller handheld video cameras, a tripod, some lights."

"You made a list?" I put on a kettle for tea. I always thought better with a warm drink in my hands.

She shrugged and sat down at the kitchen table. "Melanie always did inventory when we moved stuff from one place to another. Equipment gets smaller and smaller, but it's still expensive. It's easy to leave something behind or misplace it." She paused. "She also said it deterred people from helping themselves. Everyone knew she did the inventory. Everyone knew that if they took something, it wouldn't go unnoticed."

"When did the things go missing? Do you know?" I asked.

Lucy twisted the list in her hands. "Most of them went missing between landing in Cleveland and checking into our hotel. She did an inventory that night, the night she . . . her last night. She circled the missing items in red."

"No one else has mentioned this. How come?" I put the loose tea in the infuser and put that into a china pot.

"I don't think they know. I don't think she had a chance to tell anyone." She twisted the piece of paper harder. "At least, not all of us."

The water boiled and I poured it into the pot. "What do you mean?" I asked, gathering mugs and a pitcher of cream and some honey to set on the table.

"Melanie could be harsh, but she was usually fair. She'd always give a person a chance to, you know, come clean. I heard her do it one time when she didn't know I could hear. She took the person aside and asked if they'd maybe forgotten to return a piece of equipment and if they wanted to make sure to return it then," Lucy said.

"So whoever she thought stole the equipment might have known she'd discovered missing items on the inventory?" I sat down across from her.

"Exactly." Her list was basically origami by this point, she'd twisted it so much. "So what if that person didn't want to return the missing items? What if that person decided to shut Melanie up?"

"Wouldn't the items be missed anyway?" Eventually the crew would need the items that were missing.

"Eventually, but who knows how long that would take without Melanie doing inventory? Days? Weeks? A month, even?" She bit her lip.

Would covering up the theft of some video equipment be sufficient motive to kill someone? "Did everyone know about the inventory?"

"We did the inventory together sometimes, Melanie and me. I'd come to her room before we started shooting and we'd go over the list." Lucy wiped at her cheek with the back of her hand. "I so wish I had that last night, but I was tired. I just wanted to lie down in bed and watch bad TV."

It all made sense, but I had one more question. "I'm still

not sure what you want me to do about it, Lucy." I poured tea for both of us.

"I want you to call that sheriff guy, the one you're all buddy-buddy with. Tell him about it and get him to figure out who took the stuff." She added cream to her tea.

"Why don't you call him yourself?" It was pretty easy to get hold of Dan. The Sheriff's Department didn't exactly keep their phone number unlisted.

She returned to twisting her list. I'd heard of people making shivs out of twisted paper. I really hoped she wasn't intending on stabbing me. "I don't want the crew to know. I don't want anyone to think I turned them in. Plus . . ."

"Plus what?"

"They kind of think of him as the enemy, what with him arresting Antoine and all and being your friend. I don't want them to think I'm, you know, consorting."

I could see that. "Okay. I'll call him."

He answered on the second ring. "What's up, Bec?"

I filled him in on the situation.

He said, "Your sister isn't going to be pleased. She made meatloaf."

"Tell her it reheats really well and that you'll take it on a sandwich tomorrow."

"I doubt that will make her any happier, but I'll tell her and I'll be at your shop in ten minutes."

Approximately twenty minutes after that, Dan was calling Judge Romero for a search warrant and then calling Huerta to move out the troops. They had a search to do, but not before Dan banned me from being there as he walked to the back door.

"What? I don't get to watch? Why not?" I felt like the only kid not being invited to the birthday party.

"First of all, this is official police business. There is no reason for you to be there." Dan knocked his hat back on his head.

"Are you forgetting that I'm the one who clued you in?" I followed behind him.

He turned to me. "To be really fair, I'm pretty sure it was Lucy who clued me in."

"Through me!" I protested.

"Bec, that's like giving the phone credit when you get good news, which brings me to my next point. Haley is about to start chewing wallpaper off the walls. She's antsy. Go keep her happy so I can focus on doing my job. She's not so bad during the day. She expects both of us to be gone then. Evenings and nights? Not so much."

I hadn't thought of that. "Fine. I'll go home. It's not like my cell phone doesn't work at the hotel, though. Just saying."

"Just hearing. Just trying to explain to you that rational explanations on this one aren't going to cut it. She's spent nearly nine months growing a human being inside her own body. We're about to launch into the scariest part of the whole process, a part she's been preparing for the whole nine months. Humor her a little. Humor me. Go make a bowl of popcorn and watch an old movie with your sister while I work and, I might add, maybe find some clues to clear that ex-husband of yours that you're so damn convinced didn't kill his assistant." And with that he walked out the door.

Despite Lucy and Dan going out the back door of my shop, the media caught on to the action. Or they followed the cars from the Sheriff's Department. Or they simply materialized from the ground like some kind of creepy insect infestation. However they figured it out, they were at the hotel in full force. Instead of watching an old movie, Haley and I drank hot chocolate and watched news coverage of the search at the hotel. We probably had a better view than if we'd been on the scene, plus we were warm. It had dropped down into the thirties for the night and the reporters were all making white puffs of steam with each breath.

On the television, a brown-haired man sitting warm and cozy behind a desk said, "There are a lot of hidden dangers in hotels, aren't there, Lisa?"

The screen switched to the face of a dark-haired woman with a pale oval face. A breeze blew her hair across her face. She struggled to control the strands as she held her mike. "Yes, there are, Kurt. We did a report not long ago on some of those dangers." I took an ever-so-slight malicious pleasure in how red her nose was. It looked like her eyes might be watering, too.

"That's right. For those of you interested in seeing Lisa's report, 'Is Your Hotel Hallway Trying to Kill You?' visit our website: www.News15.com. We have the link posted there," Kurt said. The link flashed and the camera cut away from Lisa with her unruly hair.

"Tell the truth," I said to Haley. "You just wanted me to come over to make hot chocolate, didn't you?"

She smiled over the rim of her mug. "It was an added benefit."

We sat at opposite ends of the couch with our feet touching together in the middle. An afghan made by our great-aunt Dorothy was spread over our legs. I picked at a strand of yarn. "This thing is coming apart."

She sighed. "I know. I don't know how much longer it

will last. It's not so easy keeping this place together some-times."

My head shot up. I'd never heard her say something like that before. "Do you want to move? Maybe buy someplace newer?" There was a whole set of McMansions set to go in near Orchard and Railroad Avenue. I could see Haley liking someplace crisp and new.

She looked affronted. "Of course not." She straightened up a little. "I like keeping it together. I like the connection. I like feeling like I'm part of a line of people, a link in the chain."

Was that really how she saw herself? "You are so much more than a link in a chain!"

"I'm not saying it like it's a bad thing." She stopped. "Wait. Something's happening on the television."

Nothing had happened for a really long time, although Haley and I enjoyed watching the various reporters and anchors trying to find something to talk about while they waited for the eight deputies that had gone into the hotel to come out with someone or something.

"I've heard that an arrest has been made," Lisa said, excitement in her voice.

The camera panned away from Lisa's smooth oval face to the front of the hotel. Two officers came out. Between them was another man with his hands cuffed behind his back, his head down. He was a young white man who looked to be a little under six feet tall and was wearing khaki pants and a polo shirt. He kept his face turned from the camera. I craned my head forward as if that would make it easier to see him. "Who is that?" He was definitely not one of Antoine's crew.

Haley leaned forward, too. "That's Derek Wade, Barry and Patti's son. He's the night clerk at the hotel. Patti was telling me how great it was for him because it's so quiet there at night. He can study and get paid for it. He has a room there, too."

"I'm guessing his mama's not so proud now," I said. Nothing like watching your baby do a perp walk to piss on your parade.

"I'm guessing she's on her way down to the station to punch Dan in the nose and then open a can of whoop ass on Derek's behind." Haley chuckled. "She's a force to be reckoned with. Last year at the Valentine's Day Festival she thought Olive Hicks had said something behind her back and Patti pulled her hair."

"Just came up and yanked it?" My hand flew involuntarily to my own curls.

"Yep. In front of everybody. I think she wanted to start a fight." Haley grinned. "She almost did."

Then Dan was on the screen. "His nose looks fine so far," I said.

"It is a nice nose, isn't it?" Haley smiled at her husband's face on the screen.

"You know the only reason it isn't crooked is that I threw myself between him and Timmy Chandler when Timmy wanted to fight him over a call he didn't like in a flag football game." I deserved some credit for Dan's handsomeness and I intended to get it.

"I do know that. I remember you were grounded for the rest of the week for fighting, but when you weren't watching Mom and Dad high-fived each other over having raised a wildcat." Haley balanced her mug on her tummy.

I turned to stare at her. Haley almost never brought up Mom and Dad. It's not like they were a taboo subject. She was living in their house, after all. She just never raised the topic herself and she never brought up little anecdotes like that one. "You never told me that."

"Hush," she said. "Dan's about to talk."

The reporter shoved a giant microphone in Dan's face. "Sheriff Cooper, is this arrest related to the homicide that occurred at this hotel last week?"

"No comment." Dan stared right into the camera. I felt like he was looking into my soul.

Haley clutched the mug she was holding tighter and winced.

"Are you Braxton-Hicksing again?" I asked.

"I said hush." She waved her hand at me like I was a fly trying to land on the marshmallows in her hot chocolate.

I hushed again.

"Can you tell us what the charges are that are being leveled against this young man?" the reporter asked.

"No comment," Dan said.

"Ooh. Scintillating," I said.

Haley threw a pillow at me. I guess there's a reason they're called throw pillows.

The rest of the interview continued that way. Dan no commented a few more times and then the reporter turned back to the camera. "There you have it. We cannot at this time confirm whether or not the arrest of what appears to be a hotel employee is any way connected to the murder of Melanie Fitzgerald, assistant to celebrity chef Antoine Belanger."

"Thank you, Lisa," the anchorperson said.

Haley picked up the remote and clicked the television off.

I bit back a yawn. "I think it's bedtime, sis."

"Me, too." She stood and stretched. "Is your phone charged?"

"Yes."

She held her hand out and wiggled her fingers. "Show me."

"You're not a very trusting person, you know." I handed her the phone.

She hit a few buttons. "Eighty percent battery power. Very nice. You may go to bed."

I tried to. I really did. I'd had a long day and would have to be up at five to get to the shop to make the breakfast bars and coffee, but I couldn't stop tossing and turning. Did Derek's arrest have any impact on Antoine's case? Stealing was wrong. Absolutely. But it was a far cry from murder. There's no way that Melanie's death was any kind of accident. Most people didn't carry around modified blow-dryers with them, so having it there would have to be preplanned. I punched my pillow and rolled over. I still didn't sleep.

Finally, I did what Dan did for me. I got up, grabbed some blankets and some beers and sat down on the front porch to wait.

It was nearly two in the morning when he finally came up the walk. "I think it's past your curfew, young lady."

"You're not the boss of me, old man." I popped off the top of his beer and handed it to him.

"You're right, but if I were I would have told you to do precisely this." He sat down with a groan.

"Freeze my ass off on your front porch?" Even Sprocket hadn't been enough to keep me truly warm.

"No. Just the beer part." He let me drape one of the

blankets around his shoulders while he opened the bottle and drank.

"Long night?" I asked.

He took a second long swallow from the bottle. "Indeed."

That sounded interesting. "Care to dish?"

"Depends. Who am I talking to? My best friend Bec or Antoine Belanger's ex-, but still somehow helpful, wife?" He turned those clear blue eyes on me and I had a flash of not ever wanting to break the law in Grand Lake. Or at least not in a serious way. Dan could be scary when he felt like it.

"I can't be both?"

He let his head loll back and stretched his neck. "It looks like a pretty fine tightrope line to walk from down here on the ground."

"I've walked fine lines before. Remember when Timmy dared me to walk along the fence between the Harrisons' and the Grays'?" Timmy had offended my sensibilities in a number of ways. I realized now that he'd probably been doing it on purpose. At the time, though, there wasn't a dare he'd throw out that I'd back down from.

He nodded. "I do. I also remember the sling you had to wear for three weeks."

"Yeah, but I made it more than halfway before I fell." I hadn't made it the entire way, but farther than anyone else had.

Dan leaned forward, elbows on knees and let the beer bottle dangle. "We found one of the cameras, a tripod, some lights in the night clerk's room."

I whistled. "That's pretty ballsy. Did he really think he wouldn't get caught?"

"He claims he didn't think he would get caught because

he didn't actually steal those items. He says that Melanie gave them to him to sell for her. Back-door kind of stuff. According to him, Melanie was planning on saying the items were stolen out of the van somewhere else and collecting the insurance money to replace them later," he said.

"Wait. What?"

"He claims that . . ."

"Stop it. I heard what you said. It's just a lot to absorb." How many different ways was Melanie stealing from Antoine? His crew seemed loyal to him. Was there more going on under the surface? How would I tell? I'd certainly never sensed even a whiff of Melanie's treachery.

He took another long drink. "Not really. It's part and parcel of the way she was trying to deal with her debt problems."

I pulled the blanket tighter around my shoulders and drank some of my beer, too. "Why this kid, though?"

"Well, that's where things get a little dicier for Mr. Wade. Melanie chose that kid because she caught him stealing from the hotel." Dan shook his head.

"What's there to steal from the hotel that's not bolted down? Towels?" It wasn't like the Grand Lake Inn featured pricey artwork. Beyond the flat screens in the rooms, I couldn't imagine what someone might steal.

"More like credit card information from guests. What she actually caught him doing was marking one of the rooms as canceled and then instead of refunding the money to Antoine's credit card, he pocketed it. Not bad as schemes go. Pretty clever, really." Dan smiled, but it seemed forced.

"Well, he is a college boy," I observed, pulling the blanket tighter around me.

"So his mother informed me." Dan rubbed his forehead

with his thumb. "A college boy with a future, supposedly. Or one who had a future before he started stealing credit card numbers and being a complete idiot. I wasn't even planning on searching his room, but we caught him sneaking out the side door with an armful of equipment."

"Why?"

Dan shrugged. "He panicked. Figured we'd search his room once we didn't find any of the stuff in the crew's rooms. He might have been right about that, but he definitely jumped out of the frying pan and straight into the fire."

I thought about what he'd told me. "Let me get this straight, then. Melanie caught him stealing from the hotel and figured he'd be up for fencing some video equipment?"

"Video equipment and some jewelry that appears to have belonged to Melanie. That's his version of events." He'd gone all cop face again. At least, in profile. He tapped his index finger on his knee.

I knew what that meant. There was something he wasn't saying. "And your version is?" I asked.

"What makes you think I have a version?" He turned toward me, one eyebrow cocked.

I turned to look at him and batted my eyes. "Because I know you and I know what it means when you tap your finger like that."

He snorted. "Don't tell Haley. I'll never get away with another surprise for her."

"Don't count on her not knowing, dude. She might be willing to play along so she keeps getting the surprises." If I knew my sister, that was exactly what was happening. She didn't miss much.

His brows shot up. "Damn. You're probably right."

"Now stop dodging. What makes you think his version isn't the real deal?" I punched him—lightly—in the shoulder.

"It might be. I can see other possibilities, though. Like what if he decided it would be better business to pocket all the money from fencing those items himself and decided to get rid of Melanie? He would have a key to her room. He does minor repairs around the place as part of his job. He had the tools and the know-how to alter that blow-dryer," he said.

There were even more possibilities. "Or what if the whole thing is made up and he actually did steal those items?"

Dan made a face. "That part I believe. She apparently told him something about needing to have a big sum of money fast. She needed to pay someone back for something."

"I thought she had to pay a lot of people back."

"This sounded like it could be different. She did have one big lump sum come in about a month or so ago. It was gone practically before it hit her bank account. Maybe it was some kind of loan that's come due," he said. "It was after that that she started siphoning money out of Antoine's account."

"Who was the lump sum from?" I sat up straighter.

"Not traceable. It was a money order. I'm thinking that if it was a loan, it wasn't from what you might call a reputable source."

"Disreputable enough that they might kill if they didn't get their money back?" There were bad places to borrow money from and then there were some really bad places to borrow money from.

Dan rubbed his chin. "That crossed my mind, too. That would also explain the bruising on her body."

"What bruising?"

"The coroner found evidence of some damage that was a couple of weeks old. Either she took a bad fall or someone worked her over some. Whatever it was, it happened before she came to Grand Lake. I wasn't sure if it was connected, but it might be."

"You know that both those scenarios don't involve Antoine, right?" I pointed out.

There he went again. Cop face all over the place. "I'm aware, Rebecca. Don't push it. Antoine still is the best and most logical suspect in this case and generally the best and most logical suspect is the person who did it. That's true of the little crimes I have to solve here in Grand Lake like who vandalized the water tower and who killed Melanie Fitzgerald."

"Who did vandalize the water tower?"

"Norma Jenkins." He chuckled. "Who else? Oh, by the way, that stalker lady? Marie Parsons? She checked out of the hotel the morning you found Melanie. We're trying to find her, but the ID she used was fake and she gave a fake license plate number for her car. Let me know if you see her around. I'd like to talk to her, too."

He had a point about the vandalism. Norma had always had an artistic side that has been continually frustrated, most recently when her T-shirt design for the summer street fair had been rejected in favor of a second grader's more colorful work. I still didn't think it applied to the Antoine situation. "I'm glad you're keeping an open mind."

His whole body stiffened and he turned toward me. The anger in his eyes made me wish for his cop face again.

"My mind has always been open. I'm following the evidence. I'll follow it wherever it takes me. I wish you'd give me that much credit." He stood up.

I reached up to him. "I do give you credit, Dan. I'm sorry."

He shook his head. "I think you're the one who should open your mind a little bit more. There might be more of a dark side to Antoine than you're willing to admit."

He went inside without saying good night. I went back to my apartment, but I still couldn't sleep.

Nine

Dario met me at the back door of the shop at six the next morning, ready to start rocking the breakfast bars. Business at the shop had increased about twenty-five percent since I'd started offering the pumpkin-spice popcorn bars. They took a little extra time, but they were worth it. "What is it with you white girls and the pumpkin stuff?" Dario asked as he iced the popcorn bars.

"I have no idea. Asking me is probably like asking a cat why it likes catnip." I looked pointedly at my very white arm.

He chuckled, which was an awesome sound. It was like his chest was some kind of echo chamber. "It makes you high?"

"Well, not exactly, but it seems to make me happy." I'd grab whatever little slice of happy I could get at the moment.

"Based on the expressions on people's face once they take a bite, you're not the only one." He smoothed more icing on. "I'm all about spreading the happy. You eat your pumpkin spice. Eat it all year-round."

I shook my head emphatically. "Nope. Only from October first until Thanksgiving. After that, we're going to be all about the eggnog. The day after Thanksgiving, all pumpkin items turn into pillars of salt."

"I think you've got your biblical quotes mixed up. You're serious, though? About the eggnog?" he asked.

"Yep." I was, too. I loved eggnog. I was all too aware of how really good eggnog was made and knew that I needed to limit its consumption, at least calendrically.

He leaned in and whispered, "Can we put brandy in it?"

I giggled. "I like the way you think, Dario."

We opened the doors to POPS at seven and the throng rushed in. Antoine had totally brought more business to my shop—not exactly in the way he'd planned, but increased revenue is increased revenue, isn't it?

While we served them, three different reporters slipped me their business cards with their payments for breakfast, but they didn't ask any questions.

When things quieted down, I went into the kitchen to make a quiche.

"What's that for?" Dario asked as he made another pot of coffee for us.

"For Antoine," I said as I rolled out the crust.

"You know, my grand-mère always said that the way to a man's heart was through his stomach. If you don't want Antoine's heart, why are you still trying to please his stomach?" Dario asked, flipping a chair around to sit on it backward.

It was a tough question to answer. I hadn't really admitted the truth to anyone, not even Annie or Haley. I maybe hadn't even admitted the truth to myself. "I might maybe feel the slightest, tiniest bit guilty about leaving him," I blurted out. It felt good to have it out in the air.

He snorted. "You left a man with a multimillion-dollar business, refused to take support, and you somehow feel guilty about it?"

"When you say it like that it sounds stupid, but I do feel a little guilty. I knew who he was when I married him. I didn't expect to change him, either. I hadn't understood how hard it was going to be to live with who he was." I started whipping eggs.

Dario leaned his chin on his crossed arms. "I still don't see a reason for you to feel guilty."

"He never understood why I left him. Based on our conversations, I'm pretty sure he still doesn't." It was entirely possible that Antoine couldn't understand.

Dario got up and started rinsing out the dishes in the sink. "Is that it?"

"Not entirely. I feel a little responsible for him being arrested, too. If he hadn't been here in Grand Lake, maybe none of this would have happened. Or wouldn't have happened in a way that would have ended up with him in a cage being served bologna with Miracle Whip."

Dario waved a wooden spoon at me. "Miracle Whip is zesty. It has its place in the pantheon of condiments."

"Not if you're French," I responded.

Dario shrugged. "So you're making quiche and salad so he doesn't waste away to nothing while waiting for you to clear his name of a murder charge."

"It's not as simple as that. I think you're overstating." I hoped he was overstating, because when he said it like that it sounded a little crazy.

He wiped his hands off on a dish towel. "You might think I'm overstating, but no one else does."

There was a knock on the back door. Dario let Garrett in. "Smells good. What are you making?"

"Lunch for her ex-husband," Dario said with a drawl.

I shot him a look.

He sat down at the table and stared at me. "You're making a quiche for Antoine?"

"Yes." I finished rolling out the crust and started to line the pie pan. "But I am not baking bread for him. There are lines I simply won't cross."

"Well, then, that makes perfect sense." It did to me, but I could tell by his tone that it didn't to him and that perhaps his lines were in a slightly different place than mine. Judging by Dario's snort his were in a different place, too.

I decided to take his comment at face value anyway. "I'm so glad you agree." The trick with cooking a filled piecrust is to make sure the bottom bakes and doesn't remain mushy while not burning the edges. To accomplish that, I needed to be sure the bottom was thin enough. I applied my attention to that task.

He sighed. "Are you at least making two?"

I tried to hide the smile quirking at my lips. "Of course." I hadn't been, but I would now. I rolled out a second piecrust.

In front of the Sheriff's Department, a group of women carrying signs walked in a circle, chanting. The Bunnies. It was like they were everywhere. It took me a second to figure out what they were saying. Finally I got it. "Belanger. Belanger. Set him free. Do it today."

Some of the signs had Antoine's face on them. Others had *Free Antoine* in huge letters. There were a few that had pictures of me with devil horns and goatees drawn on my face in black marker. Off to the side, a woman stood with a life-sized cardboard cutout of Antoine. A sign next to her offered pictures with Antoine for five dollars to help support Antoine's defense.

I texted Dan. "I want to come in the side entrance."

He texted back, "Don't blame you. Vera will meet you there in five."

I ducked around to the side of the building before the Bunnies or the press noticed me. Sure enough, Vera was waiting for me. "Hey, Vera," I said. "Would you be willing to try something?" Quiche was not the only thing I cooked up that morning.

She narrowed her eyes at me. "Is this like a bribe?"

"Nope. More like market research." I pulled a container from the basket and handed it to her.

She stared at it like it might be a snake. "What is it?"

"Remember when you mentioned the calorie count in Coco Pop Fudge?" I asked.

She sighed. "All too well. I remember all conversations about calories." Then she stood up a little straighter.

"Well, this is a lower-calorie option. It's still chocolatey. It doesn't have the same mouth-feel, but I'd like to see what you think." I pushed it a little closer to her.

"Right now?" She glanced from side to side as if someone might be watching.

"If not now, when?" I asked.

She opened the container and took a bite. Her eyes widened. "This is low calorie?"

"Lower than the fudge, that's for sure. Kinda nice for those times when you want things sweet and salty and even a bit spicy at the same time." I smiled.

"You mean like every day all the time?" she asked.

I laughed. "It's good to know there are like-minded people out there."

She nodded at my picnic basket. "Is that for Antoine?"

"It is. It is not low calorie." Antoine was far more likely to eat less of something rather than compromise its ideal state, which generally involved copious levels of fat.

She laughed. "I'll take you back to him." She went through the basket to be sure I wasn't smuggling in any contraband and took away the usual items like cell phones and keys and, in this case, the fork and knife.

"It's a butter knife, Vera. Antoine will barely be able to cut a quiche with it much less rough up a bitch." I knew he wouldn't be thrilled.

"Rules are rules, Rebecca. We're bending plenty of them for him already." She replaced the utensils with a plastic sfork.

We were on our way down the hall when Huerta came from the direction of the cells with Antoine. "Whatever's in that basket smells good, Rebecca," Huerta said.

Antoine came to a stop and lifted his head like a hound scenting the air. "Your quiche, of course."

"As per your request," I replied. "There might be enough to share."

Huerta looked hopeful.

Antoine continued walking to the interrogation room. "Perhaps I should offer some to the man in the cell next to mine. It might make him pause in his constant complaining if his mouth was momentarily full." He shuddered. "Or perhaps not. He seems the type to speak through a full mouth."

"It might be a nice gesture," I said as I set out the quiche, salad, sparkling water and chocolate. "Are you hungry?" I put the picnic basket up on the table.

"Starving. Perhaps literally," Antoine said.

"Vera wouldn't let me bring in any silverware. Sorry about that." I gave him his sfork. "This is the best I could do."

Antoine held it up and examined it. "It is an abomination, but sometimes compromises must be made."

"Who cares what you eat it with?" Huerta asked.

Antoine opened his mouth to explain exactly how eating implements were designed to enhance the experience of various foods and beverages, a lecture that could go on for well over an hour in my experience. He could spend twenty minutes on stemware. He wasn't wrong. It was just a long time to talk about a wineglass.

Vera stuck her head in the door. "Rebecca, your cell phone is buzzing like an angry hornet. Looks like there are some texts from Haley. Dan's on the phone with her now."

"Do you think it's time?" I asked.

"Not sure. I'll make sure Dan comes to talk to you when he's off the phone."

Antoine apparently could no longer withstand Huerta's pleading eyes. They were like huge dark pools of melted chocolate. He pushed the quiche toward him and nodded.

Huerta dug in. "Rebecca, this is fantastic."

"It is excellent," Antoine said. "Not as excellent as being given my freedom back. You have no idea what it is like inside here." Antoine's shoulders drooped.

"I'm doing everything I can," I said. "So is Cynthia."

"Of course. Of course," Antoine said while managing to still look totally dejected and pathetic. "She was here earlier today. She had many questions."

"For us, too," Huerta said. "She's a feisty one." He paused. "Do you happen to know if she's single?"

Before I could answer, Dan poked his head in. "It's not time. Haley's pissed that you and I both were without our cell phones at the same time, though."

"But she called the desk and they came and got you, right?" It wasn't like we were totally unavailable.

"Yes, but that was three phone calls: one to my cell, one to yours and then one to the desk. Plus a bunch of texts. She's worried that if her labor escalates quickly she won't have time for three phone calls." Dan tapped his fingers against the doorjamb.

"Things like that only happen on television," I protested. "Labor lasts hours." I'd been reading up. I really wanted to be ready. I really wanted to support my sister.

"I'll make sure to tell her you said that," Dan said with a smirk.

"No!" If he did that, Haley might actually scorch the eyebrows right off my face using only the red-hot heat of her rage.

"What's it worth to you?" he asked.

I knew that tone of voice. He wasn't teasing. There was a deal to be struck. "What do you want?"

"Lunch for me next time you bring it for Frenchie over there." He pointed at Antoine.

Antoine shot him a look, but didn't respond. Most likely because his mouth was full of quiche.

"Deal." Easy-peasy. "So what's the deal with Derek?"

Dan blew out a breath. "He's a piece of work. Near as I can tell, he's been scamming clients of the hotel since the day he started. There's a lot of digging to be done."

"What about Melanie? Do you think he could have . . ." I couldn't bring myself to say the words out loud. Was Derek a murderer?

Dan leaned against the corridor wall. "I don't think so,

Rebecca. He seems more enamored of Melanie than angry with her. He was impressed with how quickly she turned his scam around to pull him into hers. Something about balls of brass."

"But you'll look into it. You'll make sure, right? Because it seems like he's just as viable a suspect as Antoine."

Dan straightened and his eyes narrowed. "I'm looking into it now, Rebecca. I know how to do my job." He started down the hallway and turned. "Don't forget about my lunch, okay?"

I nodded and went back to the front desk. I called Haley back as soon as I retrieved my cell phone from Vera.

"Where have you been?" she asked.

"At the jail with Antoine. I was dropping off some food."

It felt like I could hear the steam escaping from her ears into the cell phone. It was a high-pitched sound and it was painful. "You were taking food to Antoine? That's why you didn't get my texts?"

"They make you leave your cell phone at the desk when you go in. It's a rule." Haley loved rules. Usually if I said something was a rule, she'd accept that and not argue about it at all.

"You were taking food to Antoine?"

I felt as if we'd already established that point, but apparently not. "Yes. He can't eat the jail food."

"No, Rebecca. He can eat the jail food. He chooses not to eat the jail food." I could hear her anger build in her voice.

I knew she was right. To a point. "You don't understand. Food is like his religion. It's like asking him to worship at the altar of an inferior god."

"Are you listening to yourself? Have you really thought

through how crazy you're being? You are potentially going to not be there for a sweet little boy who adores you and counts on you and not be there for the sister who tries to support you in all things and not be there for the man who has been your best friend since you were in grade school because your ex-husband—ex-husband, not even current husband—doesn't like the food in the jail where he's being held on suspicion of murder."

"Well, when you put it like that . . ."

"Stop joking around! This is serious. At least it's serious to me." Her voice cracked a little.

"I'm sorry, Leelee. It's serious to me, too. It all is. I swear I will be here for you and Evan and Dan when the Peanut comes. I swear it."

"You can swear all you want. I want some cold, hard proof. Drop this business about Antoine. He has a lawyer. Let her deal with him."

I sighed. She didn't understand how pathetic Antoine looked shrinking to nothing in that hideous orange jump-suit. "I hear you."

"Good. Now pick up a gallon of milk on your way home, please."

"Will do." That's what the texts had been about? Milk? I was afraid my head was going to explode before that baby popped out of my sister.

I went out the side entrance again, hoping to avoid the crowds out front. Either someone had gotten wise or I simply wasn't as slick as I thought, because before I could take more than a step or two, I heard someone yell, "Hey, that's Rebecca!"

Suddenly, Yolanda Barnett was jogging around the corner to me. "Rebecca, have there been any developments in Antoine's case? Was last night's arrest at the hotel

related to the murder of Melanie Fitzgerald? What were
you bringing into the prison? Was it for Antoine?"

I started to open my mouth to answer, but before anything came out, one of the Belanger Bunnies was shouting,
"Are you trying to poison him, Rebecca? Isn't it enough
that you broke his heart? Must you break his spirit and
body, too?"

Yolanda turned to me, wide-eyed. "Has Antoine been
poisoned?"

"Of course not," I said. "He just doesn't like bologna.
Or Miracle Whip."

"Someone poisoned the Miracle Whip?" she asked.

"No. No poison. No poison anywhere." This was going
wrong spectacularly fast.

"You're the poison," the Belanger Bunny said, shaking
her sign at me. "You are."

That was it. I needed to get out of there. I pushed
through the mob with both Yolanda and the Bunny following me.

"Rebecca, how is Antoine? Is he keeping his spirits
up?" Rick Day (hot chocolate and a coconut breakfast bar)
yelled after me.

"That's it! Run! That's what you do best, isn't it,
Rebecca?" the Bunny yelled.

Another reporter, Dwayne Hall from the *Toledo Times*
(black coffee, two sugars, pumpkin-spice breakfast bar)
stepped into my way with a microphone. "Is there a reason
that you're bringing food in to Antoine? Is he concerned
someone might poison him?"

A third reporter, Viola Kays from WZYN (coffee with
skim milk, but lots of it, and chocolate-chip breakfast bar)
shouted a question at me, and then another Bunny joined
the first one to chant.

I turned left and then right, but couldn't see a way past the crowd. I felt like I couldn't get a full breath into my lungs and my heart pounded. Soon all I could hear was my blood pounding in my ears, and my vision started to blur a bit at the edges. For a second I thought I might faint.

Then a strong arm circled my waist. "Easy there."

Garrett. Garrett was there with his arm around my waist. He stuck his arm out in front of him like a football player blocking a rusher and marched me away from the building saying, "No comment. No comment," over and over again.

When we finally made it through the throng, I was so relieved I thought I might cry. They kept following us, though. Then suddenly a barrage of ringtones went off at once. I glanced over my shoulder. All the Bunnies were pulling their cell phones out of their pockets and purses. Then they turned back toward the jail like a school of fish all moving at once.

"What's happening?" Viola asked one of them.

"An alert. Something's happening back at the jail," she said.

Rick Day asked, "Do you know what?"

"No. But we're heading back there," another Bunny said.

The press also turned back, some of them running.

I had no idea what the scoop was and at the moment, I didn't care. "Where did you come from?" I asked Garrett.

"I was going to the courthouse when I heard the commotion." He turned to face me on the sidewalk.

"And you came over to see what was happening?" We started down the sidewalk to put more distance between us and the mob, even if their attention had turned elsewhere. They were fickle.

POP GOES THE MURDER

He shrugged. "It occurred to me that it might be related to Antoine and therefore to you. You guys are pretty much the only commotion-worthy thing happening in town."

"I wish we were a little less commotion-worthy."

"Do you?" he asked.

"What is that supposed to mean?" I stopped walking.

"It means that your involvement at this point is pretty much voluntary." He took my elbow and urged me on.

"We've been over this. I can't let him be convicted of something I'm convinced he didn't do."

"Which is why you found him a lawyer."

"Do we have to fight?"

Before he could answer, Lucy jogged up to us. "Rebecca, I was hoping to find you. What's going on? Are they going to let Antoine go?"

"I'm not sure."

"But that Derek person had our equipment and Melanie's jewelry. Obviously she caught him stealing and he killed her to keep her quiet," Lucy said. "Right?"

"It's still not certain what happened, Lucy. Dan's looking into it, but he didn't seem to think Derek would have gone that far."

"But now there's another suspect. They can't charge two people at once. They have to let Antoine go," Lucy said.

I shook my head. "Derek hasn't been charged with the murder. He's been charged with theft."

Lucy's face crumpled. "They have to let Antoine go. They just have to." She launched herself at me and began to sob against my shoulder.

Garrett rolled his eyes at me and indicated with a nod of his head that he was leaving. I didn't blame him.

Lucy finally stopped crying and looked up at me. "Could you give me a ride back to the hotel?"

I'd managed to limp back to POPS with a weeping Lucy attached to me like a limpet on a rock. When I told him where I was going, Dario shook his head. "First you make him lunch. Now you're acting as a chauffeur for his crew. Girl, you got no boundaries whatsoever when it comes to that man."

"I have tons of boundaries. At least, I used to. I used to have a pretty big chunk of the contiguous United States as a boundary."

"That's distance. It's a totally different thing," he said.

I didn't know how to argue that, so I took my dog and got into the Jeep with Lucy. She had calmed down a little. Before I started the car, my phone beeped with a text. It was from an unknown number and said only: You're Welcome.

I frowned at it, wondering what it meant.

"Who's that?" Lucy asked.

"No idea." I put the phone back in my jacket pocket and started the car.

"I don't know what to do," Lucy moaned as we made our way to the Grand Lake Inn.

"About what?" There were so many possibilities. I wasn't sure which she was talking about.

"About Antoine. I know he didn't do it." She pounded on the dashboard with her fists. Sprocket sat up in the backseat and whined.

I reached back and patted him to reassure him. Loud noises don't agree with him since the whole gunshot-in-the-lighthouse affair. "I don't think he did, either," I said, turning onto Chestnut Street.

"If they're not going to arrest Derek for it, what should we do next?" she asked as we pulled up to the hotel.

"Dan is investigating, Lucy. I think we let him do his job." He may have settled on Antoine as a suspect a little too fast, but I could see that he was considering other possibilities.

"That lawyer lady said that Dan had a thing against Antoine." She turned to me, eyes narrowed. "Because of you."

"Antoine may not be Dan's favorite person, but he still wouldn't want an innocent man to be convicted."

"If you say so." Lucy got out of the car and slammed the door. Sprocket yipped and hunkered down in the back-seat.

I watched as Lucy went into the lobby of the hotel, and patted my poor skittish dog. As I was about to put the Jeep in gear, I saw movement in the bushes over on the edge of the circular driveway. I waited and then saw more movement. Then I saw a woman walking out of the bushes and onto the sidewalk. The same woman I'd seen in the coffee shop the morning Melanie died. The same woman who'd been crying at the antique shop. The same woman who had been lurking outside my shop and outside the lighthouse when the crew was filming. I called Dan.

"I see her, Dan. I see the mystery woman."

"Where?" he asked.

"Outside the hotel. I was dropping off Lucy. The woman was hiding in the bushes in front of the hotel." How sinister was that? He had to pay attention now.

He yawned. "Does anyone else see her this time?"

"Sprocket does. Don't you, boy?" I asked him, patting him on the head.

He yipped. I put the Jeep in gear and started creeping down the driveway to keep the woman in view.

"Sprocket can't testify," Dan said.

The woman glanced over her shoulder and picked up her pace. "Damn it. I think she's seen me." I went a little faster. She broke into a run, but instead of staying on the sidewalk, she took off into the fields.

"Rebecca. Don't engage," Dan said.

I put the Jeep in park, dropped my phone, and took off after her, not even bothering to shut the car door. "Wait!" I called. "I just want to talk to you."

She picked up her pace.

I don't run. Ever. Well, maybe if I'm late for a plane, but that's about it. Antoine runs. Garrett runs. Even Dan puts in the occasional miles. I do not. I don't get it. Right then, however, I wished I'd at least jogged a few steps now and then. My breath came in gasps and the woman was increasing the distance between us. My legs felt leaden. There was no way I was going to catch her before she hit the wooded edge of the field. If she made it in there, I'd never find her. She could hide behind a tree, under a bush, almost anywhere. Then something shot past me. A furry apricot bullet intent on one thing, his prey, and for once it wasn't some toddler's toy. Sprocket caught up with the woman and leapt, knocking into her back. The woman sprawled to the ground.

I caught up with them. Sprocket stood over her, panting.

"Get him off," she said. "Please. Don't hurt me."

I didn't point out that he wasn't even growling and had

never bit anyone. He had, after all, just tackled her. It was good sense on her part to be afraid. I grabbed his collar and extended a hand down to her to help her up. By the time we'd made it back to where I'd left my car, Dan had already arrived.

Ten

The woman's name was Marisela Santos. I knew that because that was the name of the complainant on the assault charge that Dan handed me after making sure that Ms. Santos did not need medical attention.

"I can't believe you're giving me the complaint!" I stared at the official form Dan had put in my hands. "She's the one who's lurking. You should be taking her down to the station and questioning her."

He crouched down to scratch Sprocket behind the ears. "I can't believe I'm giving you a complaint, either. I should be arresting you. I should be taking you in handcuffs down to the jail and scheduling an arraignment. The only reason I'm not is I'm pretty sure your sister might leave me if I arrested you right now." He glared at me. "Or possibly stab me in my sleep. One or the other. Maybe both."

"What?" I squawked. "I am not the one at fault here."

"Really? Because as near as I can tell you chased down

a woman who claims not to know who you are and knocked her flat to the ground," he said.

"She ran from me and it was actually Sprocket who knocked her down," I protested, shrinking back a little.

"Running from you is not grounds for assault. You're lucky she doesn't want Sprocket impounded. If he'd bitten her, I wouldn't have a choice."

"Dan, she's involved somehow in this case." I kicked at the ground with my toe. "She's been lurking all over town! Why is she here?"

"Again, lurking is not grounds for assault. It's not your business to find out why she's here or anything else." He turned to walk back to his car. He called over his shoulder, "Go home, Rebecca."

I went to POPS instead. I considered taking a selfie and texting it to Dan with a caption reading, "You're not the boss of me," but thought I might be pushing my luck.

Faith and her two daughters were at the store having a post-soccer-practice hot chocolate when Sprocket and I got there.

"You look sweaty, Rebecca," Ella said.

"Be nice," Faith said, wiping her daughter's chocolate-milk mustache off her.

"She's right. I am sweaty. I ran." I collapsed down in a chair at their table.

"How far?" While Faith wiped Ella's face, Jeannette began poking her finger into her mug of hot chocolate and then licking her finger.

"I'd say at least twenty-five yards or so." It might have been farther, but I didn't want to brag.

"Were you being chased?" Faith looked up, a smile on her face.

"No. I was doing the chasing. Luckily Sprocket is better at chasing than me." Or maybe not since I was now facing an assault charge.

Faith set her mug down. "Who on earth were you chasing?"

"Remember that woman? The one you thought was shoplifting in the store? I keep seeing her everywhere. She's always skulking or lurking around here. I wanted to know who she was and why." And now I'd completely blown getting to talk to her at all. Way to keep my eyes on the prize.

"Oh, that." Faith caught Jeannette's hand and wiped hot chocolate off it. Her smile faded. "Don't play with your drink."

"I'm just trying to sink the marshmallows." Jeannette pouted.

"What do you mean, *oh, that*?" I went behind the counter to get more marshmallows for Jeannette to play Battleship with.

"I didn't really tell you the whole story the other day." Faith took a sip of her own hot chocolate.

I wasn't sure I liked the sound of that. "What? There was more?"

She shrugged. "She was spying on her husband. She thought he was having an affair."

I stared at her, not believing what I was hearing. "Do you know who her husband is?"

"Nope. I didn't then and I don't now. I just knew she was a fellow traveler so I gave her some tissues and told her to dump the rat." She wiped off both girls' faces. "Ready to go, girls?"

"Then she's not connected to Antoine at all?"

"Not that I know of. You could ask her."

"No can do. I'm pretty sure I'm not allowed within twenty-five yards of her." My face got hot at the thought of the piece of paper that Dan had handed me.

"That makes sense, too, since it's as far as you can run."

Grand Lake was the kind of town that tourists visited to see the fall. The dogwood trees turned spectacular shades of red with elm trees showing orange and yellow. The nights would get cool, but the days turned warm. The sunlight took on a golden tinge.

Well, that was over. We were heading into November. There was no light in the morning and the afternoon light was gray and it got dark way too damn early at night. I'd thought it would make me miserable. I'd thought I'd thrived on the sunshine of Northern California. I'd thought the golden hills dotted with the green of live oak was the landscape that opened my soul, the place where I could finally draw a full deep breath into my lungs.

Turned out I was a little darker than that. I enjoyed the shiver that ran through me when Sprocket and I stepped out into the cold dark night, even if there was a spit of rain coming down. I liked watching the gorgeous red and yellow leaves turn slowly brown and drop to the ground. Granted, of course, only as long as I wasn't responsible for raking them. I liked it when the golden hazy sun of summer became the sharp crisp white light of autumn.

Maybe I was a midwestern girl at heart after all. Or maybe I should wait for the first snowfall to be sure of that. It also helped that I didn't have far to walk tonight. Garrett had texted me to see if I wanted to meet him for dinner at the diner. I'd promised Garrett I would meet him. Megan did not look fondly on Sprocket coming into the restaurant so I settled him with a peanut-butter-filled Kong and walked down the street. I got to the diner before Garrett and asked for our usual booth.

"Trouble sure follows you, sweetheart," Megan said as she seated me.

I looked up, startled. "What do you mean?"

She set the water pitcher down on the table and put her hand on one hip. "Well, there was your folks dying when you were so young. That's a start."

"That was hardly my fault!" I sat back in my seat, feeling like I'd been slapped. Losing my parents when I was still in high school changed my life, changed me, changed everything. While I felt like Haley and I had managed to put our lives on good tracks, there wasn't a milestone that happened that I didn't wish my mom and dad could be there to see. To blame it on me seemed unbelievably cruel.

"Didn't say it was, sugar. Just said stink seems to stick with you like dog shit on a shoe," she said.

Fine. "What else?"

She squinted into the distance. "Well, you come back and Coco gets killed."

I didn't protest too hard that that was not my fault. I knew my return to Grand Lake played a part in what had happened to Coco. Neither Coco nor I had foreseen how badly my return would play out, but it didn't change the facts.

"Now Mr. Belanger shows up to do a show about you and his assistant is dead and he's in jail." She picked her water pitcher back up. "Now, did you want to order or did you want to wait for Mr. Garrett?"

"I'll wait." I twirled my glass. I didn't have to wait long.

"You may want to reconsider this," I said as he slid into the booth across from me. "Megan thinks I'm some kind of bad-luck magnet."

Garrett picked up his menu and read. "Yeah, but you're cute and I'm hungry. I'll take my chances."

The bell over the door chimed and I turned to see who had come in.

Jason walked in. He wasn't alone, however. He held the door open for Marisela Santos and ushered her to a booth with a hand on her lower back.

My jaw nearly dropped. Was he the husband she thought was having an affair? If so, she was very much connected with Antoine's crew and had deliberately not told Dan that information.

I sank down in the booth with a whispered, "Darn it."

"What?" Garrett asked, looking up from the menu.

"Over there. It's Antoine's cameraman and the woman I think might be his wife. I'm not supposed to be within twenty-five yards of her. How big is this room?" I glanced over my shoulder. She hadn't spotted me yet. Or if she had, she wasn't acting like it.

"Smaller than twenty-five yards. Why aren't you supposed to be around her?" Garrett set his menu down.

"I was going to get to that over dinner. I wanted to ask her some questions and she ran so I ran, too . . ."

"You ran?" Garrett interrupted. "You never run."

"Yes. I ran. She ran faster, but Sprocket ran faster than both of us and sort of knocked her down . . ."

"Sort of?" he interrupted again. "How does a dog sort of knock a person down?"

"Okay. More than sort of. Actually knocked her down. If you want to know what happened, though, you're going to have to stop interrupting." I crossed my arms over my chest and pressed my lips together.

"Fine." He mimed locking his lips with a key and throwing the key away.

"She's the woman I kept seeing that Dan thought I was making up, but I wasn't. She's real. And I think she's married to Antoine's cameraman and according to Faith she thought her husband was having an affair with someone and she was here to spy on him." It all came out in a rush.

"I think I would have understood more if I'd kept interrupting." He rubbed his forehead with his thumb. "She thought Jason was having an affair?"

"I know. Think about it. Maybe Jason is who Melanie was getting ready to meet that night. It would explain the whole date-night vibe she had going."

"Did you tell Dan that part?" Garrett asked.

"No. I only found out about the affair thing after he'd already cited me for assault, and I only found out the husband she thought was having an affair was Jason now." I gnawed on the edge of my thumb.

"Dan what?" Garrett said loudly. Too loudly. Loudly enough that all the heads in the diner turned toward us, including Jason's and Marisela's.

"And now I think I'm too close to Marisela. Dan said I had to keep twenty-five yards away, but is it my fault if she came into the place where I already am?" Megan made her way toward us. She'd thrown me out of the diner before. I was pretty sure she wouldn't hesitate to do it again.

"We need to call Dan," Garrett said. "We need to tell him the rest of what you found out."

"Okay. Go ahead."

"Why me?" Garrett asked. "You do it."

"He's mad at me."

"Well, I don't want him to be mad at me."

"I think I know one sure way to get him over here," I said. I stood up and walked over to Jason and Marisela's table.

Marisela started shrinking back into the corner of their booth when I was halfway across the room. "Stay away from me," she hissed when I got to their table. "You're not supposed to be within twenty-five yards of me. The sheriff said."

Jason looked back and forth between us. "Why can't Rebecca be within twenty-five yards of you, Marisela?"

"Because she and her filthy dog assaulted me this afternoon." Marisela's face crumpled as if she were about to cry.

"Sprocket is very clean. He's not filthy at all," I said.

Marisela pulled out her cell phone. "I'll call the sheriff. He gave me his number."

"Go ahead," I said. "Do it. Maybe once he gets here we can get this all cleared up."

"You assaulted my wife?" Jason asked, starting to get up from the table.

I took a step back and bumped into Garrett, who literally had my back. "I didn't assault her. I wanted to talk to her. She ran."

"Why did you want to talk to Marisela?"

"I will call the sheriff," Marisela said loudly.

Megan said, "I already called him." I knew she wouldn't hesitate for a second to turn me in.

"Never mind," Jason said. "We're leaving."

Jason helped Marisela with her jacket after she got out of the booth, and they were both headed for the door when Dan walked in. For a second I thought Jason was going to

POP GOES THE MURDER

try to bolt. I'm not sure whether or not he saw Huerta out on the sidewalk or decided that it wouldn't do to leave Marisela holding the bag, but he seemed to think better of it.

Dan walked up to me. "Rebecca, I told you to leave that woman alone."

"Thank you, Sheriff," Jason said.

"Yes, if you'll all come down to the station now I can take your statements," Dan said.

"That's okay," Marisela said quickly. "I just want her to leave us alone."

Dan's phone buzzed in his pocket. He frowned. I knew normally he'd ignore his phone at a moment like this, but with Haley so close to going into labor he didn't dare. He pulled it out and looked at the message. His brow creased. Then he held up the phone. "Maybe you'd be able to explain this, too," he said. On his phone was a photo of Jason looming over Melanie in the parking lot of the Grand Lake Inn. His face was angry, his arms wide. They were clearly arguing and Melanie was cowering from him.

Jason sagged. "I was hoping this wouldn't come out. I knew it would look bad."

"Who sent that?" I asked Dan. I looked around the diner. Whoever had texted Dan the photo either had amazing timing or knew where he was and who he was talking to at precisely that moment.

Dan looked at the phone again. "Unknown number," he said. His eyes narrowed farther. "You're right, Jason. It does look bad. I think we should go down to the station and talk about it."

Jason nodded. He started to walk out of the diner with Marisela and Dan following. I followed after them, but then Dan turned around. "Not you," he said.

I stopped. "But . . ."

"No buts," he said. "Go have dinner."

"No," Jason interrupted. "I want her there."

Dan turned to him. "What? Why?"

Jason's chin came up. "She's the only one who seems like she really wants the truth. I need someone who's going to look deeper than the surface of this thing. I want her there or I want a lawyer."

Dan's shoulders dropped. "Fine," he said. "You can come, Rebecca."

When we walked into the Sheriff's Department, Dan pointed to some benches in the lobby. "You can wait there, Ms. Santos."

Jason's shoulders slumped. "No. She might as well know, too." He reached for her hand, but Marisela put hers in the pocket of her coat. He kept his hand out. "Please?"

It was one of those moments where I was aware that a lot more was going on than met the eye. On the surface, the stakes were pretty low. Would Marisela take his hand and accompany us into the interview room? Would she stay in the waiting area with Vera? Didn't seem like it made a lot of difference.

But I could tell it did. I could tell it was one of those marriage-defining moments. Jason was offering to show himself to Marisela at his most vulnerable. Would she say yes? Would she stand by her man? Or make him stand alone?

I held my breath. Finally, Marisela took her hand out of her pocket and tucked it into Jason's. I think the whole room exhaled at once.

I started unloading my forbidden items into the tray

and froze for a second with my cell phone in my hand. The funny way Haley had been wincing on and off crossed my mind. "Can I ask you a huge favor?" I asked.

"Depends. What kind of huge?"

"I know I can't take my cell phone back in there," I said, hoping she'd maybe tell me it was okay this one time.

"Nope. Strictly forbidden." So much for that.

I went with Option B. "What would be the possibility of you keeping an eye on it while I'm in there?"

"What kind of eye?" She narrowed her own eyes as she asked.

"Haley's due date is coming up and I'm supposed to take care of Evan when she goes into labor. She's getting a little freaky about me not having the phone with me and it's making me jumpy. If she texts a 911, would you come get me?" The words tumbled out of my mouth.

Vera laughed. "Which one of you is actually jumpy? You or her?"

"Both," I admitted.

She snorted. "I remember what waiting for my second was like. You know exactly how bad it's going to be, but you can't wait for it to get started anyway." She took the phone and tucked it in her pocket. "I'll keep an eye on it."

Then we trooped down the hallway into the room where I'd seen Antoine chained to the table.

Jason sat where Antoine had sat. Dan sat across from him and Marisela sat next to him. Huerta took up a position leaning against the door and I headed to the corner behind Dan.

"So do you want to explain to us what you were arguing with Ms. Fitzgerald about the night she was murdered?" Dan asked in a conversational tone.

Marisela made a noise of distress. Jason put his hand over hers. "It's a long story."

"I've got time." Dan tipped his chair back onto two legs and crossed his arms over his chest.

Jason sighed. "Look. It's not like I don't know how I look. I get up in the morning and my hair falls a certain way. There's not a lot I can do about it. I've never really been comfortable with it, though. I mean, I know what I look like on the outside. I've just never felt like that guy on the inside. It's why I like being behind the camera rather than in front of it."

Interesting.

"What does this have to do with Ms. Fitzgerald?" Dan asked, clearly unimpressed with Jason's existential crisis over his own good looks.

Jason glanced over at his wife, who was not looking at him. He rubbed at his temple with his thumb. "Melanie always looked at me . . . that way. She'd think I wasn't looking and I'd catch her checking me out. I figured as long as she was only looking, it was okay. I mean, they all look."

I thought back. Had I? I remembered shivering when he put my mike on. That was hardly my fault, though. It was reflex, like kicking when the doctor hit your knee with the rubber hammer.

"So you felt she was looking at you." Dan jotted down a note.

"Yeah. Like I said. I'm used to it. Then about six months ago, she started giving me extra assignments. Shooting extra B roll for segments. Asking me to archive old clips. Stuff that kept me around the office for extra hours." He turned to his wife. "You remember right? I started working a lot of overtime."

Marisela nodded. "I remember."

"And what did you do?" Dan asked.

"I did the work. First of all, time and a half does not suck, my man. Am I right?" Jason held his hand out in a fist bump. No one bumped him back. After a few awkward seconds, he let his hand drop. "So the extra money was nice. Marisela and I are thinking about starting a family soon. Babies cost money." He looked over at Marisela, who looked down at her hands, but not before I saw a glisten on her cheeks.

"And?" Dan prompted.

"And what?" Jason asked.

"You said *first of all*. That implies a second point. Maybe a third." I wasn't sure I'd ever heard Dan use that kind of condescending tone when talking with anyone.

"Second, I wanted to be known as a team player," Jason continued. "A go-to guy. If we have a baby, I'm going to want to be around more, cut down on the travel. One way to do that is to take on more responsibility. Maybe be the guy who schedules stuff and edits tape instead of the guy who's out shooting all the time."

Dan pressed his lips together and nodded. "I see. So how'd that work out for you?"

Jason slumped again. "Not so great, man. Not great at all. At first, Melanie just wanted to talk. I think she was lonely." That fit with her boyfriend dumping her and her cat dying. "She'd kind of hang around and talk at me while I did stuff. No big deal."

"But then?" Dan bumped his chair down solidly on the floor. "It did become a big deal?"

Jason didn't glance over at Marisela now. He kept his eyes studiously on Dan. "One night she opened a bottle of wine. Champagne, actually. It was a leftover bottle from the segment we did on how to pair sparkling wines with everyday foods. Antoine served that one with smoked oysters."

I knew that Antoine trick. It was a good one. The sharp sparkle of the wine cut through the oiliness of the oysters. Add a tiny touch of horseradish and a California sunset and it didn't get much better than that.

"So Ms. Fitzgerald had champagne," Dan prompted.

"Champagne doesn't store well. You really need to drink it once it's opened. She didn't want it to go to waste and she didn't want to drink a whole bottle by herself. Or, at least, that's what she said." Jason's voice was laced with disgust.

"So you made the huge sacrifice of drinking champagne on company time with an attractive woman?" Dan asked.

"See? That's why I want her here." He pointed at me again. "You see how he twisted that?"

"You did kind of give it a turn there, Dan," I said. Clearly Jason was one of those people who Dan disliked pretty much on sight. There weren't many of them.

Dan glared at me. "It's called interrogation."

"I don't care what you call it. It wasn't what he meant." I didn't see Jason being extra forthcoming because Dan was giving him a hard time.

Dan shook his head. "Fine. You took pity on her and had some champagne. What then?"

"Well, it seemed like it went to her head pretty fast. She got a little giggly and then a little unsteady on her feet. She stumbled and I caught her and then all the sudden her tongue was so deep in my mouth I thought she was fishing for my uvula." Jason leaned back in his chair like a man relieved of a terrible burden.

Marisela gasped. He reached for her. "I'm so sorry,

babe. I swear, I didn't kiss her back, but it was hard to get her off me. It was like peeling the skin off a tomato."

"Then what happened?" Dan asked.

"I got out of there as fast as I could that night. I expected her to apologize the next day. Make some excuse about the champagne going to her head. I don't know. Something. But instead she acted like it didn't happen. So I did, too." Jason licked his lips as if they were dry.

Dan cocked his head to one side. "And that was the end of it?"

Jason snorted. "I wish. No. It wasn't even close to the end of it. I figured it would be smart to stop saying yes to the overtime offers. Give her a little time to cool off. Maybe find someone else to focus on."

"Did she?" Dan asked.

"No. Instead she went and had a little talk with Antoine." He shook his head. "Told him I was slacking. Made it sound like I was leaving early and coming in late. I ended up with a reprimand and a warning. Shape up or look for another job."

"Why didn't you look for another job? Or tell Antoine what was going on with Melanie?" I asked. Dan shot me a look, but I didn't care.

"Jobs aren't so easy to come by unless we wanted to move back to Los Angeles and, frankly, I don't. That city is a huge hassle. The air sucks. The traffic sucks. It's a nightmare. We like Northern California. We wanted to stay there." Jason turned to look at Marisela. "Right, honey?"

She nodded, but it was about the tiniest nod I'd ever seen.

"And talking to Antoine?" Dan asked.

"You try talking to Antoine. If Antoine doesn't want to

hear what you have to say, good luck getting him to listen," Jason said.

I knew that all too well. Even before the Minneapolis incident that led to me walking out the door, I'd been trying to talk to Antoine about our marriage for months.

"So you went back to doing the overtime when asked?" Dan made a note on his pad.

"I did, but I tried to keep my distance. Melanie is pretty persistent, though. It's been escalating all that time and she's even worse when we're on the road." Again, Jason looked over at Marisela.

I glanced over at Dan. Had he noticed that Jason had slipped and started referring to Melanie in the present tense? It was as if her death wasn't completely real to him. I was pretty sure if he'd seen Melanie floating in that tub, it would be real to him. Unless he was that deeply in denial. Maybe seeing Melanie in the tub had been so traumatic he'd blocked it out like it hadn't happened.

If Dan noticed, he didn't give me any indication. He went on questioning Jason. "Is that what happened on Wednesday night? Did she go too far?"

Jason covered his face with his hand. "She did. She went way too far. When we got back to the hotel, she asked me to check on one of the tripods. She said she thought it wasn't stable. It was just a ruse to keep me out in the parking lot after everyone else went inside. Once we were alone, she told me that I'd better show up at her hotel room by nine o'clock ready to, uh, service her." He glanced over at Marisela, who'd let out a strangled sob, and a tear leaked out of his own eye. "She wanted me there right after she took her bath."

"Her bath?"

"Yeah. She always took one when we were on the road. It was kind of a ritual."

"So you decided to take care of her once and for all? Was that it? You were tired of being sexually harassed and decided to end it?" Dan asked, still in that conversational tone, as if he was asking Jason if he liked football.

"Yes. Wait. No. Not how you mean. I told her I wouldn't. She went nuts. She screamed at me. She told me she'd get me fired and I'd never work again. I told her I didn't care. She said she'd make me care." Jason's voice rose. "She told me she knew I'd make the right choice after I thought about it and that she would be waiting for me."

"Tell us what you did, Jason. It'll be easier for everyone." Dan kept his voice low and quiet. "Had you already bought the blow-dryer? Had you already altered it? Or did you do it that night?"

Jason looked almost surprised. "I went to my room, shut the door, put the security lock on, drank two shots of whiskey and went to bed."

"Was anyone with you?" Dan asked.

"No. That's the point. I don't want to be with anyone except Marisela." He took her hand again. She didn't pull away.

Dan shut his eyes and I could almost hear him counting to three. "Can anyone vouch for your whereabouts? Did anyone come to your room? Talk to you on the phone?"

Jason shook his head. "No. I'm not a big drinker. Two shots of whiskey and I'm out."

"So we only have your word that you went to your room and stayed there?" Dan started to shut his notebook.

"No. You don't only have his word. You have mine," Marisela said.

The attention of everyone in the room shifted to her.

Jason said, "But you didn't even get here until this morning."

She blushed. "Not exactly."

"I saw her in the coffee shop at the hotel the morning I found Melanie," I said. "I saw her in the alley behind my shop and running down the sidewalk on Main Street." I straightened up from where I'd been leaning against the wall. I looked over at Dan. "Not everyone believed me that you even existed, but I saw you."

Dan threw his hands up in the air. "Can you blame me? Until you tackled her in the field this afternoon, no one else had seen her."

"Faith saw her!" I protested.

"Faith would say she saw Santa Claus if you asked her to. Plus you were the one who insisted that you saw a ghost in the girls' bathroom in elementary school so they'd close it and let you use the teachers' bathroom."

"That was fourth grade, Dan, and that bathroom was disgusting." It had needed remodeling to even make it to nineteenth-century standards.

"Once a fabulist, always a fabulist, Rebecca."

I hated it when he called me Rebecca. "That is so . . ."

Huerta cleared his throat. Loudly. We both looked over at him. He nodded his head toward Jason and Marisela.

"You tackled my wife?" Jason asked, starting to rise from his chair.

"Technically, my dog tackled her. I was trying to get her to tell me what she was doing here and why she was always lurking."

Jason took his hand away from Marisela's. "You've been here all this time. Why didn't you tell me? What were you doing?"

She blushed even harder. "I knew something wasn't right.

The late hours. You showering when you got home. I knew. I knew." She buried her face in her hands and began to weep.

Dan pulled a handkerchief out of his pocket and handed it to Marisela. Once she settled down a little, he said, "So how do you know he stayed in his room the rest of the night?"

"Once he went into his room, he was there all night," she blurted out.

"How do you know that?"

She blushed. "I, uh, put a piece of tape across the edge of the door and the doorframe. It was still there the next morning before I went for coffee. Once he went in, he stayed in."

"You did what?" Jason turned to his wife, clearly horrified.

"I put a little piece of tape on your door. It wouldn't have stopped you from getting out if you needed to." She shrank away from him a little.

"That's not the point, Marisela. It's crazy enough that you followed me here. It's ten times crazier that you're using weird spy techniques on me." Jason pushed his hands through his hair.

She shrugged. "I didn't feel like I had a choice. I knew something was going on and you weren't telling me what it was."

"Because I didn't want to worry you," he protested.

"Yeah, well, how'd that work out for you, Jason?" she asked, a new sharpness in her tone.

He dropped his head into his hands. "I can't believe this."

Dan shut his notepad. "You might not, but I do. You maybe should say thank you. She just made sure you were cleared of any murder charges."

"You didn't seriously think I could have killed Melanie?" Jason's eyes widened.

Dan stared at Jason until Jason looked back down. Then Dan looked around at the group, then threw his hands in the air. "Is there anyone who didn't want to kill that woman? Anyone at all?"

I resisted the urge to say, "Bueller?" when no one answered.

"Well, I can tell you who else came to see her," Marisela said.

Dan sighed and picked up his pen. "Who?"

"Sunny Coronado."

I must have made some kind of funny noise, a squeak or a squeal, because everyone turned to look at me. "Excuse me. Hiccups."

"The Sunshine Chef?" Huerta asked. "What would he be doing going to see Melanie? Aren't he and Antoine bitter rivals?"

Marisela shrugged. "I don't know. I just know that after Jason went into his room, Sunny showed up."

"Did he go into Melanie's room?"

"I don't know. I went back to mine. He could have done anything. I just saw him knocking on her door." Marisela pressed her lips together as if she was literally keeping herself from saying anything else about men knocking on Melanie's door.

"What about Antoine?" Dan asked. "Did you see Antoine that evening?"

She laughed. "It's hard to miss Antoine."

Didn't I know it.

Marisela continued, "He banged on her door before Sunny showed up."

Dan turned to me. "Did you know anything about this?"

I bit my lip. "I heard Sunny on the radio the other day, but I didn't know anything about him coming to see Melanie."

"Are you sure, Rebecca?" Dan leaned in toward me.

I was sure. I just wasn't sure that Antoine didn't know anything about Sunny coming to see Melanie. "Maybe I should talk to Antoine."

Eleven

Huerta ushered Jason and Marisela out, leaving Dan and me alone in the conference room. "Do you believe her?" I asked.

"I do," he said.

"It would explain why Melanie's room looked like she was getting ready for a date. She was expecting Jason to show up." I chewed on the edge of my thumbnail.

"Except he didn't. Someone else showed up and whoever that someone else was killed her," Dan said.

I shivered. Then a thought occurred to me. "Dan, how did whoever killed Melanie get into her room?"

"You said the door was ajar when you got there. Maybe she'd left it that way."

I shook my head. "I don't think so. Antoine said he tried the door when he knocked on it. It was locked."

"We still don't have a definitive time of death," Dan said, rubbing his chin. "We don't know if she was still alive when Antoine knocked on her door and was just hiding from him or if she was already dead."

"Who else had the key card?"

"Derek Wade would have," Dan said.

"I thought we believed him about not being involved with Melanie's death, just with her thievery."

"If evidence points me in another direction, I'll follow that faster than I'll follow my gut," Dan said.

As a chef, I wasn't sure that was a good plan. People following their guts was my bread and butter.

"And what does that mean for me, *mon ami*?" Antoine said as he walked into the room accompanied by Huerta.

Dan looked at me and shook his head, then looked back at Antoine. "It means you're damn lucky, *mon ami*," he said with a sarcastic edge to the *ami*. "Because my gut says that you're still not coming clean about something, but I don't have any proof of that yet."

Antoine smiled. "So you will be letting me go?"

"Not yet," Dan said. "You're still a flight risk and you're still the main suspect. Means, motive and opportunity, Antoine. They all add up to something."

Antoine opened his mouth to speak, but I cut him off. I knew he wouldn't back down and the only thing he would accomplish would be irritating Dan, which wasn't in his best interests whether he could see that or not. "Dan, could I talk to Antoine alone for a minute?"

Dan looked back and forth between us and shrugged. "Why not?"

I waited until he left and the door clicked shut behind him. I stared at Antoine for a minute or two. If you've ever done it, you'll know how long that can feel like. The first ten seconds rush by, but then time slows. At first, Antoine apparently thought I was ready to profess my love for him again and reached across the table to try to take my hands.

I moved them away.

Truth was, I was thinking. Dan was right. There was something that Antoine wasn't telling us, something that had to do with Sunny Coronado, something that had to do with Melanie.

I knew him. I knew him so well. Not just as a person, either. I knew who he was as a chef and as a businessman. I'd been there as he'd made the business plan he was still following.

Then I thought about all the things I'd learned recently. I'd learned that Melanie was short for cash, that there'd been a big payment not too long ago.

"Melanie sold your spice mix formulas to Sunny, didn't she?" Antoine's pasta sauces had launched a few months ago. His business plan called for him to launch a new product line every two years. We hadn't specified exactly what those product lines would be—Antoine hadn't wanted to have his creativity hemmed in—but spice mixes had been on the long list of products he was considering. Antoine was precise, nearly scientific, in his approach to cooking. He didn't rush the development process. He would have already been working on his next products already.

Antoine's face went ashy. "How did you know?"

"I didn't. It all just fell into place for me now. That's what your phone message was about. Not money. The spice mixes." I felt a little pang. I had actually been the one to encourage Antoine into starting his first product line. I'd been in on the ground floor of all of them, even the pasta sauces that launched after we'd divorced. I knew nothing about these new spices. "Sunny has always wanted to expand his business the way you have, he's just never managed to come up with anything before you did. No way he would scoop you without some serious help."

Antoine leaned forward. "Yes. That's exactly what I thought when I saw the announcement of his new line. I was going to confront Melanie and then contact the police, but she didn't answer her door and by the next morning she was dead."

"This is bad, Antoine. You realize that this gives you a heck of a reason to kill Melanie." We would have to get Cynthia in here right away.

He nodded miserably. "On the surface, yes, if her death looked like a crime of passion, of anger. Rewiring a blow-dryer and dropping it into the tub during her nightly bath? That requires planning."

I rubbed my forehead. He was right. "You're sure it was her?"

He slumped down in his chair. "Yes. We two were the only ones with access to the formulas. We were still that early in our development phase."

"But Sunny is already going to market!" Generally, these things take time.

"He must have rushed it through. Crashed it, as they say. All done to scoop me so I can never introduce spices of my own without looking like I'm copying him." Antoine looked like he might be sick at the thought. "What's more important is finding out why Sunny is here. Why would he be anywhere close to where we were filming? I would think he would want to be far, far away, to disassociate himself completely."

He had a point and it was sharper than the tip of a boning knife. What was Sunny doing here?

There was a knock on the conference room door. I opened it and Vera held out my phone. "It's buzzing like crazy."

Five messages from Haley. I sighed. "I'll see what I can find out," I told Antoine, and headed out.

I slid out the side door more successfully this time and called Haley.

She didn't even say hello. "Please don't tell me you were visiting Antoine again."

I didn't say anything.

"Rebecca, are you there?"

"Yes, but I'm not sure what I'm supposed to say since I'm not supposed to tell you I was visiting Antoine."

"You were, weren't you? You were visiting Antoine."

"To be fair, it didn't start that way. I started out helping Dan question someone."

She sighed. "Are you out now?"

"Yes. Are you in labor?"

"No. I still want you to come home, though."

"I have to pick up Sprocket from Garrett."

"You have your boyfriend dogsitting while you visit your ex-husband in jail? Rebecca, what are you thinking?"

Again, I didn't have an answer. "See you in a little bit."

I called Cynthia's office and left a message for her to call me in the morning and headed to Garrett's place.

Garrett lived on Birch Street in a two-flat that had once been a two-story Craftsman bungalow. Mrs. Patrick, who had been my eighth grade homeroom teacher, had the bottom flat and Garrett lived on the top floor. Mrs. Patrick hadn't liked me in eighth grade and she didn't like me much better now. I felt she'd been inordinately interested in exactly when I arrived at school in eighth grade and she seemed to take an even more inordinate interest in exactly when I arrived at Garrett's apartment. And, of course, when I left.

The walk over to Garrett's from Dan's office helped clear my head. I tried to make my way as quietly as possible, but the heels of my boots echoed on the sidewalks. There's something about cold night air that makes everything sharper. Smells, sounds, sights, all of it seemed to have harder edges. The streetlights left pools of yellow on the cracked sidewalks that made the dark seem all that much darker as I passed. Someone had a fire going. I could smell the smoke of it over the scent of the fall leaves that crunched underfoot.

I felt a little bad now about assaulting Marisela. She'd only been doing what she thought she had to do to save her marriage. Of course, a lot of it could have been avoided if Jason had told her what was going on with Melanie. It wasn't good to keep secrets. At least, not from the people you cared most about. Except, of course, the kind I was keeping from Dan. That was okay, right? That tight feeling in my chest didn't mean anything.

Garrett's entrance was on the left side of the house. The blue light of a television flickered from Mrs. Patrick's living room window. What did she watch? Was she a true-crime aficionado? Did she like cop shows? Lawyer shows? Doctor shows? I tried to peek into the window, but couldn't quite make out what it was. I really wanted it to be Kardashian related.

I went up the stairs, avoiding the fourth step because it creaked crazy loud, and knocked on the door. I heard one small yip and then Garrett opened the door. I kissed him hello and then bent down to get kisses from Sprocket, too.

"How are my men doing?" I asked.

Garrett raised his eyebrows. "Maybe I should ask you that?"

I stood and leaned my head against his chest. "Please don't," I said.

His arms wrapped around me. "Okay," he whispered into my hair.

He was cozy and warm, wearing sweats and socks and not looking corporate at all.

"We need to talk," I said into his chest.

I felt the tension in his arms, but all he said was another quiet, "Okay." We sat down on his couch—which was shockingly not leather. At one point, I had a theory that all single men must own leather couches.

He sat down next to me and I felt my heart do a little dance move. I liked him. Maybe a little more than I'd realized or even wanted to. I also hadn't realized that while my life was an open book—you don't get to divorce even a minor celebrity like Antoine without it showing up in a few tabloids—Garrett's was one of those diaries with a lock on the outside. It might not be too hard to break in, but it made you want to stop and respect his privacy. Until there was a reason not to. Like, you know, the diary's ex-girlfriend being in town and making everyone make choking noises every time you mentioned it.

"You know, there are very few sentences that strike more fear into a guy's heart than *We need to talk*." He rested his elbows behind him and stretched his long legs out in front of himself. He didn't look at me, which allowed me to study his profile for a moment. Like Dan, he played his cards pretty close to his chest. It was hard to know exactly what was going on behind those dark eyes.

"I'm not pregnant, if that helps any." I leaned back, too.

He laughed. "It doesn't hurt. What's up?"

"I want to know about Cynthia," I said, turning to look straight ahead instead of looking at him.

"She's a great lawyer." His response was instant.

I was fairly certain he knew that wasn't what I was asking. "I was hoping to hear more about the personal side."

"Oh, that." His voice was flat. It was impossible to read anything from those two words.

"Yes, that." I sat up and opened the container next to me and handed him a cookie.

He laughed. "Aren't you supposed to save the reward for after I cooperate?" He took it anyway.

"I trust you." I did. I just needed to know.

"But you still want to know about Cynthia. I don't suppose it would be enough to tell you not to worry about it." He bit into the cookie. "Gingersnap?"

"It seemed like a solid autumnal choice and no, you can't just tell me not to worry about it after seeing Haley's face the night Antoine was arrested."

"You Anderson girls and your glass faces." He shook his head. "Neither of you should be lawyers or poker players."

"Noted. Now cough up the goods."

Garrett straightened up and leaned forward on his elbows. Tension bunched his shoulders. "We had a client, one we were both pretty sure was guilty."

"That can't be the first time that happened." Defense attorneys probably ran across that scenario every day.

He laughed. "Oh, no. No indeed. Not everyone accused of a crime is guilty, but a fair number of them are. That doesn't mean they shouldn't have a good defense. It's how the system was constructed."

"I get that." Maybe even a little more now with Antoine sitting in jail. "But this client was somehow different?"

"He wasn't. Not really. We'd represented a dozen people like him. What he had was a brother that looked enough like him to almost be his twin."

I felt like I had a glimmer of where this was going. "Was there eyewitness testimony against him?"

"Close. Security camera video." He let out a deep breath. "You know how footage from those cameras is always at an odd angle because the cameras are up high in corners?"

"Yeah."

"And they're kind of fuzzy? Not the best definition?" he asked.

I nodded.

"Well, looking at the video, it could have been this guy or his brother. Plus it just so happened that the brother was visiting. Home from school on fall break." He sighed.

"So you used the brother to create reasonable doubt?" I watched almost as many legal thrillers as psychological thrillers.

He nodded. "Yes, Counselor. That's precisely what we did."

"Did it work?"

"A little too well. The brother came under suspicion, too. All of a sudden the cops were asking for his alibi—he didn't have one—and interviewing his coaches and teachers at the university." Garrett rubbed his face. "It wasn't him. We all knew it wasn't him. We all pretended like it could be him and because of how good Cynthia and I were at pretending, he was kicked off the basketball team and lost his scholarship."

"They can do that?" I sat up.

"They had some kind of ethics clause. They felt he'd violated it." Garrett remained slumped.

"Because his brother committed a crime?" Bastards.

"Or maybe him. We'd muddied the waters sufficiently that no one was really clear on that anymore," Garrett pointed out.

"So your client went free." It wasn't a question.

"He did. Cynthia was ecstatic." He took a deep breath and blew it out.

"And you?" I asked.

He winced. "Not so much."

"And you broke up over that?"

"Yes and no."

"That is such a lawyerly response. I'm pretty sure you have to pick one." I shifted away from him on the couch.

"But I can't. It started a whole set of conversations that made both of us realize that we didn't see the world the same way." He rubbed his face. "It made me realize that there were parts of the law I would do better staying away from."

"Like defense attorney-ing?"

"I'm not sure that verb exists, but yes."

"You represented Jasper and you represented me."

"I represented Jasper as a favor to Dan."

"And me?"

He looped his arm around me. "Let's just say I was hoping there would be fringe benefits." He sighed again. "It made me realize that we had to make some choices, and Cynthia didn't choose me." The words came out calm, almost flat.

Looking at his profile, you'd never know what it cost him to say that out loud. No veins bulged in his forehead. His jaw wasn't clenched. His hands weren't fisted.

We hadn't been together long, but I had been getting to know my man. There was a quality to his stillness that spoke volumes. There was something he was holding very close and very deep inside himself. It made me want to wrap my arms around him and hold him close until he let that stillness go.

I laid my head on his shoulder and he kissed my forehead. "So you broke up with Cynthia, gave up your practice with her and moved to Grand Lake?"

He shrugged. "Pretty much."

"You could have gone anywhere, but you chose Grand Lake." I shook my head.

He nudged. "Uh, pot? Kettle?"

He had a point, except for one detail. "I have family here." At least, that was my story and I was sticking to it.

Garrett stared straight ahead. "I don't have family anywhere."

I'd known his parents were dead. It seemed like something we had in common. But no family anywhere? That was a cold world to survive in. "Not even a long-lost cousin?"

"If there is one, he or she has been extremely lost for a long time." He cracked his knuckles. "Dan always talked about Grand Lake like it was a little oasis of goodness in a crazy world. I figured I'd give it a try. If it didn't work out, what would I lose except some time?"

I would not have described Grand Lake in the same glowing terms that Dan would have. Despite growing up side by side, we'd seen things a little differently. Funny how your perspective changes when you get older and hopefully wiser. What felt constricting to me in high school felt like an embrace now. What had been claustrophobic was now cozy. "How do you think it's going?"

He put an arm around my shoulder and pulled me in close, his sweatshirt warm and soft against my cheek. "I think it's going all right," he said, and kissed the top of my head.

When Sprocket and I got home, Haley was sitting on the porch wrapped in a blanket. "How do you and Dan stand sitting out here for all those hours? It's freezing."

I slipped inside the blanket, cuddling up to her. "It grows on you." Sprocket settled on her other side and put his head on her lap.

"I guess I can see that," she grumbled. She held out her hand like an irritated schoolteacher confiscating gum. "Give me your phone."

"Why? I have plenty of battery power."

"Just hand it over." She nudged me with her knee.

I handed it over.

"What's your security code?"

I told her. She punched in the numbers and then started tapping away.

"What are you doing?" I asked.

"I'm installing a program on your phone that will let me keep track of where you are." My phone beeped and she tapped in a few more numbers. "There. You've given me the okay to track you with your phone."

I sat up a little straighter. "I have?"

"Damn skippy you have. Now if I text you or call you and you don't answer, I'll at least know where you are." She handed the phone back to me.

I stared at her. "You're LoJacking my phone?"

"Actually, sweet sister, I'm LoJacking you." She stood

up, wrapped the blanket tighter around herself and went inside the house.

Sprocket looked around as if he was expecting more, like maybe a treat. Haley had a lot to learn about front porch–sitting etiquette. "That's it tonight, I guess," I told him. I stood up and stepped down off the porch.

Twelve

During the night, someone had spray-painted "Popcorn Whore" across the front display window of POPS. It had taken me a minute or two to figure out what it said since I was trying to read it backward from inside the store. "I don't even know what that is," I told Dario. "Does it mean that I'll do anything for popcorn? Or that I do something dirty with popcorn?"

Dario stood looking at it, hands on hips. "You may once again be overthinking. How about we leave it at it not being a compliment?"

I sighed. "Yeah. It'll make great copy to show a photo of me washing it off the window, won't it?"

"Which is why you won't." He went into the kitchen and came back a minute later with a bucket and some sponges. "Can you handle prep without me?"

"It won't be as much fun, but I'll handle it." I went into

the kitchen and put on the oldies station and started to dance while I popped and mixed, stirred and measured. Dario was back in before I finished making the pumpkin breakfast bars. He put away the scrub brushes and bucket and tied on an apron, which he somehow managed to make look studly.

"So what's up with not-your-man?" he asked.

"Why do you think something is up?" I set the timer and stared at the caramel sauce as it bubbled.

"First because something always seems to be up, but also because the morning headlines said that someone else was being questioned."

I dropped my head a bit. The press didn't miss much, did it? "Dan had some questions for Jason."

"The cute one?" he asked, a smile quirking at his lips.

"Yes, the cute one."

"And?"

I glanced at the timer. One more minute. "Melanie was trying to force him to sleep with her."

Dario's eyebrows went up and he snorted. "At least she had good taste. Does Dan think he had anything to do with it?"

The timer finally went off and I started to stir the caramel and then poured it over the popcorn. Dario already had his hands greased and started to mix the sauce into the popcorn.

"No, but it does explain the clothes all being laid out like she was getting ready for a date. She was."

"Was she planning on receiving him while she was still in the tub?"

I frowned. It was a good question. Whoever had killed Melanie had come in while she was in the tub and she hadn't gotten out when whoever it was came into the room.

Haley and I had had more than our fair share of conversations with one of us in the tub and the other perched on the edge, but we were sisters. Was there anyone in Grand Lake who felt as close as a sister to Melanie?

Faith and Annie stopped in for their mid-morning coffee break at about the same time the rush ended. I filled them in on what had happened the night before with Jason and Marisela.

"So where did the text that Dan received with the picture of Jason arguing with Melanie come from?" Annie asked.

"Dan didn't know. He said it was a blocked number." That still didn't sit right.

"Whoever it was had good timing," Faith observed. "Dan could have arrested you for being within twenty-five yards of that poor woman."

"Poor woman?" Annie snorted. "How about her poor husband?"

"Oh, please. He may be saying he hated it, but I bet he liked the attention." Faith waved her hand in the air as if to dismiss the notion that Jason might have actually been distressed.

Annie shook her head. "You don't give many men much credit for anything."

"I don't know what you're talking about." Faith sat back in her chair and crossed her arms over her chest.

Annie rolled her eyes. "You do, too. You're letting one lying, cheating bastard make you hate an entire gender."

"You're letting one smooth-talking silver fox convince you that men aren't pigs," Faith countered.

"They're not. At least, not inherently."

"I beg to differ."

"Beg as much as you want."

I put my head down on the kitchen table and kept it there until they stopped.

That morning, I drove into Cleveland to meet with Cynthia. I stepped into her office and immediately felt inferior. It was tasteful. I knew that sounded like a compliment, but honestly that kind of tasteful makes me feel a little itchy. Everything was muted. Everything was soft. Everything had rounded edges.

It reminded me a little too much of the house I'd shared with Antoine. There'd been a lot of shades of beige in there, too. It's true I may have overcompensated at my shop and in my apartment, but now I'd grown accustomed to color and a lot of it.

The receptionist looked vaguely horrified at Sprocket, but I couldn't leave him in the car and I knew he wouldn't do anything socially reprehensible. "May I help you?" she asked in a tone more suited to asking if she needed to call security to escort me out.

"I'm here to see Ms. Harlen. It's regarding Antoine Belanger. I have an appointment."

"Oh, yes. Rebecca. Just a minute." She pushed a few buttons on her phone and then spoke in a hushed voice into her headset, but not hushed enough that I didn't hear the word *dog*.

She hung up. "Ms. Harlen will be just a moment."

I sat down on the couch and Sprocket lay down on my feet. I patted his head. It was more than a moment before Cynthia came out, but what can you expect from a busy lawyer's office?

"Rebecca," she said striding in the room. "Is something wrong? Is Antoine okay?"

"Mainly. He's getting a little skinny."

"Oh, well, I can't imagine that jail food agrees with him." She sat down on the couch next to me and patted Sprocket on the head. "What's up, then?"

I looked around to see who might overhear. There was only the receptionist. Just in case, I leaned in and whispered, "Remember that chef, Sunny Coronado? The one Antoine doesn't like?"

"Of course."

"Well, he's here in Cleveland," I said, leaning back in the chair to let my words have full drama.

I was not disappointed. Cynthia leaned forward. "Really? How long has he been here?"

"Not sure. Long enough to have set up a radio interview and long enough that he could drive to Grand Lake and back." Now came the hard part. "There's more you should know."

"More?"

I nodded. "Antoine thinks that the line of spices Sunny is launching are based on recipes of Antoine's."

"Does he know how Sunny got the recipes?"

"He thinks Melanie stole them and sold them to Sunny. That's what that voice mail he left on Melanie's phone was all about. He didn't even know about the money she was embezzling. He read online about Sunny's spices and saw how similar they were to his. According to Antoine, the only other person with access was Melanie."

Cynthia rubbed at her lower lip. "Sunny and Melanie spoke the day before she was killed."

Now I sat up straight. "They did? How do you know?"

"Cell phone records. The police requested Melanie's cell phone records when they were investigating so they were discoverable. Anyway, Sunny and Melanie spoke for close to five minutes. I wondered what that conversation was about." She leaned back on the couch. Sprocket rested his chin on her leg. "We need to talk to this Sunny. Do you know how to reach him?"

"I have an e-mail address."

"Send him a note and try to arrange something non-threatening. Like a coffee or something."

"He's going to be suspicious. We've never socialized. Mainly because Antoine hates him so much and I suspect the feeling is mutual." Sunny didn't show it as much as Antoine did, but I saw the way his muscles tightened up when Antoine was in the room.

"Yes, but he doesn't hate you. Maybe it would be some kind of coup to be dating the ex-wife of his hated rival?"

"Dating? You want me to ask him out on a date?" Garrett was literally going to pop something. A gasket or a blood vessel or something.

She shrugged. "It won't be a real date, but maybe he could think it was."

"I'll try him, but I'm only asking him to meet me for coffee."

She snapped her fingers. "Better yet. Why don't you see if he'll visit Antoine in jail? Play the pity card. Talk about how lonely Antoine is and how depressed. If they really hate each other, Sunny might want to get an eyeful of that!"

"Talk about appealing to someone's basest instincts," I said.

She leaned forward to scratch Sprocket under the chin.

"Because people so rarely disappoint when I do that. Right, Sprocket?"

The traitor licked her nose.

The phone call to lure Sunny to visit Antoine in Grand Lake was both easier and harder than I'd expected. My heart was beating so hard as I dialed his number I was afraid the assistant who answered the phone would be able to hear it. I managed to talk my way past that assistant plus one other and finally got to speak to Sunny himself. That's when things got complicated.

"Antoine has specifically asked that I visit him?" Sunny asked, the incredulity plain in his voice.

I leaned back in my office chair. "Yes. I told him that you were nearby and he looked really wistful. Sunny"—I dropped my voice—"he's not eating. I'm sure you can imagine what the food in prison is like."

There was a little gasp. "The poor man. It must be like torture to someone with as refined a palate as Antoine."

"Bologna with Miracle Whip, Sunny. Miracle Whip."

This time there was absolute silence for at least two beats, then he said, "I will be there by two this afternoon. I will bring a clafouti."

"I can't imagine anything that would raise his spirits more," I said. More like his ire. The custard had better be smooth as silk or Antoine would be more likely to spit it across the room than swallow it.

As it turned out, it didn't matter. We never managed to get to the clafouti. I wasn't even that sad. You really need to serve those still warm from the oven before they fall and I didn't want to eat one with a sfork anyway.

* * *

I met Sunny down the street from the Sheriff's Department. He saw me and waved, his face brightening for a moment. "Rebecca, so lovely to see you. You were always Antoine's better half."

I couldn't help but smile. Sunny had that effect on people. "How are you, Sunny?"

"Excellent, as always." Sunny was, indeed, always excellent. At least, that's what he told people.

"I had no idea you were in Ohio until I heard you on the radio. What brings you here?" I asked.

He blushed. "Oh, this and that. You know how it is when you have a television show. You must go here. You must go there. A trip gets planned and somehow you don't even know why."

I did know how it was to work on a television show. Trips don't just get planned. Sunny's schedule was as packed as Antoine's. He probably didn't go to the bathroom without an agenda. "Congratulations on the new spice line. I didn't know you were moving into product lines." That had always been much more of an Antoine thing. His precision in the kitchen lent itself to reproduction more than Sunny's more freewheeling ways.

"Yes, yes. Always trying something new." Sunny started to look a little like I had after chasing Marisela Santos, a little sweaty. I took Sunny around the back way into the Sheriff's Department. Vera met us and went through the basket Sunny carried, then walked us down the corridor to the interrogation room where Antoine and Cynthia were waiting. He froze just a step into the room. I quickly shut the door behind us.

"What is this?" he asked. "Who is this woman?"

Cynthia stood. "Nice to meet you, Mr. Coronado. I'm Monsieur Belanger's attorney. We have a few questions for you about your dealings with Melanie Fitzgerald."

"With who?" Sunny asked, but none of us were fooled by his feigned nonchalance.

"Antoine's assistant. The one from whom you purchased the formulas for the spice line that Monsieur Belanger was planning." Cynthia pulled out a chair. "Please. Sit down. We have much to discuss."

Sunny turned around. "I don't think we have anything to discuss."

I leaned against the closed door with my arms crossed over my chest. "You'll have to go through me to leave," I said. "Antoine has been accused of murder. Murder! This is serious stuff. We know what you did. We need to ask you some questions."

Sunny's shoulders slumped. "How do I know you won't have me brought up on industrial espionage charges?"

"Largely because I am here in a jail cell and do not really have the means to do so," Antoine said. Not exactly comforting words, but he did have a point.

"Fine. I bought the formulas from her, but it's not like they did me any good." Sunny plopped down in the chair Cynthia had offered him.

"What do you mean?" I asked.

Sunny ignored me and directed his answer directly to Antoine. "Either you, Antoine, have lost your touch or Melanie was more of a thieving little bitch than either of us knew."

"The spices were no good?" Antoine sat up straight.

"Bah! They were terrible. They made the marinades and meats inedible. I can't even describe what they did to the fish," he said. "We rushed the announcement of the line to make sure to beat you to the punch. I've spent tens of thousands of dollars on advertising and promotion already."

"Didn't you test it?" Antoine asked.

"Of course I tested it! Do I look like an idiot?"

No one said anything for a moment. Then Cynthia spoke up. "Mr. Coronado, if you tested it, why didn't you realize it wasn't any good?"

He waved his hand in the air. "I figured I'd messed up the proportions." He pointed at Antoine. "He's such a stickler for *exactly this* and *exactly that* and *make sure this* and *never ever that*. I'm not so big on the exact measuring thing. I go more by feel. I figured my feeling had been wrong this time. Plus I thought he would have tested it all before me! Why would I waste time? I had a ticking clock. I needed to get my line of spices on the shelves before he even announced his so he would look like a second-best copycat." Sunny pulled a small glass bottle out of his basket. "Here. Taste this."

Antoine dipped a pinky finger into the bottle and licked it. Then he nearly spat it out. "Vile! Disgusting! Who would put so much tarragon in anything?"

"I asked myself the same question when I saw the recipes, but decided you were probably starting some new tarragon trend and instead I would be the promoter of tarragon." He sat up straighter, as if he were about to receive a medal. "Everyone would talk about how I started the tarragon fad."

"You are an idiot," Antoine said, sounding tired. "A greedy idiot."

Sunny shrugged. "But generally a successful greedy idiot."

"So you realized that there was something wrong with the recipes that Melanie had sold to you and you decided to confront her." Cynthia said this as a statement, not a question.

"I wanted my money back. I could still come up with spice mixes on my own, but no way did I want that little liar and cheat to have my money if I was still going to have to do all the work," Sunny said.

"What did she say when you asked her to return the money?" Cynthia looked up from her tablet on which she was taking notes.

Sunny shook his head. "She said it was all gone. That she'd used it to pay other debts. That I couldn't get blood from a stone."

"And what was your response?" Cynthia asked.

Sunny shrugged. "I know some people."

I stared at him. "What kind of people?"

He leaned back in his chair and crossed his arms over his chest. It wasn't a good look on him. It gave him a little bit of cleavage. "The kind of people who know how to get people to pay their debts."

"You had someone beat her up?" I couldn't keep the shock out of my voice. It was so brutal. So animalistic.

"*Beat* is an ugly word. I had someone convince Melanie that it would be in her best interests to find the money she owed me quickly," he said.

I looked over at Cynthia. "That would explain the old bruises on Melanie."

She nodded. "But Melanie didn't pay, did she?" she asked.

"She begged for two more weeks to try to come up with the money. The two weeks were up last Wednesday."

Wednesday. The night she was killed.

"And that's why you came to Grand Lake? To collect your money?" Cynthia asked. "What happened when you got to Melanie's room?"

Sunny looked down and tapped on the table with his index finger. "What do you mean?"

Cynthia cocked her head to one side. "You drove all the way to Grand Lake. Surely you at least knocked on the door of Melanie's hotel room."

He nodded. "I did. Well, I didn't exactly knock."

"What does that mean?" Cynthia asked.

"Melanie had, uh, sent me a key." He looked down at his hands on the table, a faint flush on his cheeks.

"Why would she do that?" I asked. "Why wouldn't she just answer her door if she was expecting you?"

Antoine made a little noise in the back of his throat.

I turned to him. "What?"

He shrugged and said, "Nothing."

Sunny snorted. "Is she truly that naïve?" he asked.

"Perhaps. I did not give her a reason to not be trusting and naïve," Antoine replied.

"Excuse me. What am I being naïve about?" I hated when people talked about me like I wasn't in the room.

Antoine glanced over at Cynthia, who laughed a little and said, "Explain it to her."

Antoine shifted his chair so he was facing me more directly. "It is a thing some women do. They send their hotel room key to a man with the room number on a note. It is . . . an invitation."

I felt like several gears had shifted. I turned to Sunny. "Melanie was going to sleep with you to get you to forget about the money you'd paid her?" Maybe she'd been getting dressed up for Sunny rather than Jason.

He shrugged. "I believe that was her intent. But fifty thousand dollars for something I can get for free so many other places?" He shook his head. "Not a good deal for me."

"Wait. It was only her intent? Nothing happened?" I asked.

"Nothing could happen. She was already dead when I walked into the hotel room."

I gasped. "And you did nothing?"

Sunny's eyes suddenly didn't look like warm deep pools of dark chocolate. They looked like a shark's eyes. Utterly without light or feeling or connection. "What was there to be done, Rebecca? She was dead."

"You need to talk to Dan," I said. "You need to tell him what you saw."

"Dan?"

Cynthia sighed. "Sheriff Dan Cooper. I'll go get him now."

"No!" Sunny jumped up to block Cynthia's way out the door.

She cocked one hip and rested her fisted hand on it. "Please move out of my way, Mr. Coronado."

"No. I cannot allow it. I will not say any of this to the sheriff. None of it." He shook his head like an angry bull.

"I'm afraid you must," Cynthia said, her voice calm.

He shook his head again, then looked around wildly. "I will deny everything I have told you. There will be no proof. No one will believe the three of you. You are all in cahoots together, trying to frame me for the murder that Antoine committed."

"If that's the way you want to play this, Mr. Coronado, that's your prerogative. I am, however, turning over this information to the sheriff." Cynthia pushed past Sunny, but as she did, he grabbed her arm and twisted it up behind her and then slammed her down on the table. She did something with her foot, hooking it around Sunny's calf and shifting her weight back to throw him off balance. It looked like she might get the better of him, but I knew who could take him down in two seconds.

I opened the door and yelled into the hallway. "Huerta! Hurry!"

Dan arrested Sunny on assault charges, although by the time Huerta made it to the room, it was a little unclear to me who was assaulting whom. Cynthia had Sunny on the floor with her elbow across his windpipe.

Huerta looked her up and down as she straightened the skirt of her suit and tucked a loose lock of hair back into its bun. "Where'd you learn to do that?"

She shrugged. "I spend a fair amount of time going in and out of some less-than-savory places visiting clients. It made sense to learn how to protect myself."

"Smart," he said, but the look in his eye didn't really seem to be about Cynthia's intellect.

"Little help here," Dan said, hauling Sunny to his feet after handcuffing him.

"Sure, boss." Huerta took hold of Sunny and marched him out of the room, but he spared one backward look for Cynthia, who gave him a little finger wave.

Then she turned to Dan. "We need to talk, Sheriff Cooper."

"Why am I not surprised?" He indicated the door with a nod of his head and sauntered out with Cynthia following.

I turned to Antoine. "Why would Melanie sell Sunny bad formulas for the spice mixes?"

"I'm not sure. Perhaps her loyalty prevailed at the last moment. She could not bear to betray me." Antoine slumped in his seat, seemingly as deflated by this idea as by any of the other outrageous things we'd heard.

"But she did betray you," I pointed out. "Just because she didn't do it well doesn't exonerate her."

"Not fully. Perhaps her intention counts for something. Poor girl. She must have been truly tortured." Antoine took in a deep breath and straightened. "Do you think your Sheriff Dan will now let me out of this hellhole?"

"I think if anyone can get him to do it, Cynthia can." I sat back in my chair and tried to make sense of it all in my head. The crew had arrived back at the hotel after dinner. Melanie then kept Jason back in the parking lot, where they argued. They both went inside to their separate rooms. Then Antoine saw the announcement about Sunny's spice line and realized that Melanie had stolen the formulas and sold them. He phoned her and left a voice mail and then went to her room. Some time after that, Sunny arrived and found Melanie dead.

Which meant someone else had to have gone to her room, someone who knew she took a bath every night, someone who knew how to rewire a blow-dryer to remove the GFCI protection, someone who was mad enough to kill.

When Cynthia came back in, she told us that we would be going in front of Judge Romero the next day. We said good night to Antoine and headed for the exit. Cynthia wouldn't let me sneak out the side door.

"You don't understand," I said. "One of the Bunnies chased me down the street. Garrett had to rescue me."

Her left eyebrow went up. "Garrett rescued you? How very knight-in-shining-armor of him." She patted me on the shoulder. "It will be different this time. Trust me."

"Sure. What could possibly go wrong?" I said with an eye roll.

"Exactly," she said and threw open the door.

The reporters swarmed us. By this time, I recognized quite a few of them and their breakfast orders.

"What's happening, Cynthia?" Yolanda called. "Have there been further developments in Antoine's case?"

"Is Antoine turning his show over to Sunny Coronado?" Rick yelled.

Lisa shouldered her way into the front row. "What is going on between you and Antoine, Rebecca? Are you getting back together?"

I opened my mouth to reply, but Cynthia elbowed me hard in the ribs. After seeing how quickly she took Sunny down, I wasn't going to argue further.

"Monsieur Belanger will be going before Judge Romero tomorrow morning at ten. Further information has come to light that we believe exonerates Monsieur Belanger. We are certain that a man as reasonable and intelligent as Judge Romero will see that these charges should never have been brought and release Monsieur Belanger." Then she hooked her arm through mine and plowed through the reporters to the bottom of the stairs. They parted like a loaf of bread under a sharp serrated knife.

"How do you do that?" I asked, amazed.

She smiled. "You need to learn to own your space, Rebecca."

"Do you give lessons?"

She laughed that deep throaty laugh. "Maybe it'll be my retirement plan. See you tomorrow." Then she pivoted and walked away.

Thirteen

Lucy was waiting for me by the steps of POPS when I arrived the next morning. "What the heck, Rebecca? Antoine is going before the judge again and I hear about it on the news?" She leaned toward me. She did not need Cynthia's lessons in owning her space.

I was not in the mood to be menaced by a mousey production assistant, even if she did know how to own her space. "How did you think you would be informed? I don't think it's my job to keep you up to date and I seriously doubt that's high on Cynthia's priority list, either."

Lucy harrumphed. "Well, it would have been nice to have a heads-up. What's going on, anyway?"

I unlocked the door and gestured for her to come in. "Have a seat. It's kind of a long story."

When I hit the part of the story where Melanie sold the formula for Antoine's spice mixes to Sunny Coronado, all the blood drained out of Lucy's face. "She did what?" she asked in almost a whisper.

Somehow the whisper was scarier than if she'd started screaming. I knew she didn't need me to repeat what I'd said so I gave her a moment to let it sink in.

She shook her head. "Melanie was a classic narcissist. She really thought the world owed her everything she wanted. I've known that practically since I started working with her, but I never thought she'd sink to these kinds of depths."

"What depths are those?" Dario asked as he came in. He looked from me to Lucy. "Does this have to do with Antoine's hearing today?"

I nodded. Lucy gave me a reproachful look. "I should have heard about it before him, Rebecca. If you are going to be Antoine's eyes and ears . . ."

"I am not going to be Antoine's anything, Lucy. As soon as he's out of prison, he's out of Grand Lake and then out of my life," I protested.

"Sing it, sister," Dario said, holding out his fist to be bumped. I obliged.

Lucy nodded. "Good. I'm glad I know where you stand. See you this morning at the hearing?"

I nodded.

After she left, Dario asked, "So do I want to know what's happening or should I wait to hear it on the news?"

"Intrigue and prevarication on a level that I didn't think was even possible." I stood up and put on my apron. People were still going to need coffee and breakfast bars.

Dario poured himself a cup of coffee and started pouring honey into a bowl. "Do tell."

I filled him in.

"Was there anybody who didn't want this chick gone?" he asked.

"It doesn't seem like it. I'm hoping that there are enough

of them that Judge Romero drops the charges against Antoine and he can leave." And let me get my life back on track.

If anything, the courtroom was even louder than it had been at Antoine's original hearing. The buzz was higher in pitch and more frantic. Lucy, Brooke and Jason were already in the front row when I arrived. I walked in braced for invectives from the Bunnies. Instead, a weird hush came over their section of the courtroom. I heard the whisper of, "It's her" spread across the rows. Then one of the Bunnies was thrust out into the aisle by her fellow fans. I flinched away from her. There was a metal detector before you could come into the courtroom. Surely she didn't have a weapon, but I didn't feel like I could be too careful.

"We, uh, want to apologize," she said.

I stared at her. "Really?"

"Yeah. We understand that you're the one who found the information that might exonerate Antoine."

I nodded, not wanting to commit myself to too much with this lunatic.

"Thank you. Maybe you're not, you know, as bad as we thought."

If I'd ever been damned with faint praise, this was the moment. It was kind of like being told the dress I was wearing wasn't nearly as unattractive as the one I'd worn the day before. Gotta take what you can get some days, though.

"Got it," I said. "By the way, the gifts you left for Antoine were really nice. He appreciated them. I'm not sure he's been able to communicate that to you."

"Gifts?" she asked, head cocked to one side.

"The magazines. The decks of cards. The shaving cream." I couldn't remember what else he had said was in the box.

"I don't think that was us. At least not official us," she said.

"Well, probably one of you going rogue, then." I continued down the aisle, shaking my head over the vagaries of Antoine's fans.

Judge Romero made his entrance. It was no less regal than the last time. Again, he glared around the courtroom and warned everyone about being held in contempt. Then he banged the gavel and Cynthia and Ron Ramsey popped up like lawyer versions of jacks-in-the-box. Both started talking at once.

Judge Romero banged his gavel again and they both stopped talking at the same time. "One of you at a time," he said. He flipped the gavel around and pointed at Ron. "You first."

"Your Honor, after consulting with Sheriff Dan Cooper, we feel it would be in everyone's best interests to dismiss the charges against Mr. Belanger without prejudice," he said.

Romero pointed his gavel at Cynthia. "Now you."

"Your Honor, the charges should be dismissed with prejudice. Monsieur Belanger deserves to have his name cleared. The district attorney's decision to dismiss charges at all indicates how very precarious his case is and how very slipshod this investigation was to start." Cynthia placed her hand on Antoine's shoulder. "My client is innocent, Judge Romero. You and I know that it is an entirely different animal from not guilty. In the name of justice, please dismiss these charges with prejudice."

"Anything more from you?" Romero asked Ron.

"Yes, Your Honor. Mr. Belanger has not been cleared in this case. Until the investigation is complete, he is still under suspicion and he is still the same flight risk he was at our last hearing."

Romero rubbed at his beard. I leaned forward, breath held. "Dismissed without prejudice." He banged his gavel and stood.

Antoine collapsed backward in his chair and clasped his hands in prayer position while looking at the ceiling. Cameras went wild. The Bunnies went wild. Lucy began to sob.

Three hours later, Antoine stood outside the Sheriff's Department on the steps, flung his arms wide, leaned back his head and said, "Oh, freedom. There is no marzipan as sweet as you."

"Melodramatic much?" I asked, knowing the answer.

"No, *chérie*. I am not being melodramatic. My emotions are not in excess of what this means." He straightened up and let his arms drop. "I was fighting for my very life inside those walls."

I walked down the stairs, not looking to see if he was following. "I'm pretty sure I was doing most of the fighting," I muttered under my breath.

Within seconds, I couldn't even see Antoine through the crowd of reporters and Bunnies. I got into my car and waited. My phone beeped its text alert. "Good job." It was from a blocked number. A blocked number like the one that had sent Dan the photo of Jason threatening Melanie. The one that had sent me the "you're welcome" text when someone had distracted the reporters and Belanger Bunnies away from me.

Someone was watching. That didn't make me feel very comfortable.

Eventually, Antoine shouldered his way through the crowd and got into the passenger seat. Sprocket growled from his spot in the backseat. I snuck him a treat and he settled.

"Where shall we go first?" Antoine asked. "Your shop or your apartment?"

I froze with my keys partway to the ignition. "Neither. I'm taking you to your hotel and dropping you off there."

"But I need food," he protested.

That was true. He'd lost even more weight despite my bringing him quiche. It had to stop being my problem, though. "Then go get food."

He gave me a baleful look. "Where? Tell me, where in this town outside of your kitchens am I to get something edible?"

"Antoine, this has to not be my problem. Everybody's already pissed enough at me because of you." I thumped the steering wheel in frustration. Sprocket stiffened and growled again.

Antoine jerked back, clearly affronted. "Because of me? Why?"

I held up one finger. "Dan's mad at me for interfering in his investigation." I held up a second finger. "Haley's mad at me because she's worried I'll be too busy with you to be there for Evan when she goes into labor." I held up a third finger. "Garrett's pissed at me because, well, because you're still you and he's feeling competitive." I held up a fourth finger. "Faith's mad at me because she thinks you're probably spawn of Satan and I'm not avoiding you the way a good ex-wife should." I dropped my hand. "I could probably come up with more people who are irritated with me because of you, but I think you see my point."

He took my hand. "I am sorry, darling. I never meant my presence here in Grand Lake to be anything but good for you. You know that, don't you?"

I sighed. "I know. I know you were trying to do me a solid with the promo piece on the shop, but honestly I'm exhausted. Maybe we should can the whole thing."

"Never. We have already invested too much time and effort. We will do the piece. It will be amazing. But first, really, I must eat. Your shop or your apartment?" He smiled at me as if his choices were the only logical ones, as if I had already agreed, as if my resistance would be futile.

Somehow I couldn't figure out how to argue with him. I sighed. This was how our marriage had gone, too. Somehow he always made the most outlandish things sound totally reasonable. "The shop."

More than a few people have asked me why I had to go all the way back to the Midwest after Antoine and I split up. Did I really need to run that far?

The short answer was yes. The longer answer was definitely absolutely positively yes. Our marriage wasn't a good one. It needed to end. But the troubles didn't happen in the kitchen or, to go totally TMI, in the bedroom. When it had to do with our senses, taste and touch and scent, sight and sound, Antoine and I were an excellent match. Take us off the kitchen counter or the mattress, disaster struck.

But here we were again, together in a kitchen, and all those senses took back over. The rhythm we made with each other, moving back and forth, giving each other tastes, appreciating the aroma of what the other was doing. It was like a dance and my heart provided the percussion.

I didn't exactly have dinner stuff in the refrigerator at the shop. I kept a few staples around for the nights I worked late and wanted to make myself dinner. It didn't matter. There wasn't much that Antoine liked more than throwing together a dinner from unexpected ingredients.

It took me a minute or two after he started pulling ingredients out of the refrigerator and pantry to see where he was going. I couldn't help myself. When I did figure it out, I laughed out loud. He was making a shakshuka, a Tunisian dish with a spicy tomato sauce and eggs. As he cooked, I caught him sneaking a few bits of cheese to Sprocket, who accepted them without growling. Damn it. The man was even charming my dog.

I chopped the bell pepper and crumbled the feta while he sautéed the garlic and tomatoes. "I doubt anyone in Grand Lake even knows that shakshuka is something edible. They probably think it's something you might catch if you don't have proper vaccinations when you travel abroad."

He held the spoon up to my mouth for me to taste. "It's a little mild."

I took a small taste. "Ohio isn't exactly known for its spicy chiles."

He laughed. "No. Nor its bread. Do you have anything to use for dipping?"

I looked in the freezer and pulled out a ciabatta. "It's not challah, but it'll do, I think."

"Indeed." He turned the dial on the oven.

The long oak table dominated the center of my kitchen. I did everything there. Food prep. Menu planning. Ordering supplies. Talking to friends. It took up a lot of room, which is probably why at one point while we were cooking,

Antoine and I both turned in such a way that we came face-to-face. Like almost-touching face-to-face. Chests pressed against each other, gazes locked on each other, his lavender and yeast scent tickling my nose.

It was unfortunate that that was the precise moment that Garrett decided to walk in the back door of the kitchen.

I froze. My face flushed. My mouth went dry. I felt an awful lot like I had when I got caught breaking into the lighthouse to make out back in high school.

But I wasn't fifteen and I wasn't committing a misdemeanor. I was thirty-three years old and I was cooking in my own shop kitchen with my ex-husband.

Then I remembered how I felt when I'd watched Cynthia straightening Garrett's tie. There was wrong and right and wrong and right. Why did being a grown-up have to be so damn complicated?

"Antoine wanted to make dinner before he went back to his hotel," I said, hearing exactly how lame that sounded.

Garrett said, "I saw the light on and wanted to make sure you were okay." His shoulders were stiff.

"I'm fine," I said.

"I see that. Good night, then." And he was gone.

"Damn it." I dropped the wooden spoon I was holding and ran out into the night after him. I caught up with him at the end of the alley. He must have wanted me to catch up. He has seriously long legs and an ability to use them. I couldn't believe that it was the second time in a week that I actually ran. "That wasn't what it looked like."

He stopped. "Look. I have no claim on you."

"You do, too," I protested, starting to shiver in the cold night air.

He shook his head. "Not really. Maybe we should take a little break while you figure things out."

"I already figured all of it out," I insisted, wishing he would put his arms around me for warmth if not for reassurance.

His jaw stayed hard and he stayed aloof. "It didn't look like it back there."

My cheeks burned again, which at least heated me up a little. "I know, and I know how you must feel."

He snorted.

"No. Seriously. That day that Cynthia was straightening your tie and you were smiling and . . ." I didn't want to go on. I didn't want to describe the combination of anger and shame that the whole scene had evoked in me.

"That made you jealous?" He was smiling now.

If there was ever a time for honesty, I figured it was now. "Yes. Like green-eyed slasher jealous."

"That's pretty jealous." He opened his jacket and let me step inside its warmth.

I spoke into his chest. "I know. So I'm sorry for putting you in that position. Antoine just has this way of . . ."

"Getting what he wants?" he asked, cutting me off.

I nodded my head. "Yes."

"The problem with that is what he wants is you." He rested his chin on the top of my head.

"I know. He won't get me, though. He can have my shakshuka, but not my heart."

Garrett chuckled. I felt the vibrations in my cheek. "I don't know what that means," he said. "But I think I like it anyway."

When I returned to the kitchen, Antoine was sitting at the table eating the shakshuka with Sprocket sitting on his feet. Somehow, my appetite had disappeared. So had the chemistry between us, although Antoine seemed oblivious to that. "Is everything all right?" He smiled and pushed a plate toward me.

"Not really." I sat down across from him.

"May I help in some way?" he asked, sopping up some of the spicy tomato sauce with the bread.

"You can go home." I swirled my fork around in my plate.

"Alas, I cannot. You heard what your Judge Romero said. I am not allowed to leave quite yet. Plus, we have to finish the segment." His tone was matter-of-fact, but his eyes lost a little of their twinkle.

"Forget the segment." I dipped a piece of bread in the sauce and took a bite. Damn it. It was really good. It had a little of the sharp bright edges that characterized Antoine's cooking and a little of the heat and sweetness of mine. It was a great combination.

"Pah. Then all this would have been for nothing. Trust me, my production company will not allow that to happen. Too much time and money have already been invested." He pushed back from the table, his meal only half eaten. "We will go forward and finish the segment and perhaps by the time we finish Sheriff Dan will have found sufficient evidence to arrest Sunny for the murder of my cherished Melanie."

"She's still cherished? Even after she sold your spice secrets? After she stole equipment from the show? After she sexually harassed one of the crew members?" One of Antoine's great skills was creating his own reality. He figured out what he wanted and then forced his world to conform to those wishes. Even for him, though, painting Melanie as a cherished martyr was a stretch.

"She also kept my show and my travel schedule running smoothly for five years. That is, as you say, not nothing."

He returned to his plate and finished the last few bites of his food. "I don't suppose you have any more cheese?"

I shook my head. "No. I don't. What I do have is an early day tomorrow. Let's get you back to your hotel. I'll clean this up tomorrow when I get here."

As I drove Antoine to the hotel, he texted the crew asking them to meet him in the conference room. They'd reserved it for the entire time they were expecting to be at the hotel. I was going to drop him at the door and go home, but he asked me to come inside with him for a few moments. Then he insisted on holding the door for me and having me walk into the conference room first. It sounded gentlemanly, chivalrous, courtly. Maybe it was. I was also fairly certain that part of his motivation was to make his entry more gasp-worthy. The crew would turn, see Sprocket and me, be disappointed. Then I would step aside and they would see him and they would go wild.

Which is precisely what happened.

Antoine was a good chef. No. That's not right. Antoine was a great chef. There were, however, lots of great chefs in the world. Not to take anything away from him, but there were other people who were absolutely one hundred percent as good or even better than him in a kitchen.

I've already mentioned Antoine's charisma. That didn't hurt him at all. He walked into a room and people were instantly drawn to him. Not all of them were charmed, but no one could ignore him. He also knew a lot about presentation, on the table and the plate, but in life as well. He knew how to stage an event and he definitely knew how to stage an entrance, which is what he had just done.

In seconds, the crew was in a circle around him, laughing and crying and hugging. I thought Lucy might faint for a second. Antoine was the eye of the storm, the calm center of the swirl of emotions, the glue that held the group together, the person they couldn't live without.

Watching it from the outside was . . . instructive. I'd been well aware that I'd been manipulated any number of times during my marriage to Antoine and, frankly, after my marriage to him as well. I wasn't aware of how completely innate it was to him. I wondered if he even knew he was doing it or if it was as much of a reflex as blinking when you sneeze.

"Come, everyone," he said. "Let's sit. We need to talk. We have plans to make."

Everyone settled around the conference table, but each crew member managed to touch Antoine in some way as they went to their seats. Jason clapped him on the shoulder. Brooke gave his hand a squeeze and Lucy rested her hand on his back for a moment. I took a step backward toward the door, hoping to make an unobtrusive exit.

"Rebecca, my darling, come to the table," Antoine said, making that dream a non-reality. "This will affect you as well. We will need your input."

Sprocket and I trudged over to the table and sat down at the far end, well out of hand-holding distance.

"Obviously," he said, "we are behind schedule. What have you been able to accomplish while I was . . . detained?" Leave it to Antoine to find a classy word to describe being locked up for murdering your thieving assistant.

Both Lucy and Brooke started talking at once. Antoine held up his hand and pointed to Lucy. "You first."

Lucy sat up straighter. "We've done several shots of Rebecca in her kitchen with her assistant Dario. The shots of people coming through the shop have been trickier because the place has been so mobbed. We've also gotten a lot of video of the area. It would have been better with you in the shots, but you can do a voice-over for them."

Antoine put his hand over hers and said, "Excellent."

I thought she was going to swoon.

Then he nodded to Brooke. "Now you."

"We've interviewed Anastasia Bloom, Barbara Werner and Mayor Allen Thompson to hear about POPS's effect on downtown Grand Lake. We also interviewed her sister about what it was like to have Rebecca come back." She glanced over at me and then away. "Her brother-in-law, the sheriff, has refused to do an interview."

I hadn't known that, but wasn't terribly surprised. Dan's idea of a good television interview was the one he'd done in front of the hotel the other night. Basically someone would ask him questions and he would say "No comment" until they got bored and went away.

"Good. Very good." He rubbed at his chin for a moment, thinking. "So really all we need is a segment with Rebecca and me together in the kitchen?"

"That's right," Brooke said. "We can do the rest in the studio at home."

Antoine sighed. "Yes. Home. In some ways, I will not be sorry to leave this town. It has brought us all a great deal of sorrow. How have all of you been operating without Melanie?"

"It's been okay," Brooke said. "We've managed."

"I can see that. Perhaps you would like to take on the scheduling and arrangement of the shoot at Rebecca's shop, Brooke?" Antoine asked.

Brooke flushed to the roots of her hair. "I . . . I would

be honored, Antoine. Thank you for your trust. I'll make sure it runs completely smoothly."

Antoine laughed. "There is no such thing as a shoot running completely smoothly. I'm sure you know that by now. I appreciate the sentiment, though. Now let's set the schedule."

"I think it would be best if we shot at Rebecca's kitchen in the morning. The light is tricky in there," Lucy said, not looking up from her notepad.

Again, Antoine put his hand over hers. "That is Brooke's decision to make, Lucy."

"Of course," she said. "Sorry." There was a little plopping noise. It took me a second to realize that it was a tear that had dropped from Lucy's face to her notepad. She was crying. Was she still that overcome about Antoine being home and about him touching her? Her hand gripped harder around her pen. Or was she upset that Antoine had chosen Brooke instead of her to succeed Melanie?

"Brooke?" Antoine prompted, not turning to look at Lucy.

"Lucy's right. We should shoot in the morning. Will tomorrow work for you, Rebecca?" Brooke asked, also not looking at Lucy.

Tomorrow wasn't completely convenient, but I was pretty sure that the sooner Antoine and his crew finished shooting at POPS, the sooner they would be out of my way if not out of town. "Sure. We can make that work."

"Excellent. How about our equipment situation?" Antoine asked.

I hazed out of the discussion about cameras and lights. I really didn't care what they used to light my kitchen.

"So that's it, then?" Antoine finally said, snapping me back to the present.

"I think that covers it," Brooke said, nodding while checking over her list. Lucy still had not looked up from her paper.

I nearly leapt to my feet. "So see you bright and early tomorrow then. Can't wait."

"Wait," Antoine called as I headed to the door. I stopped. He walked over and stood next to me at the conference room door. "If it were not for you, I would be still locked in that cage."

"I'm not so sure about that. Dan would have realized eventually that he had the wrong man." He might have leapt to some conclusions about Antoine, but he was a thorough man. He would have seen that there were other people involved.

"Maybe. Maybe not. At the very least, you led him to that conclusion faster than he would have gotten there himself. You brought me food. You kept my spirits up, and tonight with you in the kitchen . . ." He dropped his shoulders and looked up at the acoustic tile ceiling. "Tonight was magic. I cooked better and with more heart than I have in months. Maybe years. Thank you for helping me find my soul again."

"Antoine, that had nothing to do with me." Even as I said the words, I wondered if they were true. I'd felt the magic that the two of us made in the kitchen, too.

"You are wrong. You are a wonderful person, but you are wrong. Thank you, my sweet Rebecca. I will see you tomorrow. Sleep well." He kissed my cheek and returned to the crew at the conference table.

He might as well have told me to grow wings and fly.

Fourteen

There hadn't been anyone waiting for me on the porch when I got home. I took Sprocket for a quick walk since he'd been cooped up inside most of the evening. While we walked, I received a text from the "You're welcome" and "Good job" number. This one had a photo of Antoine and me in POPS's kitchen clearly taken from the alley with a note that said, "Careful."

I texted back: Srsly who is this?

No one answered again.

I got back to my granny flat and fell into bed completely exhausted. When I woke up, bleary and sticky-eyed, I had the idea that maybe it had all been a dream, but the dirty dishes waiting for me in the sink when I got to POPS made it clear that the whole thing had been an absolute reality.

I sighed, filled the sink with hot water and started scrubbing—not that there was that much to scrub. Shakshuka doesn't make a lot of dirty dishes. Dario arrived about ten minutes later and we got to work on the real preparations for the day.

"Good news about your . . . ex," he said, as he sprinkled coconut into a big mixing bowl.

I nodded. "Maybe this will all be over soon."

I would remember those words later when Antoine and his crew showed up to shoot.

"Um, Lucy, could you please move that light over to that corner?" Brooke pointed to the corner of the kitchen by the pantry.

Lucy grimaced, her hand resting lightly on the light's stand. "Are you sure, Brooke? I think that might throw too much shadow on Antoine's face."

"I'm sure, Lucy." Brooke's voice had gotten a hard note in it. The tension in the room was getting as stiff as whipped egg whites.

Lucy moved the light, setting it down in the corner with a hard thump. "Fine," she said in that tone of voice that made it clear that it was anything but fine.

I glanced over at Antoine, but he seemed oblivious to the tension. I suspected he wasn't, but I was fairly certain he wasn't going to do anything about it, either. At least not at the moment.

It didn't stop with the lighting. It went on to mikes and when we should have close-ups of the food and when we should have shots of our hands. At one point Jason walked behind me and whispered, "I kind of wish you'd let them lock me up. Prison time would have been less unpleasant than this." I snorted, which got me dirty looks from Antoine, Brooke and Lucy and a wink from Jason.

* * *

Finally, it was over. I retreated to a corner with Dario while they packed up. Jason, Antoine and Brooke headed to the door. Lucy said, "I'll catch up with you guys."

"What's up, Lucy?" I asked after they'd gone.

"Nothing. I just needed a little space." She sat down at the table and looked at me expectantly.

"Would you like some hot chocolate?" I asked.

She practically clapped her hands. Dario took off for the day while I was making our drinks. Finally, I sat down across from Lucy, each of us with a full mug.

"I can't believe Sunny was going to let Antoine take the rap for a murder he committed," Lucy said.

I shook my head. "I'm not one hundred percent sure that Sunny did it." I would have said that he wasn't capable of violence, but watching him try to attack Cynthia made me reconsider that. Still, it was a long way from there to premeditated murder, and it had to be premeditated. No way you could alter a blow-dryer like that on the fly.

"Who else could have?" Lucy asked, wide-eyed.

"I don't know. It seems like every time I turn around there's a new suspect. Melanie pissed a lot of people off along the way." I hoped that when I left my kitchen for the final time not so many people would be cheering.

"You know Melanie's whole goal from the start was to replace you," Lucy said, taking a long sip of hot chocolate.

"Excuse me?" I said, startled by what felt like a change of subject.

"That stunt in Minneapolis? Stranding you there? That was all her," Lucy said.

I'd had my suspicions, but I also knew her stunt wouldn't

have worked if Antoine had spared any thought about me. "That's water under the bridge now, Lucy."

"Her hair wasn't even curly," she blurted out.

"What?"

"That was a perm. She did it so she would look more like you."

"Lots of women get perms," I said.

She shook her head. "Lots of women in the eighties had perms. Maybe even the nineties. Nobody does that now. She permed it and dyed it so she'd look more like you."

"There are lots of reasons people perm and dye their hair, Lucy." Just because someone had her hair done like yours didn't mean she was trying to *Single White Female* you.

Lucy leaned her elbows on the table. "She told me."

That stopped me short. "She what?"

"One night when we were working late, she opened a bottle of wine and got kind of . . . loose," Lucy said.

If this story was going the same direction that Jason's story about Melanie getting soused after work hours went, it was going to add quite an interesting twist to the story. "And?"

"And she told me that when she got the interview with Antoine, she looked for pictures of you and then made herself look as much like you as she could." She sipped her hot chocolate and looked at me with her brows arched over the rim.

I remembered when Melanie interviewed for the job. Antoine had gone on and on about her qualifications and her references. She didn't get the job because of her looks. "That's weird, but it didn't help her."

"It didn't help you, either. Did you ever wonder why so many of your evenings with Antoine were interrupted with work emergencies? Or how often your plans had to be canceled because something came up with the show or with the products or with the books?" she asked.

Antoine's work was demanding. You didn't marry a chef without knowing that things like that could happen.

"She did it on purpose. She wanted you out and her in."

"Why are you telling me all this now?" I didn't know if it would have made any difference if I'd realized all this sooner, but I knew it definitely didn't make any difference now. Antoine and I were over.

"You cleared Antoine. The charges against him were dropped. Why keep pushing to figure out who killed Melanie? What difference does it make? Whoever did it did all of us a favor, Antoine included."

I drew back. "You can't mean that, Lucy."

"I'm only saying what everyone else is thinking. You know why there are so many suspects? Because everyone hated her. You know why everyone hated her? Because she was a bad person. It's that simple, Rebecca." She stood up from the table. "You should leave it alone. Or if you figure out who did it, you should give that person a medal."

Then she was gone.

Dan stopped by the shop in the afternoon. I made him a cup of coffee and got him a big plate of my newest addition to POPS's menu: bacon pecan popcorn. I set it down in front of him.

"I don't think Sunny killed Melanie," he said, staring at the popcorn but not eating it.

I had my doubts, too, but wanted to hear his first. "Any particular reason?"

"I don't think he would be able to rewire that blow-dryer." He took a bite of the popcorn. It made me feel warm inside to see his eyes close for a second. I'd gotten it right that time. I'd take some to Garrett before my late afternoon rush started.

"Sunny has a television show like Antoine's. He has to know some of that stuff."

Dan washed his popcorn down with a slurp of coffee. "I interviewed some of his crew. They all said they do everything they can to keep Sunny away from anything electrical. Or mechanical." He frowned. "Or really almost anything that isn't cooking. They said he's a menace on the set."

That didn't totally surprise me. Antoine's persnickety ways might seem anal-retentive to some, but it also kept everyone on his set safe. If Sunny's approach to mechanical and electrical things was like his approach to cooking, all hell could break loose at any point. "Also," I said, pulling out my cell phone to show Dan the text I'd gotten the night before, "Sunny was locked up when I got this."

Dan took the phone and looked. His eyebrows shot up. Then he started scrolling through. "This isn't the first text you've gotten from a blocked number."

"Yeah, but the other ones were all nice. You know. *Good job. You're welcome.*" I liked praise. I wasn't always fussy about where it came from.

"And you don't know who it is?" He stared at the photo as if it might hold some kind of answer.

I shook my head. "I asked, but whoever it is didn't answer."

He jotted a note down then took out his phone and held it next to mine. "And I got that photo of Jason and Melanie from a blocked number."

An uncomfortable prickling sensation ran up my spine. Someone was watching us. Someone who was damn good at staying hidden. "Do you know who it is?" I asked.

He shook his head. "Huerta's checking into it. So far all we know is it was a burner phone purchased with cash in Cleveland."

The phone rang in Dan's hand. He looked at the caller ID and frowned, then handed the phone to me. Antoine. I considered letting it go to voice mail, but then I would dread retrieving that. I might as well deal with it like ripping off a bandage. Do it fast and get it over with.

"What?" I asked.

"Good afternoon, darling," he replied. "Would you be able to stop by the hotel this evening?"

"Why?" I was starting to sound like a Journalism 101 class.

"Just one last meeting to make sure we have everything we need."

I really didn't want to go, but anything I could do to wrap things up faster seemed like a good idea. "What time?"

"Seven."

I hung up. Dan shook his head. "Just make sure you leave your cell phone on or Haley will go supernova."

"How much longer, do you think?" I wasn't sure which of us was going to burst sooner. Well, technically, she was going to be doing the bursting, but I was going to have sympathy bursts at this rate.

"Any minute. The house is spotless. Evan is carrying around one of his teddy bears and calling it his baby. There's enough food to feed us for a month in the freezer. Her bag is packed." He grimaced. "Last night she handed me a three-page typewritten single-spaced birth plan so I would be ready for any and all contingencies."

"Wow." That was intense even by Haley standards.

"I'm not sure what else she can do, but I'm afraid if she doesn't go into labor soon, we'll find out."

After I closed the shop, I walked Sprocket home. I let him into the apartment and then turned to leave. He sprinted back to the door and stood between me and it.

"Sorry, boy. I've got to go," I said, trying to skirt around him.

He feinted and stayed between me and the way out.

"Sprocket, sit."

He did.

"Now stay," I said, and tried to go around him.

He didn't. It was as if he knew where I was going and thought it was a bad idea. He was right. I had no idea what I was walking into. I knew Antoine was cooking up something and I didn't mean a new dish. As usual, however, Antoine had somehow coaxed me into doing something I wasn't sure was a good idea.

Bad idea or not, I had to go and I was not going to be outsmarted by a dog, even if he was a poodle, a notoriously smart breed. I sauntered over to the kitchen area and casually opened the cupboard where I kept the liver snacks, Sprocket's favorite treat. He instantly sat and watched as I pulled two out of the box. I gave him one. He picked it up and then trotted after me to the door, once again making sure to maneuver himself so he was between me and the way out.

I pulled the second liver snack out of my pocket and held it up so I was sure he saw it. I waved it around in the air a little bit, watching his head bobble as he followed the snack with his eyes. Then I tossed it behind me.

He leapt for it and I leapt for the door. I was out with

the door slammed behind me before he knew it. I heard the first howl when I reached the bottom of the stairs. I winced. Maybe he'd stop after a minute or two.

Antoine was waiting for me in the lobby of the hotel when I arrived. He ushered me toward the conference room where we'd met with the crew the night before.

"Come in, Rebecca. Come in." Antoine waved me into the room. The furniture had been moved around in the conference room. Everything had been pushed up against one of the far walls, leaving a big open space where there were three high canvas chairs set up with lights peppered around them. It looked like an interview set.

"What are you shooting in here?" I asked.

"I'll explain." There was something wrong with Antoine's smile. It was stretched a little too far and he was showing too many teeth. It was his television smile.

I slowed my steps down. "What's wrong?"

"Nothing, *chérie*. Nothing is wrong. Everything is just as it should be." He put his arm around my shoulders to draw me farther in.

I shrugged him off. "Cut it out, Antoine."

Lisa Elliott of WOHH News walked into the room. "Is there a problem?" she asked.

I looked from her to Antoine to the three chairs. I'd been ambushed. Antoine had booked an interview with Lisa and had tricked me into showing up for it. I should have listened to Sprocket and stayed home.

"No problem," Antoine said, his big, hearty, fake smile plastered on his face. He turned to me and whispered, "Please."

"Why should I?" I crossed my arms over my chest and didn't bother to whisper.

"Think of the publicity," he said. "The extra revenue will help me pay for Ms. Harlen's fees. They were substantial and in no way contingent on me being innocent."

I softened. I'd seen the number. I knew what he'd paid her. She had been totally worth it, but that didn't mean it wouldn't hurt a little when it was time to pay up. "What do I have to do?"

"Nothing. Sit next to me. Answer a few questions." He stepped in closer and looked me in the eyes with that steady sharp gaze of his.

Lisa walked over to us and pursed her lips. "Well, I guess it's good you showed up with no makeup on. It gives Tanya a blank canvas to work with." She turned and in a sharp tone said, "Tanya! We need some work here."

In moments I was seated at the table, facing a woman with lashes so long it looked like spiders were sitting on her eyes. "So, what will you be wearing?" she asked.

I looked down at the long-sleeved cotton shell I was wearing under a cardigan.

"Oh," she said. "The casual look is great. Makes you relatable to the audience. Good choice."

I wondered what she'd say if I was wearing a sweatshirt, which I very well could have been. She spent the next fifteen minutes in a state of constant chatter, asking questions about my skin care regime, my preferred eyeliner and my opinion on lip liner. I didn't answer a single question. She didn't seem to notice. Finally, she stepped, looked at me with her head cocked to one side and yelled out, "Ready!"

As she walked away, I was pretty sure I heard her say "Or as ready as she'll ever be."

I was led to the chair farthest to the right. Antoine sat in the center with Lisa in the far left chair. We were miked up and somebody said, "Speed" and we were rolling.

"We often hear about women who stand by their men, and of course there's always the adage that behind every great man is a great woman. It's not often, however, that the great woman is the great man's ex-wife." Lisa turned to Antoine. "Tell us how you happened to be here in Grand Lake, Ohio, in the first place, Antoine."

"It was, of course, to help my beautiful Rebecca let the world know about her amazing shop, POPS." He reached across, took my hand and then lifted our clasped hands to his lips.

First I tried to pull away, but his grip was too strong. Instead I pushed forward and bumped into his lips. Hard. He twitched and put our hands back down.

Lisa laughed. "And it is amazing. I know I'm getting addicted to the pumpkin-spice breakfast bars. I'm trying to stay away from that fudge, though! It looks dangerous."

"Uh, thanks," I said, trying to smile. "I'm working on a lower-calorie chocolate popcorn as well."

"Sounds great. Rebecca, you were key in getting the charges brought against Antoine dropped. Not many ex-wives would step up to do that for an ex. What led you to lead that fight?"

I stared down at his hand on my hand. I tried to wiggle my hand out from under his, but he gripped tighter. "I didn't think he did it," I said, still trying to wriggle loose.

"That's it? You thought he was innocent? That's the only reason?" She seemed surprised.

I finally managed to jerk my hand from Antoine's grip and threw it in the air. "Can you think of a better reason?"

Lisa turned back to the camera. "Well, there you have

it. A woman's belief in her ex-husband's innocence. It all comes down to that." She froze for a few seconds, staring at the camera with a fixed smile on her face.

"And we're out," the camera operator said.

I shoved back my chair and stuck my finger right in Antoine's face. "Don't you ever do that to me again. Try it and you will regret it. I swear."

"Don't be angry. It will be great press for you and for me. You'll see." He laughed. Laughed! As if my concerns, my priorities, my life that I'd built were unimportant. Worse. That they were funny.

I wasn't laughing. "I'm beginning not to care about press. It's not worth it, Antoine."

"It's always worth it. It wasn't so bad, was it? Sitting next to me? Holding hands? We could be like that again." He took another step toward me.

I could smell the scent of lavender with warm baked bread tones beneath. Today, it turned my stomach. "No, we couldn't. Why is it you want me back so much, Antoine? There are dozens—maybe hundreds or thousands—of women who would be happy to take my place. Women who would forgive you for ditching them in less time than it takes to cook a three-minute egg. Leave me alone and find one of them."

He dropped his head in his hands. "You don't understand."

"You're right. I don't. Enlighten me." He looked pathetic, but I didn't budge.

He raised his head and fixed me with those bright blue eyes. "Since you left, I have not developed one new recipe. Not one."

I'd been gone more than two years. It's not like Antoine whipped up new recipes for his television show or his cookbook on a daily basis, but in the kitchen at L'Oiseau Gris? He tried something new nearly every week. "Not anything new at all?"

"Not even a variation on something I've done before. Nothing. At least, nothing that has worked." He slumped against the wall.

That was a heck of a dry spell. "What does that have to do with me?" I had been an educated palate for him to try new ideas out with, but it wasn't like I'd developed recipes for Antoine.

"It's because you are not by my side. You were my muse."

It wasn't the first time I'd been granted muse status. There'd been a musician, a bassist and a composer. Being his muse hadn't kept him from sleeping with several other lesser women (lesser according to him). I'd decided then that as the horse thief said about being run out of town on the rails, but for the honor, I'd just as soon walk. "There is no such thing as a muse," I told Antoine. "There is hard work and study."

"Yes, yes. For years I thought the same thing. I still do. There are no divine beings that will come out of the sky to grant inspiration. There are people, however, who by their very presence inspire us." He grabbed both my hands and kissed his way across my knuckles. "You inspire me, my darling. You make me want to be my very best. You must come back to me so I can begin to create again."

I slid my hands out of his. "No way, José."

"You don't understand how bad it has become," he said. "I'm afraid that Melanie did not switch the formulas for the spice mixes when she sold them to Sunny. I think they were simply bad. How am I supposed to start a new product line when I cannot cook? How am I supposed to do anything without you by my side?"

"You cooked before I came into your life. You don't need me." I backed away from him, but he still held my hands.

"You are wrong. I may have cooked before you came into my life, but somehow you have ruined me. I need you, Rebecca."

"No."

Antoine flung his hands wide. "But why? You cannot possibly mean to spend the rest of your days in this dreary little town making popcorn. I don't believe it. I won't believe it."

"What you believe doesn't matter to me, Antoine. I don't know why you're not coming up with new recipes, but I doubt it has anything to do with me." In fact, I did not fail to notice that the reason Antoine wanted me back had nothing to do with me at all. He didn't want my input. He didn't want my opinion. He didn't want my help. He wanted my presence, a weird passive presence at that. The reason he wanted me back had nothing to do with me and everything to do with him. Once I realized that, it all became very clear.

I'd often thought that Antoine wanting me back had to do with the fact that he'd never actually failed at anything before. He didn't know how. He'd failed at marriage—at least marriage to me—and it had shaken his confidence.

Antoine was smart. He studied food. He understood the science behind what makes a sauce come together or become a gloppy mess. He knew the chemistry involved in making a cake. On a certain level, however, like all artists, there was a magic that happened because of his unique take on the sauce or the cake or the marinade. That came from a place that science couldn't touch. It came from his gut. Somehow when I'd left, I'd apparently sucker punched him in that gut and he didn't trust it anymore.

It was the first time I'd ever felt sorry for Antoine. It was also the first time I'd felt regret about leaving him based on something other than how hard I was making my own life. I took his hands now. He looked up at me, a horrible hope in his eyes.

"Antoine," I said. "I am so sorry. I am so sorry that you aren't coming up with new recipes and that I might have had something to do with that. I don't want to be married to you, but I think your gifts in the kitchen are gifts to the world. Forget me. Reach inward. You'll find the inspiration there. I know you will." Then I let go of his hands and left.

I thought that would be the end of it. I thought we were done with taping the segment of *Cooking the Belanger Way*. I thought Antoine had gotten his interview.

I should have thought about who was listening to us. I should have remembered that Lisa was actually a reporter and not just a talking head on the television set. I should have remembered what a live mic was. If I had, I wouldn't have been so surprised when the headlines the next morning read:

FAMOUS CHEF SAYS
EX-WIFE IS HIS MUSE

Followed by an article that began like this:

Antoine Belanger made an emotional plea to Grand Lake popcorn entrepreneur Rebecca Anderson. According to Belanger, he has been unable to create new recipes or execute old ones well since the two split up. Anderson has promised to consider returning to him.

* * *

The second I saw the headline I called Garrett. "It's not what it looks like. They twisted everything."

"What?" he asked, sounding groggy and confused.

Then I remembered how early I get up. "Sorry. When you get up, try to remember this phone call. It will make more sense later."

"What?" he repeated.

"Also, I want some kind of relationship points for calling. I mean, it's not a dead body, but it's something, right?"

"What?" He was very repetitive when he was sleepy. I'd have to remember that.

I clicked the phone off. This was not going to be good. I did the only thing I could figure out to do. I got dressed and went to work. I nearly tripped over a rake that Dan had left across my stairs for some reason. It was lucky that Sprocket went down the stairs first and growled at it. I might not have seen it since it was still dark when I left the apartment. Dan usually wasn't that careless. The combination of the Melanie Fitzgerald murder and the incipient arrival of the Peanut were clearly getting to him.

As we were setting up, Dario said, "I have an idea, by the way. Something that might make the morning easier."

"I'm all ears."

"We set up a self-serve coffee station in the corner. Get those big thermos things and to-go cups. It would save us a lot of time and move the line through faster."

"Brilliant. I'll go out this afternoon and get what we need." I thanked my lucky stars for him every day. Who knew getting clobbered over the head would set in motion a string of events that would end up with me getting great kitchen help?

We finished setting up and I opened the doors. A barrage of flashes half blinded me. Then someone yelled, "Rebecca, is it true? Are you getting back together with Antoine?"

"Do you really think you're his muse?" someone else called.

I put my fists on my hips and waited for everyone to quiet. "Do any of you out there want coffee and breakfast bars?"

A forest of hands went up.

"The original deal still stands. Hold the questions. Anyone who asks me or Dario a question about Antoine or anything else regarding this case will be immediately ejected from the shop. Try to ask a second question and you will be banned for life. Understood?" I gave them all my best glare, the one I'd seen Haley give Evan when he colored on the walls in the hallway outside his room.

The microphones lowered. I propped the door open and went back in the shop. We were mobbed by the time I made it behind the counter, but no one said a word that wasn't popcorn or coffee related.

The morning rush finally ran its course and within minutes there was a knock at the back door. The days of leaving it unlocked were long gone. I twitched the curtain aside to see who it was. Annie. I unlocked the door and ushered her in.

"Interested in a pumpkin breakfast bar?" I asked.

"Nothing to experiment on me with today?" she asked, sliding into a seat at the table.

"I didn't say that." I pulled out some of the new low-calorie chocolate popcorn and some Bacon Pecan Popcorn.

"Hey, girl," Dario said. "Coffee?"

"Yes, please. So, Rebecca, what was the deal during that interview? You looked like you had to go to the bathroom," Annie asked.

"You saw it?" I cringed.

Annie looked up at me, blue eyes crinkling at the edges a bit. "Are you serious? I'm pretty sure everyone saw it. So what was your problem?"

"I was trying to get my hand away from Antoine. He wouldn't let go." I sank down in a chair and rested my head in my hands.

"And then the two of you argued while forgetting that you had hot mikes?" Annie asked.

I nodded without looking up.

"And then the headlines hit this morning."

I nodded again.

"And you talked to Garrett already?"

This time I shook my head. "I called him the second I saw them, but I woke him up. I told him I'd talk to him later."

"And he hasn't been by?"

I shook my head again.

Annie sat back in her chair and took a long sip of coffee. "Well, being single isn't so bad."

I threw a wadded-up napkin at her.

Fifteen

Right before I locked up the shop at the end of the day, I got a text from Haley: "Come to the house when you get home. Please."

I texted back: Is it time?

She answered: No. Still need you to come home.

Sprocket and I skipped our lighthouse visit. It might not be time yet, but it sounded like Haley wanted me home sooner rather than later. I let myself into the house. It was filled with an amazing aroma. Sprocket growled. "Something smells amazing. What are you making, Haley?"

Haley peeked around the corner of the living room. "It's not me."

Haley and Dan were the only grown-ups living in the house so if Haley wasn't cooking, that left Dan. Dan is great at a lot of things. He can throw a baseball straighter than anyone I've ever seen. He can fix a flat bike tire with chewing gum and a ballpoint pen. He can make me feel better about nearly anything by simply looping his arm across my shoulders. He can't, however, really cook that well. Plus, his car wasn't in the driveway. "Then who is it?"

Before she could answer, I heard Antoine call from the kitchen. "Miss Haley, do you not have a proper zester? If not, we must rectify this as soon as possible. You need the right tools to get the right results."

I turned to Haley, speechless for a moment. Then I whispered, "Why is my ex-husband making a daube in your kitchen?" Between the aroma and his need for a zester, it had to be a daube. It really couldn't be anything else.

She shrank back a little into the living room, motioning for me to follow her. Evan was splayed out on the floor pushing cars around a plastic track. I picked one up and ran it down his back and over his bottom. He giggled. "Auntie Bec, there's a funny man in our kitchen. Mama says he knows you so it's okay."

I looked up at Haley. She shrugged as she sank down onto the couch. "It was the best I could come up with on short notice."

"Why are you letting him do this?" I knew how Antoine manipulated me and his crew. I hadn't thought he'd have the same hold over Haley. She didn't like him. She'd never liked him. She hadn't even liked him before we got married.

"I couldn't stop him. He showed up with all these things. He said he thought maybe if he cooked in the kitchen where you were brought up, he would soak in some of your essence and get his mojo back." She crammed a pillow behind her lower back.

"He said *mojo*?" He really must be losing it.

"No, he said a bunch of other stuff about you being his muse, but I'm pretty sure what he meant was mojo." She patted the couch next to her and Sprocket came over and put his head on her leg. She scratched behind his ears.

She was right. He meant mojo. "Does Dan know?" I asked.

She shook her head. "I was hoping Antoine would be done before Dan got home. Dan's been so tense. I'm afraid it would push him right over the edge if he comes home and finds Antoine trying to soak in essences in our kitchen."

"Dan really isn't himself, is he? He left a rake on my steps sometime last night. So not like him." Even as a kid Dan had been an a-place-for-everything-and-everything-in-its-place kind of guy. His Hot Wheels collection was legendary in its organization.

"A rake? Really? Weird. He hasn't even been doing any yard work." She shook her head. "Can you get Antoine out of here before Dan gets home?"

A daube takes a while, but Antoine might make it. Or he might very deliberately not. "Rebecca," he called from the kitchen. "Come taste this."

I went to the kitchen because I really didn't know what else to do.

Dan came home minutes before the daube was done. "Wow. Who's cooking?" he called as he walked in. The door slammed and I heard his footsteps coming through the entryway. I made sure the swinging door between the kitchen and the dining room was swung shut, but it didn't help.

"It is I, Sheriff Dan!" Antoine called back before I could stuff something in his mouth to stop him.

The footsteps stopped. I went out into the dining room, letting the door swing shut behind me. Maybe he hadn't heard Antoine. Maybe the door muffled the sound. Maybe pigs were flying again. "Hi, Dan. Welcome home."

He stared at me. "What is he doing here?" he asked in a whisper.

"Making a daube." I knew it wasn't what he was asking, but it was actually the best answer I could come up with. I wasn't sure if Dan knew what a daube was or how much effort and energy went into making one. I'm not sure he'd care.

"Of course." His forehead creased. "Why?"

"Well, they are really delicious. I mean, smell that. Makes your mouth water, doesn't it?" I sniffed at the air.

Dan sighed and sank down into one of the dining room chairs. "Why here? In my house?"

"To soak in my essence and get his mojo back." Dan might as well know how crazy the whole thing was.

He shook his head. "You really need to set some boundaries with that man."

"You try it! He has no respect for them. I put most of a very large country between us and it still has no effect!" I really had tried in so many ways and so many different times. Antoine was like the irresistible force. Or maybe the immovable object. I'd nearly flunked physics in high school and they don't make you take it in culinary school, so it was a little fuzzy.

Antoine might have been immovable and irresistible, but Dan was implacable. "You need to get him out of here."

"I've been trying for an hour. The daube needs maybe five more minutes and it will be done." I checked my watch.

Dan crossed his arms over his chest. "And in fifteen, Garrett will be here."

I grabbed my bag and my car keys and went back to the

kitchen. No way was I going to make Garrett feel like I'd made him feel the night before. "You're done," I said.

Antoine pulled the daube from the oven. "Yes. Yes, I am."

I put the food in a container and hustled him out the door.

I managed to drop Antoine at the hotel without going in, despite his protests. The food would be ruined if it wasn't served correctly. It wouldn't be the right temperature. It would pick up the flavors of the plastic container.

I kept repeating that it wasn't my problem.

"Here," he said when I came to a stop at the door. "Taste it."

I let him feed me a small bite. It was sensational. "What did you do to it?"

He laughed. "I added a new spice combination. Isn't it wonderful?"

There was nothing to do but agree with him. "So do you think your cold streak is over?"

He turned suddenly serious. "Only because I was near you."

"You made most of that while I was still at POPS," I pointed out.

"But I was in your kitchen," he countered.

"Haley's kitchen," I corrected.

He shrugged. "The kitchen where you learned to cook."

"That would actually be Coco's kitchen," I corrected.

He waved a hand at me. "You may nitpick and argue all you want. It was your influence that allowed me to do this."

"Fine. I take all the credit. Now get out of my car, okay?" I made a shooing gesture with my hands.

He went.

I turned the Jeep around and squealed out of the parking lot. There was no way I'd make it back to the house before Garrett got there, but I could be close. Maybe we wouldn't have to explain anything to him. It wouldn't be lying to not mention Antoine being in the house, right?

It didn't end up mattering. I didn't have time to explain. I had barely made it back inside the house when my cell phone rang.

"Rebecca, I need you," Antoine said.

I banged my head softly against the doorframe. "We've been over this and over this, Antoine. You do not need me. Your cooking block is all in your head. I was joking when I said I took credit for the daube. Get over it."

"No. No. It's not the cooking. It's . . . it's Brooke." He sounded rattled.

She was a pushy little thing. Maybe he was regretting promoting her. Lucy seemed more tractable and more in Antoine's thrall. "What about her?"

"She's . . . I think she might be dead."

"I'm on my way. Call 911."

I arrived pretty much simultaneously with the paramedics. I saw Eric Gladstone hustling into the hotel and hustled right after him. They raced for the stairs, not waiting for the elevator, so I did, too. Sprocket leapt up the stairs behind me. I'd dashed out of the house so fast, I didn't even think about taking him or not taking him, so he was just there.

I burst out of the stairwell right behind the paramedics,

breathing hard. How the heck did those guys do that carrying all that equipment? None of them were even panting. They thundered into the open door of the room. I stopped at the threshold.

Brooke lay on the floor, pale with sweat beaded on her forehead. The paramedics swarmed her. I swiveled back into the hallway, back pressed against the wall, heart pounding. I shut my eyes. Let her be okay. Let her be okay. Let her be okay. Maybe if I kept thinking it, it would come true. I didn't like Brooke, but I couldn't take another dead body. I just couldn't.

"She's still breathing," Eric yelled. "Heart is tachy. Starting an IV now. Then let's get her to the hospital."

I blew out a breath of relief. She was alive.

In minutes, they were rolling Brooke out of the room strapped to a gurney with tubes going into her arms and oxygen going into her nose. They were still moving fast, but not as fast as they had on the way up the stairs. They actually waited for the elevator to go back down. It seemed strangely quiet once they were gone. I peeked into the hotel room. Antoine stood in the center of it, looking bewildered and sad.

I pulled out my phone and dialed Garrett.

He answered on the first ring. "Dead body?" he asked.

"Not quite yet." There was a catch in my voice.

"Do you need me there?"

"No, not yet at least. Will you explain everything to Haley?"

"Count on it." I hung up and turned back to Antoine. "Tell me what happened."

"I needed to discuss the next steps in the production of the episode. I texted her, but didn't get a reply. So I came to her room and knocked. She didn't answer. All I could think of was Melanie. How she had been inside that room all night with no one. I called the front desk and they came up with a key." Antoine dropped his face into his hands.

"Does she have family you should call?" I asked.

Antoine thought. "Probably. Maybe she mentioned something. A mother? A sister?"

"Do you have any kind of emergency contact information?" I asked.

"Melanie always kept all of those forms," he said, looking helpless.

"So if Brooke is the new Melanie, they should be here in this room." We both looked around. Between the mess the paramedics left and the general detritus of a woman living on the road, it felt hopeless.

Antoine looked up suddenly. "Lucy would know. She would know where to look. I'll call her right now."

Lucy arrived, breathless and flushed, in less than two minutes. "What happened? Where's Brooke?"

Antoine opened his mouth to speak and for once words appeared to fail him. He looked over at me.

"She's ill. Very ill. The paramedics have taken her to the hospital," I said.

Lucy took a step back. "What happened?"

"We have no idea, but we think someone should contact her family and then Antoine and I are going to the hospital," I said.

Lucy put her hands on either side of Antoine's face. "You poor, poor man. This is awful. Go to the hospital. I'll find the emergency contact information and her insurance information and meet you there. Don't worry about anything. I'll take care of it."

Antoine slid Lucy's hands off his face, but kept them between his two hands. "Thank goodness for you, Lucy."

Her face flushed pink.

I made a noise and indicated the door with a head nod. Antoine nodded back. Lucy was already going through the papers on Brooke's desk before we were out the door.

Three hours later, Brooke was out of the woods. Her stomach had been pumped. Her heart had stabilized. I left Antoine and Lucy sitting by her bed and went outside the hospital. Relief washed through me. I didn't have to see another dead body. Not yet. Maybe not ever.

I seriously hoped not ever.

I felt more tired than I'd felt for a very long time. I pulled out my phone and dialed.

"Hello," Garrett said after one ring.

"Now," I said. "I need you now."

He was there in five minutes.

Dario took one look at me the next morning and said, "You look rougher than chipped beef on toast."

"I feel rougher than chipped beef on toast." I unlocked the door and we went in. "I spent most of the night at the hospital."

Dario straightened. "Did Haley have her baby? What flavor? How big? Is she doing okay?"

I shook my head. "No Peanut. Not yet. Brooke was poisoned."

Dario stared at me. "How?"

"They're not certain yet." I slumped down at the kitchen table and rested my head in my hands.

"Will she be okay?"

A vision of Brooke's pale face loomed in my mind.

"They're not certain about that yet, either. If Antoine hadn't called the front desk and demanded to be let into her room, she'd probably be dead."

Dario ground coffee beans. The noise of the grinder made my head pound, but the scent of coffee in the air was the first promise of the world still having good in it that I'd seen since Antoine called me the night before.

"You should go home," he said. "You're going to be useless here."

"No. I can do it." I stood up and tied my apron on. We generally got an influx of people after church. "I'll go home for a nap later if you can stay."

He nodded. "You got it."

Dario probably would have been better off without me. I dropped bowls, spilled honey all over the counter and burned my thumb on a hot pan. Right before we opened the doors, Dan showed up with Sprocket. I sank to the floor and buried my face in his fur. He licked my ear. About half my heartache leaked away. I looked up at Dan. "Thanks for bringing my dog." I'd had to leave him at home before we went to the hospital and then Garrett had taken me back to his place before dropping me at work this morning.

"It's embarrassing when the local constabulary gets noise complaints from neighbors. He was going to howl until he saw you." Dan patted Sprocket's head.

"Sorry." I winced. Sprocket could be loud when he was displeased.

He shook his head. "It's okay. I'm glad I'm not the only one trying to look after you. It's nice to have a brother in arms." He scratched Sprocket's ears. "How are you doing?"

I shrugged. "I'm okay."

"She's a mess," Dario said over his shoulder as he continued to mix the white-chocolate cranberry bars. "Doesn't know her knee from nutmeg this morning."

"How about you?" I asked Dan. He hadn't had any more sleep than I had.

"Riding a little rough," he admitted. Dario handed him a mug of coffee and the look of gratitude on Dan's face was nearly heartbreaking. He sank down into a chair, closed his eyes, and took a long sip.

"Do we know what happened to Brooke?" I asked. "How she was poisoned?"

Dan set his mug down very carefully. "We don't know anything because there is no *we* investigating this case, Rebecca. Got that? No we. This is the second woman close to Antoine who has been attacked. I'm not going to wait for a third one to be attacked to say that there's a pattern here."

I wasn't stupid. It had occurred to me, too. Melanie was his personal assistant, his go-to person. Then Brooke stepped into her place and someone poisoned her. "What kind of psycho would do something like that?"

"A seriously deranged psycho, I'm afraid." Dan scratched Sprocket behind the ears. I suspected he would like to be down on the floor with his face in Sprocket's fur, too. Sometimes dignity was overrated.

Something that had been bothering me in the back of my mind finally made its way to the foreground. "What about Antoine's stalker?"

"No one's seen her since that night at the hotel," Dan said.

"Just because we haven't seen her doesn't mean she's not out there. Isn't that one of the things stalkers are good at?" I pointed out.

"We've been circulating her description, but haven't

had any hits. I thought maybe Melanie's murder scared her off. I know if I was Antoine's stalker and that happened when I was mid-stalk, I'd want to stalk from a distance for a while." Dan rubbed his eyes.

"But what if she didn't run away? What if she's just really good at staying hidden? She could have cut her hair, dyed it, bought fake glasses, put on a baseball cap. There would be tons of easy ways to disguise herself and still stay in the area." Sprocket licked my ear.

"I'm not sure I like how quickly you came up with ways to disguise yourself," Dan said. "But you're right. It makes a sick kind of sense. She could be getting rid of the women close to Antoine, thinking that she could step into their places. Didn't she try to move into Antoine's place after you moved out?"

I nodded. "Showed up with a U-Haul on a Tuesday afternoon. Before that, she brought little gifts. Antoine's been getting little gifts that no one is taking credit for." The cards, the brioche, the magazines. Someone had left them.

Suddenly Dan jolted upward. "Then Lucy is in danger. She's next in line behind Brooke, isn't she?"

"She is. Poor thing. She's so crazy in love with Antoine herself. She's finally getting what she wanted and it's putting her smack-dab in a killer's crosshairs." Sometimes the worst thing that can happen is to get what you thought you wanted.

"I'll go warn her. Tell her to pack her things and leave town. She should stay away from Antoine until we catch Marie Parsons." Dan shoved his chair back from the table.

I doubted she'd do it. Her allegiance to Antoine was so extreme she wouldn't leave him here even if her life literally depended on it. "I have a better idea."

"I'm all ears."

"Use me as bait." If the killer was getting rid of people close to Antoine, there could hardly be a better target than me.

"No."

"Hear me out." The plan had burst into my head. I could see exactly how it should unfold.

"No."

"Dan, it makes perfect sense. After that television interview and the coverage afterward, half the country thinks Antoine and I are getting back together already. It wouldn't be hard to convince Marie Parsons that it was really true. You could be watching. When she comes after me, you'll catch her and then this whole nightmare will be over." And Antoine could leave town and I could go on with my life. We all could go on with our lives.

"No."

"Dan, be reasonable."

He stood. "No," he yelled. "I will not put you in danger. I will not use you as bait for a delusional psychopath. No."

Dan never yelled. He barely ever even raised his voice. He didn't generally have to. He had that quiet command sense that made people stop and listen to him. Dario, Sprocket and I shrank back.

He sagged. "I'm sorry. I'm tired. I shouldn't have yelled, but no, Rebecca. Just no. Okay?" He took one last swig of coffee.

Another possibility occurred to me. "Dan, did you rake the other day?" I asked.

"Are you kidding? I've been so busy I've barely had time to go to the bathroom, much less rake." He shook his head.

"What about Haley? Was she raking?"

"Have you looked at her lately? She can barely walk. How is she supposed to rake?"

"Then who left the rake on my steps?"

"What rake?" he asked.

"The one that I nearly tripped over going down my stairs in the dark the other night," I said. If Sprocket hadn't growled at it, I never would have seen it. The stairs were steep. If I had tripped over it . . . Well, it might not have been fatal, but it certainly wouldn't have been pretty.

"Do you remember what color the handle was?" he asked.

I shut my eyes. "Red."

"Ours is blue," he said, his voice quiet.

"Dan, I think it's possible that Marie Parsons is already after me. I'm already bait. Let's use that against her." It made so much sense I couldn't believe that Dan was hesitating.

Dario waited two beats and then said, "She's going to do it anyway. You might as well help her. At least that way she stands half a chance of surviving."

"Is that true, Rebecca?" Dan asked.

I kept my face in Sprocket's neck. "Probably, although not right at this very second."

"Fine," Dan said, getting up and walking toward the door. "We can talk about it later."

Dario and I went back to work. Or as much work as I was able to do. My hands shook. My eyes blurred. I was a walking disaster. At one-thirty, Dario finally benched me. "Please go home? You're making more work than you're doing."

"That's some tough love, Dario." I knew he was right, though.

He laughed. "It's the best kind. I've got things here covered. Take a nap and be back by three thirty, okay?"

There wasn't time for napping, though. Sprocket and I walked over to Dan's office instead, carrying two take-out coffees and a bag of popcorn bars. Sugar and caffeine can get me through a lot of very bad days.

The Bunnies were gone from the sidewalk. The press had left, too. Once Antoine was no longer in jail, people had lost interest. Besides, a reality-show star had had a nip slip on an afternoon talk show. Nobody was interested in Melanie's murder anymore.

Vera let me in to see Dan.

He looked up from the papers on his desk, pinched the bridge of his nose for a moment, then took a big breath and said, "Let's make a plan."

We spent the next hour mapping out exactly how we'd convince Marie Parsons that I was back in Antoine's life for real and forever and how we'd keep her from killing me.

"I still don't like it," Dan said, looking over what we'd sketched out.

"Do you want this to be over?"

"Of course."

"Do you want Antoine to leave town?"

"Absolutely."

"Got a better plan?"

He put his head down on the desk and said, "Lord help me, but no."

I pulled out my phone and called Garrett.

"Dead body?" he asked.

"Nope. At least not yet. Can you come over to Dan's office? There's something we want to tell you about."

Fifteen minutes later, Garrett sat next to me and across from Dan. He looked back and forth between the two of us and said, "No."

"It was my first response, too," Dan said.

"Not only no, but hell no," Garrett said.

"It was my second response, too." Dan looked sad.

"He even yelled at me," I interjected.

Garrett swiveled his head and stared at me. "Dan yelled? Dan never yells."

"I know."

Now Garrett did the thing with pinching the bridge of his nose. I wasn't sure what that meant. "I saw you almost get shot," he said, his voice ragged at the edges. "I still have bad dreams about that."

I hadn't known about the bad dreams. I put my hand on his. "I'm sorry."

"But not sorry enough to not put yourself in danger." He didn't say it like it was a question.

"I won't really be in danger. It will just look like I'm in danger." I'd be protected.

"This woman has already killed once and come damn close to killing a second time. She's not going to hesitate." Garrett turned my hand over as if he was about to tell my fortune.

"Good. I want this over. I'm sick of it. I'm sick of all this craziness and the media and everything else. Aren't you?" I asked.

He nodded. "I am. Very sick of it. I think I was sick of it before it started." He lifted my hand and dropped a kiss into the palm. "Okay. Let's do it."

The next person I needed to get on board with my plan was Antoine. I arranged to meet him at the hotel. It was too far to walk, so Sprocket and I went home to get my car. It was around Evan's nap time, which these days was also Haley's nap time. Again, that whole building a human being thing apparently took some energy.

No such luck. She walked out onto the porch as I walked up the driveway. "What are you doing home?" she asked.

Then I realized there was one more person I needed to agree to the plan before I tried to talk Antoine into it. Or maybe two. She kind of counted for two these days. I sat down on the steps and laid it all out for her.

Haley pressed the palms of her hands into her eyes. "You think this will end it?" she asked. "Fast?"

"That's the plan."

"And Dan's okay with it?" She dropped her hands back to what there was of her lap.

"Totally." She didn't need to know about his reservations. It wouldn't help.

She sighed. "Okay, then. I'm in. What do I need to do to help?"

"Hold off on that whole going-into-labor thing for a day or two." She wasn't due for a couple of more weeks. It shouldn't be a problem.

"I'll try crossing my legs. I've heard that's effective." She snorted, then stood up and made a shooing gesture. "Well, go on already. Get this over with."

I drove over to the hotel and made my way to Antoine's room. He opened the door and let us in. Sprocket didn't growl, then I realized he was chewing something. "What did you give him?" I asked.

"A wee piece of cheese. Nothing more." Antoine ushered us in. "It is just you and me, my sweet," he said. "Your *beau-frère* has arranged to have Lucy taken to the airport."

"Jason's still here," I pointed out.

"With everyone else gone, I told him he could also go. He and his wife have decided to take a brief vacation together to rekindle their romance." He paused. "It is a nice idea, is it not? Rekindling a love between a husband and wife?"

"I'm not your wife anymore, Antoine. I have actual legal papers that say so." I sat down on the couch.

"Papers that could be torn up. Or trumped by different papers," he suggested.

"Antoine, no."

He sighed. "I knew that's what you would say. I had to try, though."

"I need a favor from you, though. I need you to act like that wasn't what I said."

By four o'clock that afternoon we were back in the conference room with Lisa from WOHH. This time, I did my own makeup. I might not wear it everyday, but I knew how to put it on and I wasn't going to let Tanya turn me into Tammy Faye Bakker again.

Once the cameras were rolling, Lisa looked directly into the camera and said, "We have an update on the status of Antoine Belanger." Then she turned to me.

"These terrible tragedies have made me stop and take stock of my life. It's too short not to go with your heart. Antoine and I are getting back together." I took his hand and smiled up into his eyes.

He leaned down and kissed me on the lips. "I am so grateful, my darling. I vow to cherish you forever as you deserve to be cherished."

For a second, it all felt a little too real. Antoine had seduced me away from all of them before. He hadn't even broken a sweat doing it. It wasn't a big stretch for him to think he could do it again. I wasn't one hundred percent certain he couldn't, either. All that charisma was seductive.

But too many people had sacrificed too much with my return to Grand Lake. Coco had ended up sacrificing her life because of it. There was no way I was giving up now.

The interview went on with me prattling about how in love with Antoine I was and Antoine making big googly eyes at me.

"Thanks for the scoop, guys," Lisa said as we wrapped up.

"Oh, the pleasure is all ours," I said, trying to smile. "When will this air?"

"We're teasing it for this evening's broadcast." Lisa smiled. "We're going to trounce WCLV in the ratings."

After she left, Antoine turned to me. "Now what?"

"Now we act like the ickiest most loviest-doviest couple Grand Lake has ever seen."

First we went to the lighthouse, where we strolled along the lake holding hands and stopping to smooch along the way with Sprocket trotting happily beside us. Then we dropped Sprocket off at my apartment. I picked up some clothes and my toothbrush. We went over to Winnie's Tavern for a drink. Antoine made the mistake of asking for a glass of wine, which he nearly spit back into his glass after the first sip.

"You should have tried a cocktail," I said.

"Probably best not to drink at all," he said. "Probably smarter to keep our wits about us."

He had a point. We were trying to draw out a woman who had killed once and attempted to kill a second time just to get close to Antoine.

* * *

The piece on us aired, and the Belanger Bunny social media world went wild. Even if Marie Parsons didn't see the show, she'd know what was going on. Antoine and I had dinner at the diner. Megan Templeton was nicer to me than she'd ever been before. "How soon you leaving?" she asked when she brought our orders.

"We haven't made specific plans yet," I said.

"Soon, though?"

I looked up at her. "Do you want it to be soon?"

"Things were calmer before you came home, Rebecca. Simpler. You go on back to California, where you belong, and let us be." She turned on her heel and walked away.

So much for having won the hearts and minds of my hometown.

We finished dinner and headed back to the hotel. I texted Dan: Anything?

He answered: Not a peep.

Once we got to the hotel, we went straight to Antoine's room. He opened the door and we both went in and then stopped.

"Well," I said. "This isn't awkward at all."

"Indeed." He gestured at the bed. "Perhaps you would want to share the bed with me? For old time's sake?"

I shook my head. "I'll take the couch."

"Suit yourself."

I went into the bathroom, brushed my teeth and changed into the pajamas I'd brought with me. Well, not exactly pajamas. More like yoga pants and a T-shirt. Antoine went next and came out in a pair of boxers.

We both settled into our respective beds. After about ten minutes, he said quietly, "Are you awake, Rebecca?"

"Yeah." I had a feeling I would be awake most of the night.

"Do you ever miss . . . us?" he asked.

I sat up. "Of course. There were a lot of good things about being married to you."

"Then why won't you come back?" He rolled onto his side and propped himself on one elbow to look at me.

"I think you probably know the answer to that by now."

He flopped onto his back. "I suppose I do."

I was awake when my alarm went off. I wasn't sure I'd managed to get any sleep. Between waiting to be attacked by a psycho stalker and my feet hanging over the end of the couch, it wasn't exactly a restful scenario.

I texted Dan: Please tell me you've spotted her.

He answered: Sorry.

I showered and dressed. Antoine was waking up as I left. "Watch your back," I said as I went to the door.

"You are the one whose back needs to be watched. Are you sure you don't want me to come with you?" he asked.

"Dan has pretty much the entire Sheriff's Department ranged around watching me. I think I'll be fine."

And I was. Nothing happened. Not in the back alley behind POPS where I parked my car. Not as I prepped for the morning rush. Not as I served coffee and breakfast bars to my much diminished crowd. I'd told Dario to stay home. I didn't want to put anyone in danger who didn't need to be in danger. Finally, at ten o'clock, my phone rang. It was Dan. "We've got her."

"Oh, thank goodness. Where? When? How?"

He laughed. "Posing as a maid at the hotel. She bribed one of the maids into giving her a uniform and keys. She was sneaking into Antoine's room. I have no idea what she intended to do once she was in and I don't want to."

"Did she confess?" I sat down heavily in a chair.

"No. At least not yet. We really haven't had time to question her yet. It'll come. I'm sure of it."

"What a relief." That didn't begin to sum it up, but it was all I had at the moment.

"I know. Antoine can go back to California. Things can finally go back to normal."

Normal sounded very, very good at the moment.

I opened the back door. "Free coffee and snacks to anyone who was trying to keep me from getting killed."

Huerta, Stephens and Vera converged from three separate spots and jogged toward the door. Annie appeared in her own doorway. "I would totally have thrown myself between you and a bullet."

"Sure you would have." I waved for her to come in as well.

After my crew left, I sank down at the table in the kitchen myself. I called Garrett. "It's over."

"I heard." He sounded as relieved as I felt. "Dinner tonight?"

"Yes, please. I'll even let you bring in takeout. I'm so tired my eyelids feel like they have ten-pound weights on them."

I couldn't stay sitting for long, though. The room was a mess: empty coffee cups and plates everywhere. Then there was prep for the afternoon rush. I had a feeling that having been part of the arrest of Marie Parsons wasn't going to make me any less of a subject of conversation and speculation. I figured I'd better be ready for double crowds.

I was exhausted, nearly stumbling I was so tired, but it

still felt good to work in my kitchen. It just felt right to be mixing and measuring, testing and tasting, sipping and savoring as I made popcorn and fudge. I heard the tinkle of the bell signifying that someone had come in the front door. I grabbed an apron and headed to the front to meet my first afternoon customer.

It was Lucy.

"Lucy, what are you doing here? I thought you'd flown back to California."

"Just because a person goes to an airport, doesn't mean they have to get on a plane." Her tone was sarcastic.

"I don't understand."

She rolled her eyes. "What a surprise. Rebecca doesn't get it. You are so freaking dim, girlfriend. You never get anything right."

I'd never heard Lucy speak in that tone of voice before. "What are you talking about?"

"What are you talking about? What's going on? Who did this? Who did that? Why? Why? Why?" she said in a whiney singsong voice. "I don't know how anyone can stand to be around you. I really don't know what Antoine sees in you."

I didn't have an answer to that since I wasn't entirely sure what he saw in me, either.

"But he's totally smitten with you," she said. "Can't stay away from you. Can't stop talking about you. Can't stop thinking about you. Of course, there are a lot of things I don't understand about Antoine's taste in women. I mean, can you believe he promoted Brooke over me? What was that about? And after all I did to get Melanie out of the way so I could step into her place."

"Wait," I said. "What?"

Lucy rummaged in her purse and then came up with a

gun, which she pointed directly at my chest. "There you go with the stupid questions again. That's right, Rebecca. I got rid of Melanie. I altered the blow-dryer. I had it ready and waiting. She used to summon me to her room to discuss production issues all the time while she soaked in the bath. She had no more shame than a cat."

"So you didn't know she was stealing from Antoine?"

"No. That came as quite a surprise. Then Antoine was arrested and I had to team up with you to get him out of jail. Unbelievable. Then he goes and promotes Brooke over me so I had to get rid of her, too." She sounded irritated about the extra work. No regret. No guilt. Nothing.

My throat started to close. I couldn't believe what I was hearing.

"Then I figured I was home free. Brooke was gone. Melanie was gone. Sunny had been arrested and they were trying to tie him to Melanie's murder. I'd finally have Antoine all to myself. Then I see that television interview with the two of you holding hands." She started to gag a little. "Made me sick. Seriously physically sick. I actually barfed watching the two of you together."

I straightened up, prepared to bluff my way out of this one. "Then you know you still can't have Antoine. He's mine. Put the gun away and go."

She laughed. "Really, Rebecca? I've killed for him already. You think your little play for him is going to stop me? And now I have the perfect patsy. Even if they realize that your death wasn't an accident, they'll blame Marie Parsons somehow."

"Wait. My death?"

My phone rang.

"Don't even think about answering it." Her voice was flat and the gun didn't waver.

I glanced at the screen. It was Haley. "It would be better if I did."

She snorted. "Really?"

"Yeah. Really. It's my sister. She put a tracer program on my phone. If I don't answer, she will track me down." Please, I thought. Please let her send Dan to track me down. Please don't let her come herself.

"Does your big sister always take such good care of you?" she asked in a sicky-sweet voice.

I sighed. "It's not that. You've seen her. She's about to go into labor. In fact, this is probably the phone call telling me she's about to have the baby. I'm supposed to go home immediately to take care of my nephew."

The shadow of doubt flickered across Lucy's face, but it only flickered. It was replaced again by the maniacal glint. "Then we better get this party started." She turned the heat under the deep fryer to high.

"Hey! Careful!" Grease fires start fast, spread fast and are a bitch kitty to put out. If the grease gets hot enough, it can catch fire.

"Rebecca, I have a gun on you. Do you really think I'm not going to hurt you?" She laughed.

That took me aback. My worst nightmare returned. A gun in my face. "You're going to burn my shop?"

"It's going to be absolutely tragic. You were distracted. In love again with Antoine. You left the fryer going and it caught fire. Instead of trying to get out, you tried to put the fire out by throwing water on it." She said it in a singsong voice.

"Come on. I'm not that stupid." Pretty much the worst thing you can do with a grease fire is to throw water on it. The results are, shall we say, explosive. I backed toward the wall. How long would it take Haley to get frustrated and trace my phone? How long after that would she call Dan? How long would it take for Dan to get to us?

I wasn't sure of the exact numbers, but I was pretty sure they all added up to too late. The grease was already bubbling.

"Oh, I think you're pretty stupid. You had it all. You had the most perfect man in the world and you left him. Then you didn't have the sense to stay gone." She shook her head.

"I don't understand, Lucy. Why are you doing this?" I asked, hoping to buy some time.

"Because I don't want anything between me and Antoine. I figured with Melanie out of the way, he'd turn to me. Then he promoted Brooke instead." Her voice quavered and tears welled into her eyes. "I couldn't believe he didn't see how much more devoted to him I was."

He had seen it. It had alarmed him. "So you tried to kill her, too?"

"Another five minutes and it would have worked. Still, she's sick enough that I'll be firmly in place by the time she can return to work." Her eyes hardened. "As long as you're out of the way, too."

Someone knocked at the back door. Hard. "Rebecca! I know you're in there!" Haley yelled. "I'm in labor, damn it. This is not a drill. Come out and get over to the preschool to pick up Evan."

"Don't move," Lucy hissed at me.

I took a step backward and hit the shelves behind me. My hand searched behind me for anything I might use as a weapon. All the knives were safely in their block on the counter. The scissors were in the drawer. All I could feel on the shelf was the container of popcorn kernels.

Haley knocked again. Hard. Then there was a gasping

noise. "Damn it, Rebecca. Now my water's broken. Let me the hell in."

Oh, sweet caramel sauce on popcorn, if I got out of this alive Haley was going to kill me.

The grease lit. "Finally," Lucy said, as if the grease fire had chosen not to catch fire just to frustrate her. She started toward the sink.

"What are you doing?"

She smiled. "Getting the glass of water for you to throw on that fire."

I shook my head. "I won't do it."

"You'll do it or I'll shoot your sister right through that door." I shook my head hard, but behind my back I unscrewed the container of kernels.

Without taking her eyes or her gun off me, Lucy used her left hand to turn on the faucet and fill a glass with water.

"How are you going to get out of here?" I asked.

"Oh, I'll be over here by the door. As soon as I'm sure you're going to be gone, I'll go out the front. I'll tell everyone how I warned you not to throw the water and how you ignored me and sealed your own fate."

Haley pounded on the door. "Rebecca!" Then she groaned. A horrible, guttural sound. "Rebecca, this isn't funny. I think I might already be in transition. This baby is coming fast."

Lucy started toward me with the glass of water. I was only going to have one chance. As she took another step, I threw the kernels under her feet and ran for the door.

"Stop!" she screamed, and did exactly what I needed her to do. She took another step and went down like a ton of bricks on the kernels as if she was trying to run on ball bearings.

I unbolted the door. Haley was doubled over on her knees on the back porch. "Run!"

"Can't," she panted. "Contraction."

Then Lucy was on us, gun trained at my vulnerable sister. "Get back in that kitchen, Rebecca. Right now."

I bowed my head. I was beaten. I had no other tricks up my sleeve.

It turned out I didn't need any new ones. Jasper came around the corner. "Hey!" he yelled.

"What the hell, Rebecca?" Lucy asked. "Is your back alley like some kind of weird convention center?"

Her gun went back and forth between Haley and Jasper. It was the distraction I needed. I threw myself at her, knocking her back into the smoky kitchen. The gun flew from her hand, spinning across the kitchen floor. It hit the cabinet and went off. The bullet hit the fryer, providing just the spark required to ignite the grease fire.

"Jasper, get Haley out of here!" I screamed.

I leapt up and started toward the door, but Lucy just lay there.

"Lucy, get up! We have to go." My kitchen would be engulfed in flames in minutes.

"No," she cried. "It's all ruined. How many people will I have to kill to make him love me? It's just too much."

I grabbed her arm and tugged. She slapped me away. "Lucy, you'll burn. You have to get up."

"I don't care anymore." She rolled onto her side into the fetal position.

In the distance, I heard sirens. The fire caught the cupboards next to the stove. The smoke had already made me start to cough. I grabbed Lucy's feet and dragged her toward the open door.

She kicked me.

I wasn't sure exactly what happened at that point, but something inside me burst. I had had it. "Damn it, you ungrateful little turd. You have caused me enough trouble. You are not dying in my kitchen. It is my happy place and you will not ruin it. A person only gets so many of those."

I grabbed her legs again and heaved. Either I'd shocked her into cooperating or the smoke had gotten to her and she couldn't fight anymore. I managed to drag her out onto the porch just as Eric Gladstone came running up in full turnout gear.

Sixteen

The next morning, Evan and I walked into Haley's hospital room hand in hand with Garrett beside us. Even if I hadn't been on babysitting duty, I wouldn't have been able to open the shop. The kitchen was a mess. It would take weeks to clean it all up, but it was salvageable. At least, that's what Eric and Dario told me when they came over to the house. I'd had to leave the shop to pick up Evan from preschool while Dan took Haley to the hospital. Garrett had shown up with dinner and we'd settled in for an evening of reading *The Little Engine That Could* and laying down wooden train tracks. I'd felt happier than I had in weeks. I hadn't been back to the shop yet.

Glenn Huerta had had to be the one to tell Antoine about Lucy. Antoine had already been packing to leave. He had all the video he needed to put together the show. He'd been expecting to put it together with Lucy. I hadn't spoken to him, but if the series of voice mails he left on my phone were any indication, he was pretty shaken.

"I do not know how I am to go forward, Rebecca. I have always prided myself on being a good judge of character. Clearly, I know nothing. Please come help me," was what he'd said in one of them. The rest were variations on that same theme. I ignored them all.

I felt like I knew when he'd left Grand Lake, though. It was as if my lungs could suddenly expand fully. I could breathe. There was a lot of charm and charisma in Antoine, but it seemed like it would smother me if I was around him too long.

Sunny Coronado also left town. Cynthia dropped her assault charge against him and they had no reason to hold him any longer. I didn't know if Antoine would bring suit against him for trying to steal his spice formulas or not. If he did, he might have to divulge that they simply weren't very good. That would be difficult for him, especially on the heels of what had happened to his crew.

Evan had been uncharacteristically calm and quiet, agreeing not to wear his Batman cape, letting me tie his shoes. Then he saw Haley. He took off running and leapt into the bed. "Mama!"

"How's my little man?" she said, motioning me over to take the baby from her.

For the first time, I lifted my niece in my arms. I'm not sure how to describe what happened next. It was like my heart exploded into a thousand joy bubbles in my chest and all rose up my throat and into my eyes, which is totally why it looked like I was crying. "I am so glad you're here, sweet thing," I whispered against her tiny fuzzy skull. "I am so relieved you and your mama are okay."

"Can I see the baby?" Evan asked from his spot snuggled in next to Haley.

I looked at Haley, who nodded. I walked over to show

him his little sister. He reached one finger out and gently touched her cheek. "My baby," he said.

A half-strangled sob came out of my throat. That's what Haley used to call me. I looked up at her and saw that her eyes were shiny with tears, too.

Dan came in and offered to take Evan out for ice cream to celebrate having a sister. Garrett decided to join them.

I sat down in the rocking chair next to Haley's bed, holding Emily, admiring her tiny fingers, her teeny toes, her perfect little ears. "I'm so sorry I missed this with Evan," I said.

"I'm sorry you missed it, too," Haley said. "It's pretty amazing, isn't it?"

I nodded. "Totally, but you know, I'm glad I left here."

"You are?"

"Yes. I am. Because if I hadn't, I don't think I would have ever appreciated it. Coming back here makes me see it with completely new eyes." I thought how different the town seemed now, how I saw friends where I once saw enemies, how I saw comfort where I once saw restraint. "I don't think I would have ever known my happy place was right here in Grand Lake if I hadn't left to look for it somewhere else."

RECIPES

BACON PECAN POPCORN

4 cups popped popcorn (Pop ⅓ cup kernels in ¼
    cup oil)
½ cup butter
2 cups brown sugar
½ cup Karo syrup
1 teaspoon salt
½ teaspoon baking soda
1 teaspoon vanilla
1 pound bacon, cooked and chopped into bite-
    size pieces
1 cup pecans

Preheat oven to 250 degrees.

Melt butter in a medium saucepan. Add in the brown
sugar, Karo syrup and salt. Bring to a boil, stirring. Then
set the timer! Let it simmer for 5 minutes without stirring.

Then remove from heat, add in baking soda and vanilla. Pour over the popcorn and mix. Add in the bacon and the pecans.

Pour popcorn mixture into a shallow pan lined with parchment paper and bake for 1 hour, stirring occasionally. Let cool. Break apart. Store in an airtight container, if there's any left to store!

LOW-CALORIE MEXICAN CHOCOLATE POPCORN

4 cups popped popcorn (Pop ⅓ cup kernels in
   ⅛ cup oil)
3 tablespoons honey
2 tablespoons butter
2 tablespoons cocoa powder
1 tablespoon chili powder
½ teaspoon cinnamon
½ teaspoon ground cumin
¼ teaspoon cayenne
½ teaspoon salt

Preheat oven to 250 degrees.

Combine everything but the popcorn in a small saucepan over low heat and stir until butter is melted. Pour over popcorn and stir. Pour popcorn mixture into a shallow parchment-lined pan and put in oven. Bake for 20 minutes, stirring occasionally.

ABOUT THE AUTHOR

Pop Goes the Murder is Kristi's second book with Berkley Prime Crime. She has been obsessed with popcorn ever since she first tasted the caramel-cashew popcorn at Garrett's in Chicago. If you've never had it, you might want to hop on a plane and go now. Seriously, it's that good.

Kristi lives in northern California, although she was born in Ohio like the heroine of the Popcorn Shop Mysteries. She loves snack food, crocheting, her kids, and her man, not necessarily in that order.

Connect with Berkley Publishing Online!

For sneak peeks into the newest releases, news on all your favorite authors, book giveaways, and a central place to connect with fellow fans—

"Like" and follow Berkley Publishing!

facebook.com/BerkleyPub
twitter.com/BerkleyPub
instagram.com/BerkleyPub

Penguin
Random
House